The Dreamer

Fiction

By Troy C. Wagstaff

Tibble Fork Publishing
American Fork, Utah
Copyright 2017 © by Tibble Fork Publishing

ALL RIGHTS RESERVED
No part of this publication may be reproduced, distributed, or transmitted in any form or by any means, including photocopying, recording, or other electronic or mechanical methods, without the prior written permission of the publisher or author, except in the case of brief quotations embodied in critical reviews and certain other noncommercial uses permitted by copyright law.

This is a work of fiction. Names, characters, businesses, dialogs, websites, places, events and incidents are either the product of the author's imagination or used in a fictitious manner and are not to be construed as real. Any resemblance to actual persons, living or dead, blogs, locations, or actual events or places is purely coincidental. Any reference to real events, businesses, organizations and locales are intended to give the fiction a sense of reality and authenticity. Any resemblance to actual persons living or dead is purely coincidental.

Cover photography and cover design by Colette Wagstaff (ColettesCreations). Copyright © 2017 by Colette Wagstaff

DEDICATION

The Dreamer is dedicated to Dylan and Emily

Dylan a kindred spirit and Emily a beacon in the storm

Table Of Contents

Forward 7

Chapter 1: Evil Report 8

Chapter 2: Birthright 17

Chapter 3: Obedience 28

Chapter 4: Forgiveness 38

Chapter 5: Friends 46

Chapter 6: The Dreamer Cometh 53

Chapter 7: Trust In The Lord 62

Chapter 8: Sold 71

Chapter 9: Joseph's Coat 79

Chapter 10: Egyptian Slave 84

Chapter 11: Houseboy 94

Chapter 12: Mustard Tree 104

Chapter 13: Overseer 111

Chapter 14: Zeleakia 122

Chapter 15: Still A Slave 131

Chapter 16: Falsely Accused 140

Chapter 17: Prison 146

Chapter 18: Butler and Baker 156

Chapter 19: Pharaohs Dream 162

Chapter 20: Zaphnath-paaneah 172

Chapter 21: Governor 181

Chapter 22: Hebrew God 191

Chapter 23: The Joseph Canal 198

Chapter 24: Attraction 206

Chapter 25: Open Honest Heart 214

Chapter 26: Aseneth's Conversion 221

Chapter 27: Marriage 228

Chapter 28: Celebration 238

Chapter 29: Letting Go 247

Chapter 30: Brothers 253

Chapter 31: Judgement 262

Chapter 32: Obeisance 273

Chapter 33: Silver Cup 284

Book Club Discussion Questions 295

Personal Study Guide For Genesis 298

The Dreamer

Forward

      This work of historical fiction is based on the account of Joseph of Egypt found in the King James version of the Holy Bible. The historicity of the story is based on the account found in Genesis 37, 39-45 and not on ancient Egyptian historical accounts and folklore.

      While some ancient texts were consulted in the development of this story to add flavor, depth and names, the bulk of the novel is inspired by the Old Testament account.

      This historical fiction seeks to emphasize the spiritual journey of Joseph as he is beaten, betrayed and sold into slavery and his quest to live according to the teachings of his Hebrew God.

      To help promote the inspiration and the power of the story of Joseph and the coat of many colors, both a book club style list of suggested questions and a study guide have been included with the novel. You may find it fun and entertaining to read the biblical account and compare it to the fictionalized account.

      This fictionalized historical account of Joseph and the coat of many colors follows Joseph's life from the time he was seventeen until after he was married and saved his family from famine. It examines how Joseph dealt with the countless tragedies and challenges of life. He is victimized several times and yet, with the help of God, is able to overcome those wicked deeds done against him. I hope you enjoy the novel.

The Dreamer

Chapter 1: Evil Report

For I know the thoughts that I think toward you, saith the Lord, thoughts of peace, and not of evil, to give you an expected end. Then shall ye call upon me, and ye shall go and pray unto me, and I will hearken unto you. And ye shall seek me, and find me, when ye shall search for me with all your heart. Jeremiah 29:11-13

    A stinging wind of sandy grit and blackness blew. Joseph was riding his camel flat out on the trail heading for Canaan a day in front of the family flocks, he was trying to outrun a sandstorm, but couldn't run fast enough and was overtaken by the sand storm that swept in on the trail unexpectedly. Joseph's innate tendency to get the job done forced his camel onward. Eventually, it became impossible to see through the dark clouds of sand where he was going.

    In spite of fearing that he might lose the trail, he stopped when he found a steep hillside. He caused his camel to lay down so he could get off then tie the camel to a nearby bush. He positioned his camel just in front of himself with the hillside at his back creating as much shelter as possible. Joseph spent the rest of the day and all of the night in that same spot huddled, waiting for the storm to stop.

    While stuck in that position, Joseph had nothing to do but listen to the loud wind rage by as it carried the biting sand. He was alone with his memories and thoughts. He was still upset by the terrible discovery he made when he learned that four of his brothers Dan, Gad, Naphtali and

The Dreamer

Asher along with their servants, stole sheep from smaller flocks on the other side of the hill from where the family flocks were grazing. They stole enough sheep to almost double the size of their flock. The sheep herders from the smaller flocks dared not say or do anything.

Then they went to the market to sell off a part of their flock, they sold the stolen sheep as well. They skimmed off the money from the stolen sheep and when they got home, they would divide the ill-gotten profits with their brothers, except for Joseph and Benjamin.

They left Benjamin out because he was too young to participate in herding the sheep. They left out Joseph because they knew he wouldn't approve and he would likely give Father Jacob a report on their illegal deeds. Jacob would not abide their wicked ways.

Ever since the eldest brothers went after Shechem and his servants (for what they did to their sister Dinah), they knew the wrath of their father was terrible. They thought they were doing right by Dinah to go after Shechem, but they had no idea just how terrible the wrath of their father could be. Ever since that episode, the oldest ten brothers stayed as far away from their father as possible. They figured it would be much easier to keep Joseph out of their plans.

There was a terrible animosity between the ten older brothers and Joseph. Joseph was naturally inclined to do things that pleased his father, whereas the brothers seemed content to go their own way and didn't care so much about pleasing their father. There was another reason for the animosity between Joseph and his older brothers.

Father Jacob, who was also called Israel because of the covenant and because he was the Patriarch, stripped the birthright from the firstborn son Reuben because he

The Dreamer

committed sin with one of his fathers' wives.

Israel turned around and bestowed the birthright on Joseph, who was the first born son of his wife Racheal. When this happened, it added greatly to the natural divide between the older brothers and Joseph. There were many brothers who thought the birthright should have gone to Simeon, who was next in line after Reuben or to Gad, who was the first born of Zilpah, or even to Dan the first born of Bilhah. In every case, they were all older than young Joseph.

There was always pressure on Joseph with whatever he did. He lived to please his father and he was growing and maturing in his relationship with God. The other brothers didn't seem to care so much about the God of Jacob and they hated Joseph for his relationship with both God and their father.

Joseph had decided he needed to inform Father Jacob of the evil deeds his brothers had done by stealing sheep and selling them off. He left his brothers and the flocks behind and rushed on ahead of them toward Canaan to tell his father.

Joseph was only a day ahead of the returning flock. It was even possible that one or more of the brothers might have left the flocks behind and raced after Joseph to stop him from informing their father of their misconduct. If that were the case, they could be close.

It was hard for Joseph to never get any fellowship from his brothers, but he considered the love of his brother Benjamin and the love of his Father Jacob more than enough, but still, he wished he could please his brothers and get on their good side. He just wasn't willing to live like they did and do the things they did to win over their affection.

The Dreamer

Now that he knew his brothers were thieves, he assumed that his father didn't know. They might sneak around their father on occasion, but if he ever found out something bad was going on, he could put the fear of God into them. Since they were still engaged in rustling sheep, it was safe to assume that they had not yet been caught. Joseph had no idea what his brothers might do to him if they caught him before he made it home to the protection of Jacob and he didn't want to find out.

Joseph was miserable packed between a smelly camel and the side of a foothill. The wind was causing the sand to blow hard and covering everything it touched. Even though Joseph was well covered with his thick woolen clothes and scarves, somehow the sand found its way to Joseph's skin. It was dusty, dry and gloomy. He could barely see the camel lying down before him.

He wondered what his brothers would do to him if they caught him. Would they just threaten him? That probably wouldn't work. They could beat him, but would they consider killing him? After all, there was a lot of hate between some of his brothers and him.

When Joseph discovered their evil deeds, they tried to bribe him with a large portion of the profits from the stolen sheep, but he refused. He overheard Dan and Asher talking about killing him after he went to sleep, but were they serious? Dan and Asher were known to be hot heads and spouting off over anything they didn't like. Killing him would be extreme, but Joseph wasn't so sure they were kidding.

The roaring wind storm raged on and Joseph kept pulling his clothes tightly around him trying in vain to keep the sand out. *Why did Father give me the birthright*? He wondered. If given the choice of carrying the mantle of the

The Dreamer

birthright or letting one of his brothers have it, he would gladly let it go. He knew it didn't work that way and he did his best with the responsibility of the mantle because he loved and respected his father. He also loved and worshiped the God of Abraham as he was taught by his mother, and Patriarch father.

As the blinding sand storm raged on, Joseph was worried, if this storm didn't blow over soon, the landscape could change and he could easily get turned around. He knew the basic's of keeping his bearings, but he didn't have the experience his older brothers had.

These massive storms could entirely change the landscape by removing landmarks and adding new ones. He was a gifted Shepard and he could do amazing things with a large flock of sheep, he just didn't have the experience for orienteering yet. He needed to get to his father before his brothers and he needed to get there safely.

In spite of the fierce winds and the stinging sand, sleepiness finally overtook him. It wasn't a long rest, but at the time while he was asleep, he was able to experience an unusually vivid dream where he was with all of his brothers in the fields as they were gathering and binding sheaves of grain for the harvest. He noticed that his stack of grain was bigger than any of his eleven brothers bundles and it continued to grow larger with each passing minute. As his bundle grew it was surrounded by eleven stacks of grain. One for each brother.

Once Joseph's bundle was completely surrounded by his brothers' sheaves they all bowed down before his stack. They bowed down over and over before Joseph's stack of wheat as they gave obeisance to his large bundle.

At first, this concerned Joseph until he realized, surely

The Dreamer

this must be because I have the birthright and they are finally giving me the respect that it demands. While he thought, he understood the meaning of the dream, he wasn't comfortable with the reverence they were showing his sheaf of grain.

The dream repeated over in Joseph's mind vividly three times. When the third dream finished Joseph woke up to find the storm was over and the skies were clear. As he feared, the landscape was vastly different from the day before. He noticed the direction his camel's head was positioned and he took out his knife and laid the point in that same direction so he wouldn't forget which direction they were heading as he prepared to leave.

He tried in vain to shake the sand out of his clothes. He finally took out some food for both himself and the camel. While Joseph ate, he prayed to the God of his fathers and asked for divine guidance and safety on the journey. While taking a deep breath, he wrapped his scarf around his neck and head, leaving a hole for his eyes. He headed off in the direction that the knife was pointing. He hoped he could find some familiar landmarks before nightfall. He wanted to know he was on the right course to Canaan.

His camel plodded along in the loose sand. After a while, Joseph saw the heat waves coming from off the ground. He kept his eyes open for a large lone tree on top of a dune. In spite of the shifting sand, Joseph was sure that the tree would have survived the storm. He looked for that familiar landmark to verify he was on the right path home.

He thought about the dream he had and how vivid it was. It made no sense that a sheaf of grain would bow like a person to a much larger sheaf of grain, but that's what

The Dreamer

happened in his dream. Then he thought about the need to get to Canaan before his brothers. If they got their first, they would tell father Jacob a tale that would contradict his story. He needed to get there first.

As the sun got heavy on the horizon and began its descent, Joseph saw a large sand hill with a solitary tree on the top. The hill looked like nothing he could remember, but the lone tree looked familiar. He was relieved because he had no more food and only a few drops of water left. If he remembered right, he was two full days away from his fathers' estate in Canaan.

He pushed on and traveled until it was too dark to travel. He had no food to cook so he didn't bother with a fire. He was still hot from a blistering day in the sun. He let his camel wander around a little before tying him up. As Joseph prepared his small camp, he thought of his brothers and their hatred toward him. Until now he had never turned on his brothers. All he had ever done was follow the teachings of his father. When the brothers were out having fun, Joseph preferred the company of his father.

He would rather have his father tell his memories of his mother and teach him things about God, the birthright and other gospel subjects than being with his brothers. There was also an age difference between him and the youngest of his older brothers and that also contributed to him seeking company other than with his brothers. In fact, his older brothers had children that were just a little younger than Joseph and he often spent time with them.

This was his first major assignment herding sheep with his brothers in a far away pasture and he was disappointed that his brothers turned out to be thieves. He was surprised at his brother's behavior, stealing sheep and

The Dreamer

selling them. Surely he needed to let his father know what was going on.

He was only seventeen, but life didn't seem to be turning out like he thought it would. Of course, he was young and not completely sure what life should be like. He finally drifted off to sleep.

While he was asleep, he dreamed the same dream of the sheaves and his brothers. It gave him hope when he reflected on the dream in the morning. The dream made Joseph think that it was a sign from God. Why tell him in a dream that his brothers would one day respect his birthright if Joseph was going to die in the wilderness?

He kept the few drops of water for himself, the camel would have to go dry. He knew he could go a day or two without food and water. It wasn't wise, but he had done it before.

The night came and there was a full moon with clear skies. He decided to keep going for a while longer since it wasn't so bad traveling at night, it was a little cooler and he could still see where he was going. Eventually, he needed to sleep so he made camp. He had the same dream as the night before, about the sheaves of grain. In the morning he started on his journey with a throat so dry it hurt to swallow.

Everything around him was stunning in its beauty. The brilliant blue sky and the several shades of tan and brown sand on the horizon with a glowing orange disc beating down on the painted landscape. Every now and again there was a lone tree or a small stand of bushes. There were sand dunes along the way. As he examined the wonderful landscape, he licked his dry cracked lips. It didn't help. He was developing a powerful headache caused by being so thirsty and hungry. The desert was as hot as an

The Dreamer

oven they cooked bread in. But Joseph pushed on because there was so much at stake.

Later in the afternoon Joseph came upon two sets of camel tracks that came in from a different direction, but was now going in the same direction as he was. They could be from anyone, but he feared they were from two of his brothers.

How would Father Jacob react to what Joseph had to say? How would he react if his brothers got there before he did? He was used to being treated badly by his brothers, but lately, they seem to be meaner and harder toward him than they had been. Ironically, sometimes Reuben would defend Joseph to the other brothers and then other times he would be the leader in some plot against Joseph.

The sun was starting its downward decline as Joseph found himself atop of a large dune which allowed him to see for miles around. He spotted what looked like two men on camels trotting toward his father's farm in Canaan.

For the time being, he was more relieved that he was close to home rather than being upset that his brothers would get to his father first. He was tired, thirsty and hungry. His face felt as dry as the sand around him. He coughed when he tried to swallow. He was feeling weaker by the minute. He nudged his camel homeward.

The Dreamer

Chapter 2: Birthright

And he that searcheth the hearts knoweth what is the mind of the Spirit, because he maketh intercession for the saints according to the will of God. Romans 8:27

As the horizon was about to swallow the sun, Benjamin, the youngest of the twelve brothers saw Joseph in the distance and rode out to meet him. Seeing him parched and weak, he gave a fresh crock of water to Joseph. As he tried to swallow the clean, cool water, he choked and coughed, wasting much of the lifesaving water trying to quickly satisfy his ravaging thirst. He finally got enough down his throat to perk himself up. As Joseph spurred the camel on toward the barn, he found out from Benjamin that Father Jacob was not at home. He was scheduled to arrive sometime in the next two days. This was a pleasant surprise. That meant that even though Dan and Asher had arrived sooner than Joseph, they hadn't had a chance to speak with Israel. At least he was safe and could take some time to rest. He knew his brothers wouldn't dare try to hurt him in his fathers' house. Feeling safe he went into the house and ate, drank and went to sleep.

While he was asleep, he had the same dream of the sheaves. However, that dream was followed by another dream that seemed to have an even greater impact on Joseph. In his dream state his mind came upon a sea of total blackness. Then, one by one, stars started to appear until there were eleven little dots in the night sky. Shortly thereafter came a moon dimly lit in the dark expanse. Lastly, a bright sun came into view. Its radiance caused the moon and stars to shine brighter than the rest of the celestial

The Dreamer

bodies.

Joseph wondered at this dream. Why eleven stars, a moon, and a sun? What were they doing? In that dream state, Joseph floated through the vast expanse and came to where these heavenly bodies were. As he moved closer to them, they kindly moved out of his way, allowing him to pass without touching, it was as if these great heavenly bodies were showing obeisance to him, a young boy of seventeen.

It shook young Joseph seeing that such grand celestial bodies were showing such respect, even reverence to him. What could it mean? Was it similar to the sheaves he had dreamed about so frequently over the last few days? It was so much more grand and vivid than sheaves of grain that he wondered at the meaning of it all. There was one thing both dreams had in common, the first dream had eleven sheaves and the second dream had eleven stars. Was that similarity significant?

The next day came and slowly went as Joseph was, with the help of Dinah and Benjamin, nursing himself back to health. He had lost so much energy from not eating and drinking in the scorching hot desert for two days that he could hardly move. He slept a lot. When he was awake, he shared his evil report regarding his four brothers with Dinah, his older sister who was always a trusted friend and confidant.

She told Joseph to concern himself with getting rest and building up his strength. Also she advised Joseph to gain all the health and strength possible so he could be ready to lead when Father Jacob came home. She assured young Joseph that their father would believe and respect what Joseph had to say. She said it in a way that sounded like she knew more than she was letting on. She did let slip

The Dreamer

to Joseph and Benjamin that there would be a great feast for the household after Israel arrived.

Dinah's words gave confidence to Joseph's young and troubled mind. Benjamin was excited to see his father and to know there would be a grand celebration. Benjamin was young enough so as not to appreciate the intrigue between the older ten brothers and his favorite brother, Joseph. Later that day Gad and Asher, along with their servants brought the flock home and once they were settled in they met up with the other brothers to divide the profits of their ill-gotten gains. In their meeting, Gad and Dan spoke to Reuben about the venomous young Joseph finding out their secret plans. Reuben could tolerate losing the birthright. He could tolerate just about every crazy thing that Father Jacob required of them, but when it came to his wealth, that's where he drew the line. He vacillated on just about everything, but he wasn't about to let the dreamer get in their way.

They discussed how to prevent their vile younger brother from spoiling their secret plans to gain their own wealth. Reuben said that all options were fair game except for murder. Judah suggested that they take the money that Dan and Gad brought back and immediately bury it.

"Then if it becomes an issue with Father, we tell him to go ahead search our possessions and our houses and find the money that Joseph is talking about. He will not find it and we will be in the clear and Joseph will look like a fool to father."

"That is a good idea for now, but what about the next time and time after that? I do not want to have to deal with the snake every time we make our private profits. Let us kill the boy and be done with it," said Simeon.

The Dreamer

"No. Murder is not an option," said Reuben. "We can look at all other options, except killing the boy. That is not an acceptable solution."

"How do you expect us to be free from this stinking little rat?" asked Zebulon, "if we don't get rid of him permanently?"

Naphtali and Levi joined in the argument and within a matter of minutes there was a free-for-all in the debate. Judah looked to Reuben, the undisputed leader of the older brothers. Undisputed by all except their father.

"Do something Reuben, nothing will get done like this," said Judah.

Just after Reuben had regained control of the hot debate, Asher spoke up, "You know as well as I do, we have to do something extreme or we will be plagued with the little rat dreamer for the rest of our lives."

"We won't have to. In another ten years we will have more than enough wealth to strike out on our own and be free from Grandfather Isaac and Father Jacob. Maybe sooner depending on the size of the flocks, we can get our hands on," said Reuben.

"Until then, what do we do with Joseph?" asked Simeon.

There was another outbreak of voices and opinions, most of which dealt with killing Joseph in one fashion or another.

"All right, all right! Quiet down, everyone. Quiet down," Reuben regained control of the rabid group. "We will consider killing the little viper when we can all be away from the homestead. We will have to have a solid plan though," said Reuben, giving way to the demands of the mob. "Until then we stick to the plan that Judah suggested and buried

The Dreamer

the recent profits with the money we already have."

The meeting was adjourned and everyone returned to their homes on the homestead and resumed their normal routine while Zebulon and Issachar took their money and left the homestead to bury it.

The next day when the sun was high in a cloudless sky and the bleating sounds of sheep along with the guttural sounds of the cattle were heard by Father Jacob as he made his way down from a sandy berm toward his pastoral grounds in the land of Canaan. Even though he had only been away for a few days, he was always happy to see the entirety of his temporal blessings, the vast pastures and stables for his flocks and herds. He saw at a distance his youngest son on a horse running flat out toward his caravan to greet him. Benjamin, with his dark brown hair and dark brown eyes, brought him much happiness as did his stalwart son Joseph, who was getting too old for such displays of admiration.

After a joyful reunion, Benjamin joined Jacob out in front of the caravan which was laden down with food, spices, fabric and many other household goods needed to maintain a sprawling estate along with other things that could only come from the city. After settling in, Israel sent Benjamin out with a message to every son and daughter and their families, instructing them to come to a feast that evening.

Joseph was feeling much better after taking time to rest from his harrowing trip in the sandstorm. He came to the feast early to give Israel the evil report of his four brothers, Dan, Naphtali, Gad, and Asher. Father Jacob listened intently as Joseph recited all the details of the plot he had uncovered.

His response to Joseph wasn't what he expected.

The Dreamer

"You have had the birthright for nearly two years now and though you are still just a boy, but with a mans responsibility. I expect great things from you. I expect you to be able to handle yourself among your brethren. You are strong and able both physically and spiritually. I expect you to be able to deal with your brethren and see that they do right by God and by the laws of my household. It is by handling the various issues that come up that help you develop wisdom and that takes time."

"But Father, they have threatened my life. They have sought to kill me. Would you have me use physical force with my brothers?" asked a deflated Joseph.

"I would prefer my sons get along with each other, but I know very well that they do not. I know they are jealous of you and they do not agree with me and the Lord in giving you the birthright. There are, apparently times when you may have to use your size to put a few of them in their place. That is not the preferred way, but there are times when that may be the only way."

"I know I am strong and big for my age, but how can I stand against four brothers at one time? That is what I would have had to do out in the fields if I were to have responded to their rustling of sheep."

"No, no, I guess you are right about that. It is one thing to physically stand up to one or two at a time. Tonight at the feast I am making a presentation to you. I will not tell you more than that because I want you to be surprised. I expect that afterward, your brothers will see you in a different light. That may help."

Joseph left his father wondering what had just happened. His father did not seem to be upset about the evil report and his father seemed to think that the power of the

The Dreamer

birthright should always prevail. One thing Joseph was good at was having faith in God and faith in his fathers' teachings. Of course, now he was wondering about his father's teachings since his father did not seem to care about the evil afoot in his household. Didn't he care that his sons were thieves and hurting other people?

The feast was well underway and everyone was well fed and enjoying themselves. As was usual in these settings, Joseph was surrounded by many of his brothers' wives and children. Both Joseph and Benjamin enjoyed time with the nephews and nieces. In many cases, they treated their older nephews and nieces as younger siblings.

After the servants had cleared away the dishes and stoked the fires, Father Jacob stood up and stroked his long gray beard. His presence commanded everyone's attention.

"The reason why I have called this feast was to make a public presentation to your brother Joseph. As you know, in accordance with the Patriarchal laws and the will of God, Joseph is the legal and lawful bearer of the birthright that I have bestowed upon him. While he has held that lofty position for two years now, he has not yet received the symbol of the birthright. When the coat was taken from Reuben, it was tattered, torn and useless. I commissioned another coat of many colors and I have it now. Joseph come up here and received the symbol of your office."

Joseph, in his youthful vigor, short beard and broad shoulders stood up tall. He walked with his head held high to where his father stood. His father held out a dazzling new coat with long sleeves and a twelve colored stripe pattern that ran from collar to hem. He helped Joseph put on the coat. It fit perfectly. The crowded hall filled to capacity with ten families erupted into a congratulatory applause, all

The Dreamer

except for the ten older brothers.

After the noise settled, Israel called on Joseph to say a few words. Joseph cleared his throat and started to speak. He wasn't prepared to speak and wasn't sure what to say.

He cleared his throat again, "I know that you all jokingly refer to me as the dreamer. That is all right. I do not mind. I feel the need to share a dream I have had recently. I would rather not share the dream and leave it to myself, but because of the urgency with which it was given to me, I feel the need to share it with you all."

He set the stage for the dream and how the dream came to him in a setting from the fields where they would harvest grain.

"The pile of sheaves I had was large and all the sheaves in that pile came together as one very large sheaf of grain. It stood upright. It was twice as tall as I am. All of your small sheaves joined together into eleven smaller sheaves. They stood at the feet of my sheaf and bowed down to my bundle. Your sheaves worshiped my sheaf."

There was a loud murmur in the audience, which came from each of the ten oldest brothers. The murmuring turned into angry catcalls. It was one thing to see their younger brother arrayed in a glorious coat of many colors. They didn't like that, but they could deal with it. But it was another thing entirely to see him stand and tell them they would all bow down to their younger brother as if he was to be their ruler and have dominion over them.

Joseph felt awkward and insecure at his brother's response. He turned to Israel for guidance. Father Jacob put his hands together like a spire in front of his face and bowed to Joseph encouraging him to go on with his speech.

Joseph took courage from his fathers' response. He

The Dreamer

stood tall, squared his shoulders and raised his voice to a commanding tone which restored order to the fray.

"I can only speak to you from the feelings of my heart and the words and dreams given me from the God of Abraham." The crowd quieted even more after hearing such a declaration.

"I received another dream after the dream of the sheaves. This dream was even more spectacular. In this dream, I saw countless stars of the heavens, and the moon. Then when the sun came out, eleven stars shone brighter than the rest. Along with the moon, they gave of their reflected light. When I came into the scene, I saw the eleven stars, the moon and the son all bow down to me and give me obeisance—"

Joseph was cut off sharply by murmuring from the audience. Joseph turned to his father for guidance. He saw Father Jacob along with Leah, Zilpah and Bilhah and grandfather Isaac all shook their heads in disbelief.

Oh no, I've done it now, thought Joseph. I've gone too far. But what was I supposed to do? The God of my fathers gave me these great dreams to share. If I didn't share these dreams with my family who would I have shared them with, the servants?

He looked around in the great hall and saw a commotion as the brothers were talking back and forth angrily gesturing toward Joseph. Father Jacob was still shaking his head as he spoke to Grandfather Isaac. The only people in the audience that seemed unaffected by what he had to say were the nephews and nieces scattered around, along with Dinah and Benjamin.

Seeing Dinah smiling and nodding her head reassuringly toward him gave Joseph courage. He tried

The Dreamer

unsuccessfully to get the audience's attention.

What have I done? Why would God give me these dreams with the strong feeling to share them with my family only to have them turn on me?

In spite of the uproar, he put his trust in God that he had done the right thing. He wasn't sure what would happen, but he knew he was correct which gave him peace. He turned to Father Jacob to see him listening to Grandfather Isaac. Jacob seemed to be agreeing with Isaac and his countenance was changing as Isaac spoke to him emphatically. Joseph stood on the stand alone commanding no one's attention.

Joseph started to notice slowly that the audience was quieting down. He looked around to see the cause of the shift in the mood. He saw Isaac in his frail state walking with Jacob to where Joseph was standing. There was a change in the countenance of his father.

Israel motioned for Joseph to step aside. By the time Jacob was in place to speak to the crowd they were all curiously quiet waiting to hear what rebuke Jacob would give their insulting and venomous little bother.

"My children. Give an ear to my words," said Israel, "when I heard the dream of the sheaves of grain, I was in agreement with it. It went along perfectly with the birthright Joseph has. He was entitled to receive that dream. When I heard the second dream, the dream where even me and his mother bowed down to him made me bristle at the very thought. As my dear Father Isaac reminded me, as the birthright is passed down from one generation to the next, so is the authority. While Joseph is only seventeen he is worthy of the mantle placed upon him. He is the chosen one of the God of our fathers. You will, we all will give Joseph the

The Dreamer

respect of the birthright and the mantle that comes with the coat of many colors."
    There was complete silence in the room. And for a moment, there was a peaceful spirit in the air, which didn't last long as they all started to file out of the great hall. Outside of that hall, the murmuring and complaining erupted again as fast and sure as a wildfire.

The Dreamer

Chapter 3: Obedience

Charity suffereth long, and is kind; charity envieth not; charity vaunteth not itself, is not puffed up. Doth not behave itself unseemly, seeketh not her own, is not easily provoked, thinketh no evil. Rejoiceth not in iniquity, but rejoiceth in the truth. Beareth all things, believeth all things, hopeth all things, endureth all things. 1 Corinthians 13:4-7

    A month passed and it was time to round up most of the sheep and send them to greener pastures to graze. This would take several weeks of work and organization. Throughout the homestead, everything was busy. Some were gathering the flocks while others continued to shear the sheep before they left. As was customary, Israel held classes three times a week to teach his family the glorious ways of the Hebrew God.

    While the other sons had never fully appreciated these opportunities to learn about God, Joseph never missed one if he was at home. As Benjamin was growing older, his interest was growing stronger in the classes. As the hour of the next class came up, Joseph told Judah, Zebulon and some of his other brothers standing nearby that he was leaving the fields and the hot dry weather to learn at the feet of his father in the comfort of a shaded garden.

    "Who does that little slithering serpent think he is?" asked Zebulon.

    "What he thinks he is and what he is are two very different things. That little serpent will get what's coming to him the first chance we get," responded Simeon as he wiped some of the perspiration from his forehead.

    "I do not know how much more I can take from that

The Dreamer

rat," said Levi shaking his fist. Judah just shook his head in disbelief.

With each passing day, Joseph's brothers grew angrier and more hateful toward him. The only members of his fathers' household that were peaceful toward him were his younger brother Benjamin, his father Jacob, his grandfather Isaac and his sister Dinah. After sharing the dreams he had with his family, some of his brothers' wives started to turn on him. He was starting to feel like a stranger in his own home.

As Joseph, with his strong gait, was walking toward the garden where the lessons were held he could hear both of his brothers and some servants speak evil about him, saying, "How does he possibly think he can reign over us?" While he could reprimand the servants, there was virtually nothing he could effectively do toward his brothers. He swallowed his pride and made his way to the shaded garden, all the while wishing he could beat some humility into his brothers.

"I know it has been hard for you Joseph since I rightfully bestowed the birthright on you two years ago and now that you officially have the symbol of the birthright in the coat of many colors. It seems your brethren are even more upset with you than ever before. I've told you before that you need to sometimes physically stand up for yourself and that is still true. However, there are other ways to deal with those who are opposed to you. That is to love them—"

"What?" exclaimed Joseph with a look of shock on his face. "How is that possible? It makes no sense. How can you possibly love those who hate you and abuse you?"

Warmly smiling, Israel went on to say, "There are many different types of love, the love of a friend, romantic

The Dreamer

love, a type of respect that includes love. I could go on, but the one thing that those types of love have in common is what we will talk about in today's lesson."

While some of Jacobs daughters, servants and daughters-in-law were in attendance, they were not permitted to speak. Only the men of the family could actively participate. Joseph and young Benjamin were the only students who could interact with Israel as was their tradition.

"There is an element of love that is more important than any other aspect of Godly attributes. The word for it is Charity. Without charity all the gifts and blessings we have are worthless."

Looking directly at Joseph, Father Jacob went on, "You are known for your dreams. Those dreams are God's way of using you to tell of things to come. This is a prophetic blessing. It is a great gift from God. However, if you do not have charity, then you are nothing. If you don't prove yourself by exercising charity, then with time, your gifts and blessings from the Lord will be taken from you and you will be left to your own devices."

Joseph's ruggedly handsome face showed worry in the furrows of his forehead and the shallow wrinkles around the corners of his mouth and eyes. Joseph nervously ran his large, strong hands through his thick brown hair.

Sensing that Joseph was concerned, Israel went on teaching that charity was more important than faith, good works, understanding mysteries or any other godly characteristic. But charity is something that, when understood, was easily within anyone's grasp if they were humble and sought after it.

"The special kind of love we are talking about is the attribute of being long-suffering, kind, and not puffed up in

The Dreamer

our own pride. It does not envy what others have and it does not put itself above others. We are all God's children and he loves every one of us the same."

Israel paused while he took a drink of fresh, cool water and he wiped perspiration from off his face. "He doesn't always love what his children do, but he wants every one of his children to come back and live with him in the end.

"If you want to have charity, then you cannot be selfish, or think of evil things. Don't allow yourself to be easily provoked and don't behave unseemly. If you have charity you have hope and you are willing to believe all good things that come from God, and you are willing, no matter how hard it is to endure all things put before you."

Even in the shade of the garden trees it was still hot and dry, just not as hot as in the fields. Joseph took a drink of water and then asked, "Father, I have always tried to do my best, but what you are teaching me seems impossible. How can a person possibly live at that level?"

"With God all things are possible. If you put forth your best efforts and keep trying and seeking after this level of living you will be richly blessed throughout your life."

Joseph took a long, deep breath and his face seemed to relax a little as he listened to these inspired words from the family Patriarch. Joseph had learned early on that if he did not fully understand his father, he eventually would if he was patient and looked to the God of Abraham for comfort and guidance.

~

"Benjamin, run out into the fields and find Reuben

The Dreamer

and tell him that I want to talk to him," said Father Jacob.

"Do I have to? It could take hours to find him. It is so hot out there. I am afraid I will roast to death. Can you wait until the evening meal to talk to him? Please?" whined Benjamin.

"I need to talk to him now, not this evening. Now, get a drink of water and go and do as you are told."

Benjamin wasn't happy, but at last he was obedient and ran out to find Reuben. As Benjamin feared, it took two hours that seemed like five hours to find Reuben and have him report back to Israel.

"Father. You called for me?"

"Reuben. Yes, come forward and sit down."

Reuben dusted himself off and took a drink from the large bucket of fresh water as he stepped before Israel and sat down.

"It is time to take the flock to greener fields. You will be in charge of your brothers and the expedition."

"Does not that job belong to young Joseph, the bearer of the birthright?" said Reuben sardonically.

"Yes, it does, but he is not going," said Israel.

"He will never earn our respect if he does not carry his weight and work the sheep and herds with us."

"Do not worry yourself about Joseph. He will be staying behind to manage the herds and to teach Benjamin a little about the farm and the herds. He is pulling his weight just fine."

"Whatever you say, Father, you are the Patriarch of the family. Where would you like us to graze the flock?"

"I want you to take the sheep to Shechem. We have not used that land in years and it should be thick and well prepared for our flock."

The Dreamer

"Certainly you cannot be serious. I do not think it is safe for us to be there so soon after we fled out of that land," said Reuben scornfully.

"It has been several years and if we do not make an effort to use the land someone might take it for themselves. The land is legally ours. Surely you and your brothers can handle yourselves if there is any conflict. You managed to do plenty well fighting in Shechem those many years ago. Take extra servants with you if you are afraid for your safety," said Father Jacob.

"Very well. We should be ready within a week to depart," said Reuben in a tone indicating that he had given up.

"Do not rustle any sheep while you are gone."

Reuben's eyes lit up when he heard that statement.

"Joseph told me what happened when he was out with Dan, Gad, Asher, and Naphtali. That practice had better stop or you and your brothers will be without any inheritance at all," said Father Jacob sternly.

Reuben was furious when he heard what his father had just said. He got up and stomped out of the hall without saying anything more. That night at the evening meal he told his brothers, they would be having a meeting after they had finished eating. During dinner, Joseph and Benjamin were sitting by each other and talking.

"Joseph, you are so lucky to have memories of our mother. You and all the rest of my brothers all know their mothers. It is not fair that I do not know anything about her except for what I am told. I do not have any memories," sighed Benjamin.

"I never thought of that. I can understand that you would be upset. I can tell you that there will never be another

The Dreamer

woman born to this earth that is as fair and lovely as our mother was," said Joseph comfortingly.

"Beside what she looked like, what was she like?"

She was gentle and kind. I do not have as many memories of her as you might think. I was young when she died. But I do remember sitting on her lap and being held by her. She loved me and taught me some important things."

"Do you remember what those things were?"

"Not as much as I remember how she taught me."

"What do you mean by that?"

"I remember that she taught with love and she made me feel like I wanted to do what she told me to do," Joseph dabbed a tear away.

Shaking his head like he was starting to understand, Benjamin asked, "Do you think that could happen to me since I do not know how it felt to be in her presence?"

Joseph was not sure how to answer that question. As he thought about it, he took a sip of water and dabbed his forehead.

"For me, our Mother is a symbol of love and all that is right with the world. I feel her when I do good, and sometimes when I feel sad and alone. It is similar to how the Holy Spirit works with us." Joseph saw the expression of a question on Benjamin's face.

"When was the last time you did something good or right? Can you remember?" asked Joseph.

"Earlier today it seemed hotter than usual and I was tired and I did not want to finish working in a pig pen. I was ready to leave early, but I remembered a lesson that Father Jacob taught us once about honesty and so I decided to stay and finish the work."

"How did you feel after you were finished with the

The Dreamer

work?" asked Joseph.

"Hot and sweaty."

Joseph smiled at his response. "Other than that, how did you feel? You know, how did you feel inside?"

"Thinking for a moment, Benjamin said, "I felt strong and good inside, like I could be relied on."

"There you go. You felt good inside. If you had quit and walked away without finishing the job you would have felt bad or guilty for not doing it right?"

"Right," Benjamin nodded in agreement.

"Where did the good feeling come from?" Joseph asked encouragingly.

Benjamin had a look like he knew, but didn't have the words to express it. He thought a for a few moments and then looked at Joseph silently asking for some help.

"When we do something good we get a good feeling and when we do something bad we get a bad feeling. The Holy Spirit helps us with those good feelings we have."

Benjamin nodded as it dawned on him what Joseph was getting at. Joseph went on to say. "Like all that, when I do good or right things I feel good, sometimes from the Holy Spirit and other times it feels like a loving feeling from Mother Racheal. It looks like you are starting to understand and I think if you pray and ask the Lord to help you discern, maybe you can feel her. If you are not sure where that good feeling comes from just know that it is all the same because our Mother was deeply committed to the God of our Fathers."

Benjamin replied by taking a deep breath and shaking his head, which indicated that he only partially understood what Joseph was telling him.

"How about you and I go talk to Father Jacob? He

The Dreamer

might have a better answer than I do," said Joseph.

"Yes. That is a good idea. Maybe right after we are finished eating?"

"Yes, as soon as we are done eating. Now eat. My food is getting cold."

The evening meal was over and Joseph, and Benjamin were in conversation with Father Jacob, which meant that Reuben and his brothers would have to find another place to meet. They decided to go to Reuben's house. His house was the largest among the brothers.

"Father knows about our sheep rustling and keeping the profits," announced Reuben angrily.

"Let me guess, Joseph got to him after all," replied Simeon with contempt.

"Exactly. He threatened us with taking away our inheritance if we did not stop."

"That filthy venomous little serpent," said Asher red faced. "Who does he think he is?"

"We have to do something about him," said Naphtali in frustration.

"He thinks he is so wonderful that he can rule over us. That will be the day," said Issachar with a snide tone to his voice.

"Father thinks Joseph is so wonderful, such a great leader with the birthright and he cannot even keep from getting lost in a sandstorm," bellowed Gad.

"I called this meeting," said Reuben in a loud voice, "To tell you that we have a week to get everything ready to take the flock out to graze."

"Where are we taking them?" asked Levi still shaking his head in animosity.

"Shechem," answered Reuben.

The Dreamer

"Really? That should be interesting," replied Simeon with an evil grin on his face.

"That concerns me," said Dan. "What we did there and how we fled so fast, do you think those people have forgotten us?"

"I hope so. I am not afraid to fight, but I would rather not," said Judah trying to sound strong.

"Father thinks it will be all right and he thinks the grass will be thick and green and perfect for the sheep," added Reuben.

"Well, if we only have a week to get started, then we better get ourselves a good night's rest and get started early in the morning," said Judah.

Chapter 4: Forgiveness

So shall ye say unto Joseph, Forgive, I pray thee now, the trespass of thy brethren, and their sin; for they did unto thee evil: and now, we pray thee, forgive the trespass of the servants of the God of thy father. And Joseph wept when they spake unto him. Genesis 50:17

    Five months had passed since Reuben led his brothers and their thousands of sheep to their seasonal grazing in Shechem. During those five-months, Joseph and Benjamin had been regularly taught more in the ways of doctrine and the ways of managing the estate. Benjamin wasn't as interested in these topics as he was in spending time with his brother and father, but he did learn. Joseph was gaining more confidence in his responsibilities while having this extra time with his father.
    After their midday meal Dinah, Benjamin and Joseph went for a walk in the shady garden with the sky a brilliant blue and long shadows cast over the garden giving them good relief from the scorching sun. They were enjoying a nice conversation with each other when Benjamin asked, "Dinah, how come you are not married?"
    "Benjamin that is not a polite thing to ask," responded Joseph. Dinah blushed.
    "All of our brothers are married and all of our sisters except Dinah are married. Why is that not a polite thing to ask? I am just curious," replied Benjamin weakly. Dinah was still blushing.
    "You do not need to know that. Go over to the barn and feed the livestock," demanded Joseph with an air of authority.

The Dreamer

"I did not mean to do anything wrong," replied Benjamin as he got up and left the great hall.

"Thank you for that," said Dinah as Benjamin closed the door.

"You are welcome. I hope I was never like that when I was that young," said Joseph.

"You were young and foolish just like Benjamin, but in different ways. It is part of growing up. I suppose we all went through something like that when we were young," said Dinah.

"Dinah, since the topic has come up, if you do not want to talk about it, then tell me, but from what I know about your story with Shechem, I have wondered why you have not married. You did nothing wrong. So why not marry?"

"We are only suppose to marry Hebrews and since I am not a virgin, no one wants to marry me."

"Why does that part of your life matter to anyone?"

"You are young, Joseph, maybe too young for this conversation."

"I am young I know, but I do know about life and from what I know about your story, what happened should not be held against you."

"Well, I was there – "

"But from what I have heard from my brothers you were not a willing participant. Is that right?"

"That is true. I did tell him to stop and he refused. He said he wanted to marry me, but– "

"If he really wanted to marry you then why did he treat you like that?"

"I have wondered that many times before," said Dinah wistfully.

The Dreamer

"Maybe what Simeon and Levi did was not such a bad thing," observed Joseph.

"Father Jacob did not think it was a wise thing for them to do and I think I agree. I am not sure killing Shechem, and Hamor was right. I know that killing all the men in Shechem was wrong, I know that much for sure."

"I do not know if I agree. If I was old enough and understood, I may have joined my brothers, at least in killing Shechem. Maybe not all the men in the city of Shechem, but at least the man who hurt you."

"I have spent much time talking with Father and with my Mother Leah. I think forgiveness is a better way to go in the end, at least better than trying to exact revenge."

"But what he did to you still affects you making it so that you are not married and not having your own kids. He really hurt you with a pain that will last your whole life," said Joseph with a hint of rage in his voice. "How can you possibly forgive anyone who has done something like that to you?"

"Forgiveness is not easy, but it is worth it in the long run. My life is not ruined. There is more than one way to live life and who knows, I may still marry," replied Dinah hopefully.

"Maybe you are crazy or maybe I do not understand . . . How can you forgive someone like that for what they did to you?"

"What he did to me was wrong and it was terrible, but if I did not forgive him, he would still be hurting me even to this very day. Forgiving him was a smart way to get over what he did to me."

"Please forgive me Dinah, I am young I know it, but I am not dumb, but I just do not understand what you are saying, it makes no sense . . ." Joseph was getting frustrated.

"Forgiving means many things, but the most important parts of forgiving is to let go of what they did to you – "

"But – " Joseph was trying to interrupt.

"Just hear me out. Sit still and listen to me my dear young brother."

"All right, I will be quiet, go on."

"I could harbor all those terrible feelings from what Shechem did to me. If I hold onto all those angry feelings, then whenever I remember back, it would still hurt. I would be hurting all the time. Letting go of it and trying not to dwell on it freed me from being hurt again by him. I strive to not let what happened continue to hurt me or define me. What I am is not a victim to Shechem, but a daughter of God who has a lot to offer my family and my God."

There were several years just after it all happened that I felt like I was under his control even though he was dead and gone. But with the advice and counsel from Mother Leah and Father Jacob, I am free from the effect of Shechem. That is my forgiveness to him. It is strange that forgiving him helps me."

"Since you have forgiven him, does that mean he should not have been punished?" asked Joseph.

"Not at all. He should have been punished, not killed, but punished. He should not be allowed to ever do that again to any other woman."

"So maybe killing him like Simeon and Levi did was not so bad after all. Since he is dead, he can no longer hurt any other woman," suggested Joseph.

"Maybe all you brothers are alike after all, all you talk about is killing . . ." Dinah's voice trailed off.

The Dreamer

Joseph did not like being compared to his brothers. He meant what he said in the most sincere way.

"I am sorry Dinah, I will no longer mention killing Shechem. I do not want to add to your burden."

"Let us turn the tables Joseph. We both know how rotten our brothers have been to you. Do you carry that hurt feeling around, or have you forgiven them for their meanness?"

"I do not know. I have never thought of it. I know Father has talked about forgiveness before, but not like we have today. I guess I have not fully forgiven them."

"Do you think you should?" asked Dinah.

"Yes, I probably should. What they have done to me is far less than what has been done to you," said Joseph thoughtfully.

"Think about it and consider fully forgiving them. I have to go help prepare the evening meal," said Dinah as she walked up to Joseph and gave him a hug.

~

Father Jacob called Benjamin into the great hall. "Son, I need you to go find Joseph and tell him I need to see him after he was done with his work at the end of the day."

After looking around, Benjamin found Joseph working in the barn with some cows. "Father wants to see you when your work is done for the day," Benjamin said matter of factly.

"Do you know what he wants of me?" asked Joseph.

"He did not tell me. All he said was that he wanted to speak with you."

The Dreamer

"All right then, thanks for the message." Faithful to his fathers' wishes, Joseph went directly to his father's house after his last job was completed.

"It has been five months since your brothers have left for Shechem, and I have not yet received word from them. They were supposed to send a servant once a month with a report on how they are doing," said Israel with a worried tone in his voice.

"I want you to take tomorrow and prepare everything you need for a long trip and the next day rise up early and travel to the land of Shechem, and check on the flocks and your brothers and then return and bring me an update."

"Benjamin might want to come – "

"No!" declared Israel. "He will stay behind."

"I will gladly do as you wish," said Joseph eager to see if the forgiveness he had given his brothers would hold up once he saw them in person.

Joseph brought with him two servants and enough pack animals for all the required provisions. He led the small caravan. As they rode on day after day under the burning heat of the scorching sun, Joseph tried striking up a conversation with both of the servants. They were respectful yet withdrawn. In the past, he never seemed to have any trouble talking with any of the servants. This was an unusual circumstance. He wondered if he should flat out ask them why they seemed to be hesitant in speaking with them, then the thought came to him that they may have had a change of heart from all the anti Joseph feelings that his brothers had been spreading throughout the estate. The more he thought about it, the more likely it seemed. He kept to himself the rest of the trip.

Joseph had seldom experienced loneliness in the

The Dreamer

past because he always felt at home in his mind. In his mind, he felt safe, safe from the evil words and ridicule from his hateful brothers and he felt a calming, peaceful feeling as he pondered on the things of God. Sometimes in his mind, memories of his dear mother flourished.

Why has God chosen me to have the birthright? Why do my brothers hate me so badly? If they would simply follow the commandments of the Hebrew God, they would be so much happier and content, and they wouldn't have any reason to hate me so much and to treat me so badly, Joseph thought to himself.

Joseph was eight years old when his mother Racheal died while giving birth to Benjamin. He tried hard to remember what she looked like. Sometimes he would dream about her, but in the light of day, all that was left of those dreams were great memories of love. These memories had a physical quality about them. It was as if he could feel warm inside as he thought about his mother's love for him. He also reflected on the many things she taught him in his young life. Those that he remembered all centered around love.

Joseph wasn't old enough to get married, but he always knew he would marry a righteous woman favored of God. He wouldn't deliberately do anything to sin against the birthright. He knew something about the birthright that his brothers seem to overlook. The birthright blessings were not just the leadership role over the family and the flocks, herds and lands. The birthright was also a spiritual blessing.

His father told him when he gave him the birthright that is was immense responsibility. If Joseph strived to please the Lord, he would have the capacity to bare up the great responsibilities.

He yearned for a friendly relationship with his older

The Dreamer

brethren and he felt like he would do anything he possibly could to earn their acceptance, anything that is, except evil deeds. He loved his brothers dearly, but he loved God more.

The Dreamer

Chapter 5: Friends

A friend loveth at all times, and a brother is born for adversity. Proverbs 17:17

Joseph and his small caravan arrived on the outskirts of the grazing lands of Shechem. The only sign of the massive flock his brothers were herding was the grass being eaten to the roots. It was late in the day so he took his small party to a nearby hillside to set up camp. He was hoping that if he was elevated above the horizon he would have a better chance at finding his brothers in the valley below.

While the servants were preparing their nightly camp, Joseph wandered around the nearby hillside looking for trails that would take him higher up the mountainside allowing him a better view as he searched for his brothers and sheep.

The valley below was vast with scattered trees and patches of yellow and brown where the sheep had grazed too close to the earth. The valley was surrounded by mountains on three sides. The sunset was spectacular with the blazing orange disc setting beyond the brink with the shimmering heat rising up from the ground, creating a glimmering bright yellow and orange dance on the distant horizon.

The sun was about down when he ran into an older man, perhaps the age of Levi or Judah, with a small flock of sheep.

Greetings to you young fellow," said the elderly man.

"Greetings to you good sir. How are you getting along this evening?" asked Joseph. "I am doing as well as can be expected," the older man found a stump to sit on.

"My name is Joseph, son of Jacob also known as

The Dreamer

Israel."

"I am Mordecai."

"Are you out gathering strays?" Asked Joseph.

"In a manner of speaking, yes. These are not even my strays. Two months ago five men along with their servants stole my flock. They blended it in with their large flock and left in the direction of Dothan."

"Would you happen to know the names of any of these men?" asked Joseph. He had a sick feeling Mordecai may have met up with his brothers and their evil ways.

"I heard them talking between themselves and I heard two names, Dan and Levi. They are common names so I doubt it is much help to you."

"Could you describe any of these men?" asked Joseph.

"Not really." Mordecai tugged at his salt and pepper beard.

"For all I know they looked like you meaning they were Hebrew like you and me," said Mordecai.

"I have ten brothers who are grazing a large flock of thousands of sheep. They were sent here, to Shechem, by my father Israel. I have been sent to check on their condition. The only problem is I cannot find them," said Joseph as he tried to shake the grit and sand from his robe.

"There was a very large flock grazing here a few months ago, but they have long since left in the direction of Dothan," said Mordecai.

"I think the men who stole my flock were part of the great flock you are talking about," said Mordecai. "I do not know if they were your brothers, but I think they were all family."

"It is getting late, would you like to make camp with

The Dreamer

me and my servants?"

"Yes. It has been a lonely two months. When they stole my sheep, my servants left me. I would love the company."

They walked back to the camp to find the evening meal cooking on an open fire. The pleasant scent of food stirred the hunger already in their bellies. The rise and fall of the flames caused shadows to dance off of Joseph's face. As Mordecai was looking at Joseph, the feeling of familiarity came over him. Could this nice young man be related to the evil men who robbed him?

They enjoyed each others company and talked until late in the night. Mordecai had been a successful Shepard for many years, now he was reduced to gathering strays to try and rebuild his flock. It would be hard work, but he had no choice if he wanted to remain a Shepard. He had no other skills.

The more they talked the more Mordecai trusted the lad who was before him. He wanted to help him find his brothers, but he was now sure Joseph was related to the men who had ambushed him and stole his sheep. He wondered if anything would happen to him if he helped this friendly young man?

"Joseph, as I have been looking at you, I feel like I see some familiarity between you and the men that robbed me. It is almost as if you were brothers. You share some similar features with them. Your build and the way you conduct yourself. Of course, they never spoke with me, they just yelled and ordered me around threatening me."

"Among my older ten brothers, two of them are named Dan and Levi. In the past, my brothers have had problems stealing sheep from nearby flocks. I have a feeling

The Dreamer

my brothers may indeed have robbed you," said Joseph.

"Will you steal my few sheep from me?" asked a concerned Mordecai. *Is this nice young man like his brothers?*

"No. I will not. In fact, what I will do is offer to take you with me and verify my brothers rustled your sheep. I will return your stolen sheep to you along with extra sheep to make it up to you. Even though I am the youngest of my ten brothers, my father has placed me in charge and they will have to do what I tell them," said a determined Joseph.

"I appreciate that, but I think I will start over with what I can find around here. I am very afraid of your brothers and with all due respect, I do not think they will listen to you and return my sheep. I fear I may die if I see them again," said Mordecai.

The fire was low and they were growing tired so they stoked the fire and went to sleep.

That night, as was typical, Joseph's sleep was invaded with dreams. His first dream was the familiar dream of the eleven stars, the moon and the sun paying homage to him.

The next dream was a joyous one. In it, his brothers and Joseph were enjoying each others company. There was no hint of jealously or profane speech. His brothers treated him as an equal. There may have been a hint of his brothers treating him with a degree of respect. Joseph couldn't be sure because he was so surprised by the reaction of his brothers and their new attitude they were demonstrating toward him. He awoke from the dream with a smile and a heart filled with joy. Once he was awake, he realized sadly, it was only a dream and the joy that filled his heart was replaced with despair and longing.

The Dreamer

The reality of the dream served as a reminder about how he and his brothers didn't get along and the deep resentment his brothers had toward him. He had no idea how deep that resentment was, although he would soon find out.

"It is unfortunate that we do not have more time together," said Joseph, but I have to be moving on with all haste."

"If that large flock is indeed going to Dothan, it will likely take six weeks, maybe more, to make the trip. Maybe even two months, but with your small caravan you should be able to make the trip in two weeks, maybe sooner if you ride hard."

"Thank you for that information. My best wishes to you and your new flock," said Joseph as his camel made its way up onto his hooves.

After Mordecai bid Joseph farewell, he gathered his small flock and walked on. He kept close to the side of the hills so he could look for more strays in the cracks and crevices of the surrounding hillside. He was impressed with this young man and trusted that he was indeed good. He had an unusual spirit about him. How could one family produce both evil thieves and an honorable young man?

As they took off, Joseph sent one servant back to Israel with a message that he hadn't found the flocks or his brothers yet. Joseph would be heading to Dothan. He ended the message assuring his father, he would send word as soon as he could, once he caught up with his brothers.

They rode from sun up until sun down as they continued on their Journey to Dothan. Joseph had a lot of time to think about his life and where he was and where he was going. He thought of love and marriage and wondered

The Dreamer

when he might find the right one. He knew his father had many contacts that could help provide a worthy companion. He was hoping he could find the right one and avoid the trouble Father Jacob had when it came time for him to take a wife.

Jacob had to work fourteen years in order to receive permission to marry Racheal. First he worked for the agreed upon seven years to marry Racheal. Then Laban, the father of Racheal, tricked Jacob by giving him Leah to marry. After Jacob married Leah, he discovered Laban had tricked him. Laban said he could marry Racheal if he would work another seven years. Because Father Jacob was so in love with Racheal, he agreed. Young Joseph thought it was a romantic story and he was grateful his father worked that extra seven years, otherwise, Rachel would not be his mother. He loved his mother. He was grateful for his father sticking it out for seven more years. He did not want to have to go through a trial like that.

He was grateful that Father Jacob had given each of his sons a share in the massive flocks and herds he owned. Because of that, Joseph would be able to afford a complete dowry to his future father-in-law.

Now all that remained was to find a righteous woman he could marry. She would have to share in many of her traits like his dear sweet mother, Racheal. He loved the Hebrew God his Father Jacob had taught him about. He wanted to please God with the right kind of marriage. He wanted to do as his father before him had done and that was to raise his children in the ways of the Lord. He hoped his children turned out better than Jacobs oldest ten sons. He would emphasize to his children not to be to so worldly, greedy and full of pride. Joseph wondered if there was any

The Dreamer

hope for his older brothers. Would they someday repent for what they had done?

He wondered what was different between him and his brothers? His brothers were taught the ways of the Lord as Joseph was, yet they had chosen to follow a different path in their lives and Joseph had chosen to live his life dedicated to the God of Abraham, Isaac, and Jacob. Benjamin seemed to be following in Joseph's footsteps.

The days on the trail were long, hot and hard traveling from sun up until sun down and Joseph, even with his young and strong body, was getting wary of the trip. The long dusty days never seemed to end. The flaming sun was glowing hot and beat down hard on Joseph and his servant. He was covered with grit from head to toe. They hadn't come across any rivers or oasis's over the last week, so all Joseph and his servant could drink was the warm water carried on the back of their donkey.

Just as Joseph was on the verge of complaining, he noticed some haze on the horizon. As he kept a careful watch he noticed as they inched forward, there was a huge flock of sheep miles ahead of them on the horizon. Those sheep were kicking up the dry ground as they foraged on the low-lying vegetation. The size of that herd made Joseph think it could be his father's herd. After a few more miles he came to the conclusion that indeed, he had finally found his father's flock. He spurred the camel into a trot to make better time.

The Dreamer

Chapter 6: The Dreamer Cometh

The thoughts of the wicked are an abomination to the Lord: but the words of the pure are pleasant words. Proverbs 15:26

"Behold the Dreamer comes," yelled out Judah. His brothers, Levi and Issachar heard Judah and came running up to him.

"Why is that slithering snake even here? I thought Father Jacob was keeping him home safe and sound?" said Issachar, in a snide tone as he brushed his tunic with his left hand. He held a bottle of wine in the right hand.

"That is a good question. Why is the dung beetle Joseph coming?" asked Levi as he stood up.

By now the rest of the brothers who had been sitting idly in the main camp were up and milling around Judah.

"I have a great idea," said Simeon, "let us slay him, and finally be done with him like we were talking about back at home. We could rip him off the camel and beat him to death."

"Yes! I agree," said Levi. Most of the brothers also cried out in agreement.

"We can kill him and tear up his precious coat of many colors," suggested Simeon.

"Yes, then we dip it in goats' blood and tell father a wild animal killed him," added Levi.

"That is a perfect idea. Finally, after all these years we won't have to be constantly looking over our shoulders for that venomous little snake," said Gad.

They all seemed to be in agreement. When the dreamer came into camp, they would grab him and beat him

The Dreamer

and finally kill him. They were getting lathered up in their murderous furor.

"I can't wait to see him dead," said Gad, "we will just see what happens to all of his dreams when he is dead and buried."

"We will not be bowing to him that is for certain," added Simeon as he threaded his fingers through his dirty dark brown hair.

Reuben was walking up to the group and overheard their threats.

"Do not kill the boy. None of us will be guilty of shedding his blood. There is a dry well on the other side of the campfire. Throw him into the pit for now and we will figure out what to do with him, but he will not be killed. Even though Reuben no longer possessed the birthright, all of his brothers respected him and treated him as their leader.

The rest of the brothers grumbled when they heard from Reuben.

"Well, maybe we will not kill him, but we will not bring him back to Canaan. This is our chance to be rid of him once and for all," said Levi.

"Killing Joseph would kill Father. It would break his heart. We will work it out later, but do not kill the boy," commanded Reuben as he swallowed some fresh water.

Joseph was inching forward and growing closer by the minute.

"I don't care about Father's feelings. He has always loved Joseph and favored him over us for as long as the snake has been alive," said Asher accusingly.

"This is the perfect opportunity to be rid of Joseph," added Dan as he dipped his cup into a barrel of fresh water.

"I said we will resolve the matter later. I have to check

The Dreamer

on the east end of the flock. Do not kill him!" emphasized Reuben. "Just put him in the pit over there," he motioned, "and be done with it. You can remove his coat of many colors if you want, but nothing more. Do you all understand? And do some work for a change."

Reuben's brothers either nodded their head in assent or they said nothing. Reuben climbed onto his camel and headed to the east side of the sprawling flock.

"Look," exclaimed Naphtali, he's getting close. The dreamer is about here. What is our plan?"

"We will do what Reuben said and take off his coat and throw him into the dry well," said Judah. "For now, we will do nothing more."

"What if he resists?" asked Dan spitefully.

"Let us hope he does," said Simeon. "That will give us an excuse to rough him up a little."

Joseph was close enough that they all could hear his camel hooves slapping the hard-packed earth. They were all excited and aching to bring down their rage on the poor unsuspecting Joseph.

Joseph wasn't sure what to make of this crowd of brothers that seemed to surround him as he climbed off his camel. No sooner had he got his feet on the ground when his body was upended and he fell flat on his back knocking the wind out of him. He felt some ribs crack as he hit the hard ground. He saw a blinding flash of light before everything went black for a matter of seconds. While on the ground, he felt many feet kicking him in the head, shoulders, and ribs. He still couldn't breathe. He raised his arms up to try and protect his head and face only to find someone was stepping on the sleeve of his right arm. He flailed his left arm to no avail.

The Dreamer

His body was instinctively thrashing around while trying to get up and away from these angry vultures. *What is going on? Why are they doing this to me? What have I done to deserve this? I need to get up.* He finally regained his breath and was sucking in air. He was dazed and confused at the vicious assault by so many men. He felt their feet kicking him and stomping all over his body. In an instant, his right arm came loose and he was able to move his upper body enough to roll onto his side.

The intensity of the kicking and stomping increased and spread to the newly exposed shoulder and back. *Why is this happening? What have I done to deserve this?* While he was on his side, he was able to partially curl his shoulders toward his thighs, which allowed him to change positions enough that he was able to roll onto his hands and feet and quickly get up. As he got to his feet, his fists were flying all around him with no particular target.

As he was swinging his fists, everyone took a defensive step or two backward to get out of range of his arms. Suddenly there was a sticky warm salty taste in his mouth. Until then he hadn't realized he was bleeding from his nose. He was also starting to notice other cuts and scrapes on his face and exposed skin.

Joseph found himself surrounded by his brothers and maybe a few servants. He didn't take time to do a proper count. He was dancing on his feet moving side to side and then front and back trying to keep everyone off guard while he regained as much composure and strength as he could.

"Why are you doing this to me?" asked Joseph to everyone in front of him.

The only response he heard was hideous laughing and cursing directed at him. As profanity-laced the dry, hot

The Dreamer

air, Joseph tried to wipe the sweat and blood from his face.

He wanted to know what was happening? He was happy to see his brothers hoping for another chance at healing the rift between him and them.

"Tighten the circle," said Simeon, "then on my mark, we will all advance on him and take him down. One . . . two . . . three, go!"

They all lunged at Joseph at the same time, but before taking him down, he was able to knock Judah and Asher down and as he started to fall he took Gad and Levi with him.

He now had his wits about him and he was fighting with everything he had. He was rolling around on the dry packed earth trying to keep Gad and Levi with him on the hard ground while trying to pull down anyone else he could. The more men sprawled on the ground, the fewer standing to kick him. He managed to pull down Issachar, but that was all. He was rolling around trying to get out of range of their savage feet.

He starting kicking his legs in any fashion possible and he saw someone else drop. *Maybe I can beat them all. Why are they doing this? What have I done to deserve this?* There was a slight reprieve in the onslaught which was enough to get back on his feet. As he stood unsteadily on his feet, things seemed to be blurry. His eyes were already starting to swell shut from the savage kicks to his head. He was amazed that he felt no pain, just rage, and confusion. He was breathing in gulps and wincing as he did. If every rib in his body wasn't broken, they were at least severely bruised.

Because of his blurred vision, he could no longer recognize his brother's faces. One of them came up thinking

The Dreamer

to make sport of his condition and sucker punch him from the side. While he had poor vision, he still had some peripheral vision and was able to see his brothers approach. Joseph whirled around and knocked his brother down with a stinging blow to his cheek and nose. Joseph felt something crush and break beneath his fist. Was it, his fingers or his brothers face? He couldn't tell, maybe both. He fell down with the force of his swing. He was exhausted and was starting to lose energy. He was on his knees trying to suck in as much painful air as possible, trying to regain energy and composure.

"Stand him up," said Levi, "let us tear the royal robe off of him. When Joseph heard them talking about the symbol of the birthright, the coat of many colors, something stirred within him giving him fresh energy. He used Simeon to get on his feet by pulling on his clothes and as he did, he threw his fist into Simeon's gut and then followed up with a knee to Simeon's face. He fell to the ground. Then Asher came after Simeon to be knocked unconscious with another fierce blow by Joseph.

Two more brothers approached him from behind and two from in front of him. He dropped one, then the second brother only to feel someone grab him by his neck and he felt a knee forcefully burrow into his back. Against his will, his knees buckled underneath him and he dropped to the ground. Starbursts of pain coursed through his back, up his spine and exploded into his head. The searing pain caused him to moan.

Why are my brothers trying to kill me? He needed to know, to make sense of all of this violence. He felt them yanking, tugging and pulling his coat of many colors off of him. He prayed for more strength and started to thrash

The Dreamer

around trying to break free from his brother's grip. He couldn't under any circumstances allow them to take possession of the coat of many colors. It was highly symbolic and sacred. He tried to regain his footing, but what strength was left in him was not enough to stand.

As he tried to roll off of his back and onto his stomach, he saw something approaching his face very fast. He felt a dull thud on his face. He felt his nose flatten, the limited light his eyes could see turned black.

All nine of his brothers started grabbing and tearing at his coat. By the time they got it off it was torn and thrashed as if an animal had worked it over. The bloody coat lay on the ground in tatters. They turned their attention to Joseph. He was lying limp on the ground. His face was smeared with fresh blood. Dust and dirt clung to the sticky blood creating a bloody paste over most of his face.

They dragged him over to the pit and started to push him over the side into the hole when Judah cried out, "Stop! Turn him around. If he goes in head first he will break his neck."

"That would be perfect. He breaks his neck and then we can bury him down there. That is perfect," said Levi as he tentatively touched his bumps and bruises.

"No. No, we are not going to kill him," said Judah with profound determination. "For now, we toss him feet first into the pit." He looked at his eight brother's faces and wished Reuben was there to back him up. All he could see where his brothers stood was evil, seething, murderous rage in the eyes of eight angry men.

"For now just toss him feet first. We will decide later when Reuben comes back what to do with him," said Judah hoping that would be enough of a compromise. It was. They

The Dreamer

turned him around and slid him slowly into the deep dry pit. The hole in the well was just big enough for his body to fit through, but Joseph was unconscious and couldn't use his feet or arms to control his fall. He banged his head several times as he tumbled to the bottom of the pit. He made a thud when he reached the bottom. The brothers turn their evil rage to the coat of many colors.

Issachar picked up the bloody robe and started to tear it more. Gad grabbed at it. "I want a piece of that bloody cloth," he was seething in anger.

Simeon grabbed the coat away from both of them and held it up in the air. "Hold on now, hold on." In an exaggerated tone he said, "Let us all bow ourselves down to this wonderful, colorful coat and give humble obeisance. Let us worship this holy symbol, this bloody, filthy symbol of pride that Joseph will no longer wear."

"One last thing, what do we do with his servant?" asked Simeon as they all turned toward Joseph's last servant.

Joseph's frighten servant responded by spitting into the nearby pit, "You do not need to worry about me, I never respected the worm."

Levi walked up from behind the servant and slapped him on the back. "That is right," he also spat into the dry well, "he is a worm."

All nine brothers whooped and hollered and exaggerated their bows before the coat of many colors.

~

The Dreamer

It was dark when Reuben arrived back at the main camp. "What happened with the dreamer?" he asked with curiosity and disdain.

"We put him in the pit like you said to do."

Reuben walked over to the pit and yelled down, "Joseph, are you all right? You brought this all on yourself. I told you to stop with all the dreams and parading that coat of many colors around all the time, but you wouldn't listen to me." Reuben couldn't hear anything from Joseph so he called after him one more time. "Joseph?"

He turned to Simeon and Dan, "Why doesn't he respond? What have you done to him? Is he dead? Why can't he hear me?"

"I don't know," said Dan. "Maybe he's asleep." He laughed.

"We had to get a little rough with him to get him into the well," confessed Simeon with a smile of satisfaction.

Reuben drew a stick of burning wood from the fire and held it over the pit try to illuminate the well enough for him to see down to the bottom. All he could see were shadows.

Reuben got a bucket of water and threw it on Joseph. He managed to hear some moaning, but Joseph didn't respond to Reuben's questions. *Well, at least he's alive* thought Reuben. *What will tomorrow bring*?

The Dreamer

Chapter 7: Trust In The Lord

Trust in the Lord with all thine heart; and lean not unto thine own understanding. In all thy ways acknowledge him, and he shall direct thy paths. Proverbs 3:5-6

It had been three days since Joseph had been thrown in the pit. Reuben had commanded his brothers to feed him and send water down to him at least twice a day. The brothers decided to have fun with the unwanted responsibility. As they all took turns sending food and water down to him, they all took turns wearing the tattered and bloody coat of many colors. As yet, they had not killed a goat to dip the robe into, but it was still bloody from Joseph's many wounds. It almost looked as bad as if a wild animal had torn it off of Joseph.

The first day had been Simeon and Levi's turn. The next day Judah and Issachar each took turns wearing the tattered coat when they fed and watered Joseph. "Look at me young Joseph. I have the royal birthright right now," declared Issachar mocking him in the process. The third day was Zebulon and Gad. They both mocked Joseph telling him to worship them as they wore the coat of many colors.

The pit was close to the main campfire and Joseph could easily hear what his brothers talked about as they lazily gathered by the fire to eat and get drunk. His brothers seldom worked the field or tended to the flocks except for Reuben and Judah. They spent all their time drunk or getting drunk. Now with Joseph beat up and at the bottom of the pit they had reason to celebrate, which meant they drank more. They had been drunk ever since they had beaten Joseph to within an inch of his life.

The Dreamer

They talked about how they would secretly kill Joseph and show Reuben the bloodied coat of many colors. They were perplexed about why Reuben wanted Joseph alive. After the birthright was taken from Reuben and given to Joseph, it only made sense to their evil minds that Reuben would want him dead. Judah also spoke of keeping him alive, although he was not as adamant about it as was Reuben.

Why are they doing this to me? What could I have done to make them treat me like this? I know I have made them mad at me and we do not agree on much of anything, but still, this is a bit much, to beat me so near death. Joseph was in pain and felt alone, despairing, and despondent.

When Both Reuben and Judah were gone, the brothers talked about different ways they could kill him. Some said "let us fill up this pit with enough water to drown him," others said "let us bury him alive." A few of the more hardened brothers like Simeon and Levi suggested they bring the boy back up out of the well and practice their sword fighting with him. He would be in no position to fight back. All plans involved burying him in the pit.

Joseph heard every proposed scheme to kill him and even though he was angry with his brothers, he still felt a bond with them, although it was weakening. Somehow, he still loved them. It hurt him to hear all the various ways they thought of to kill him. After being beaten so badly he now thought it was a very real possibility they might kill him. They had threatened him many times with a terrible beating, and sometimes they had even threatened him with death.

The pit was dark and Joseph was in even more darkness due to his eyes being swollen shut from the beating he received. He could only breathe in short, shallow breaths due to broken ribs and the pain each gasp caused.

By the fifth day the swelling was starting to subside and he started regaining his ability to see. All he could see were shadows and a narrow circle of light straight above him. All around him in the shadows was a dry, hard brown dirt wall and floor.

Joseph heard his brothers complain about the heat above. He wanted to offer to trade places with them as it was cool so deep in the earth, but he didn't have the strength to yell loud enough.

Aside from the constant gnawing pain that filled his body, he was able to draw peace and strength as he reflected on his sweet memories of his mother, Racheal. It was enough to give him hope. She died when Joseph was young and he still had tender memories of his mother holding him in her arms, remembering well many of her teachings. The things she taught him were centered around the divine concept of love, including forgiveness. Forgiveness? Where did that idea come from? Forgiveness. How could he forgive his brothers for what they had done to him? He wondered if his mother was right about the idea of forgiveness? Of course it would be easy to forgive small things, but it seemed an impossible task to forgive his brothers, especially since they were still in a drunken rage against him.

Six days had passed by and his ability to see improved, and some of the pain was letting up. At the bottom of the pit there was barely enough room for him to sit with his legs bent sharply so his knees were against his chest. He could shake his legs enough to wake them up when they fell asleep. They often fell asleep in the confined space. There were times when he felt like he would give up.

The Dreamer

He was cramped, in pain and he didn't have the strength yet to stand up, so all he could do was sit in agony. There were times when he felt himself in the tender arms of his mother. He sometimes would drift off to sleep and imagine he was very young and small and sitting on her lap. Her arms were wrapped around him and he could feel her heart beating as she would whisper in his ear. He could feel her warm breath against his cheek and ear. It was, for a moment, like he was in heaven only to have sharp shooting pains break his dreams and bring him crashing back to painful reality.

He wasn't sure which was worse, the physical pain of the moment, or being ripped away from such a tender dream with his dear mother.

He tried to make sense of the condition he was in. He thought of the teachings of Father Jacob. It was interesting both he and his brothers were taught the same things yet his brothers were wicked and living free of constraint. He, on the other hand, was righteous and living confined in the bottom of a dry well. They were drunk and he was in writhing pain, beaten, bloody and bruised. He felt like giving up. He even looked for ways to kill himself beating his brothers to it. He had nothing with which to kill himself. The rope was let down twice a day, once to bring down the water vase and the second time bring up the empty water container. The food was thrown down to him. He ate the food off of the dirt unless he could catch some of it with his hands. It was dark and shady and that made it hard to catch the food. So he had no rope to hang himself.

He could barely stand and there was not enough room to move his arms freely. To move his arms above his head, he would have to carefully bend his arm at his elbow and with enough energy he could force his arm straight up.

The Dreamer

He thought of trying to hit himself in the head with the water vase to kill himself, but he didn't have enough room or energy to move his arm with enough force to do anything but bruise his scalp.

The days were long and slow. The minutes seemed like hours and hours seemed like days and the days had no end in sight. He knew he wouldn't die of thirst or starvation and there was no way to kill himself. Maybe he didn't really want to die. After all, they couldn't force him to eat or drink. He thought about it. He was already in so much pain he didn't want to go through the hunger pains of starving to death or of dying of thirst. He had been in the desert without food or water for long periods of time and it was a painful, miserable way to suffer. He wanted a clean, quick way to die, but that was out of his control. Everything was out of his control. He only had three things he could control. He could choose to eat, to drink and how to think.

As he thought about those three options, he thought about the third one, controlling how to think. He had already decided he would eat and drink so he had one item with which he had any control over and that was how to think.

What should I think about? Immediately he started to think how mean his brothers had been to him for about as long as he could remember. As he pondered about the past, he started to feel worse in every respect, even physically. He worked himself up into a rage. After a while a thought crept in, which helped him realize there were other things he could think about, things that were positive and inspirational.

He had been able to think of some happy thoughts, but he noticed the happiness from those thoughts was short lived and it made the bad thoughts worse because they contrasted with the dark place he was in. But he felt the

The Dreamer

need to keep trying. The first thing that came to him when he was recalling positive memories was of his mother. As he thought about his mother, he started to feel happy. He hadn't felt happy in over a week. He relished the memories, the love and the contentment his mother brought him.

He recalled another memory when he was young and some of his brothers were practicing their sword fighting with wooden swords. They offered to let him join with them as long as he could hold his own. He picked up a smaller wooden sword and stepped into the ring with Naphtali. Within less than a minute he had bruises all over his body. He was on the ground and Naphtali kept hitting him with the wooden sword.

The rule was that you were fair game unless you were out of the circle. It didn't matter if you were down on your knees or back. If you were in the circle, you could be hit or stabbed with the blunt wooden sword. Naphtali grew tired of hitting Joseph and reminded him to get out of the circle if he wanted to stop being hit. Joseph was to tired and sore to move.

Naphtali yielded his time in the circle by striking Issachar's sword. Issachar began beating Joseph with fresh strength. Joseph feared he would be beaten to death, but he couldn't move. There were two ways to get out of the circle. You could yield to anyone with their sword reached out to you or if you gave up. There was no respect for you if you gave up and no one wanted to trade places with Joseph. Father Jacob happened by and saw what was going on. Joseph was bruised and bleeding at the hands of his brothers. "Joseph, give up and get yourself out of there. You will not accomplish anything if you cannot get up and fight back."

The Dreamer

Joseph couldn't speak. He shook his head no. Father Jacob was filled with pride at the tenacity of his young son and the courage it took to not give up. No one would hold any long term ill will toward him if he tried to save himself.

"Issachar stop," said Father Jacob. "Everyone, come here, gather around and listen to what I have to teach you." Grumbling, everyone gathered around Father Jacob.

"This sparing game is designed to teach you how to conduct yourself in battle, to kill or be killed. In battle you use your limited strength to neutralize the enemy by killing or wounding him so he can no longer fight. Once he is dead or wounded you move on. In this sparing game you can learn how to fight, but you can also learn the quality of mercy."

As there is nothing to gain by continuing to beat on someone already out of the fight, in this game you have the opportunity to grant mercy, that is to stop beating someone clearly wiped out. Joseph is beaten, bruised and even a little bloodied. He has no chance against you older and bigger brothers. You can show your strength in your ability to show mercy. Never forget that. Now help your brother and clean him up. Take him back to his house and see to him until he is well enough off."

A burning pain in Joseph's knee brought him back to reality. That memory got him angry and worked up again. Where is that quality of mercy now? He forced himself to think of his kind and thoughtful mother. Suddenly he was filled with love and peace as he remembered the words his mother had spoken to him. You are a special boy sent to me from the God of our fathers. You are meant for an important responsibility in your life, a responsibility no one else can have. You must never give in to temptation and despair, and you must never give in to your anger or bad thoughts.

The Dreamer

Always ask yourself, what would the Lord have me do? If you do this, you will always be on the right side of any situation.

Joseph rolled that thought over in his mind a few times. He was about to pray and ask God what he should do then he stopped. He wondered if he would be able to do whatever the Lord asked of him? Would he be strong enough to do whatever was required of him? He knew his prayer would be answered. He was a man of faith and that scared him because he doubted whether he could do what the Lord required of him.

Both his mother and father had always taught him to trust in the Lord in all things. If he did, he would never drift too far to the side, but would always be on the straight and narrow path.

Joseph took a deep breath and started to pray. He had barely got into his prayer when he had thoughts and ideas placed in his mind that didn't come from his own thinking. *In spite of all your brothers have done against you, you need to forgive them. Do not dwell on what they are doing to you, but rather keep your mind focused on what you can do to serve me. You will be delivered from your hardship in my own due time.*

Joseph thought about what had flashed in his mind. It was as if he heard someone wonderful speaking to him. Someone heavenly. He wondered how it was possible to forgive them. Then a very distinct thought flashed in his mind, trust in the Lord and you will be blessed.

Joseph thought to himself, how can I forgive them? "Dear God, I want to do what thou would have me do. Please help me forgive my brothers. I need thy help. I do not think I can do it on my own."

The Dreamer

He waited and listened for an answer, then he realized the answer would likely come, not in words, but in divine help from within his soul. "Dear God, help me to understand and to feel thy help as I struggle to forgive them."

He took a deep breath and strived from that point forward to have a spirit of forgiveness toward his oldest ten brothers even though he was mad at them.

Chapter 8: Sold

Fear not: for they that be with us are more than they that be with them. 2 Kings 6:16

Joseph's hunger and thirst were the only physical activities that measured time, otherwise, it had no meaning as Joseph was held against his will in the dark abyss of the dry well.

It was the seventh day for Joseph being kidnapped and held in the pit. Most of his swelling was gone and many of his bruises were changing from dark blue to an ugly dark green. For the sake of survival, he spent almost all of his time wrapped up in the comfort of his thoughts and dreams. This helped pass the time yet the contrast between pleasant memories and the suffering he was in frustrated Joseph. He reflected on his Father Jacob and his teachings many of which dealt with the responsibilities of the birthright and being faithful to God. Jacob taught Joseph that the Hebrew God was a jealous God, meaning that no one should worship false idols and false gods, but only worship the true and living God of Israel. Worship him in thought and deed.

As Joseph thought about the responsibilities of bearing up the mantle of the birthright, he wondered if it was worth it considering where he was at the moment. Because of his nature, Joseph was true and loyal and he had always been to Israel and his teachings. But all that had led him to being held prisoner against his will in the bottom of a pit in some far off land that he had never been to before, Dothan.

He wondered if the birthright was worth all the suffering he had been through and all that he was now going through. He knew he was to trust in the Lord and he knew

The Dreamer

that he needed to forgive his brothers and he was trying, but he really wasn't sure at all that the birthright was worth it. His memories took him back to the time when Father Jacob had taken the birthright from Reuben and given it to Joseph. There was a wonderful, glorious feeling that came over Joseph bearing witness to him that he really was Gods chosen bearer of the royal birthright. He knew down deep in his heart that the birthright was more than just temporal blessings. The main component to the birthright was spiritual. That was something Reuben and the other brothers never really understood. To them it was just a temporal wealth and a power thing to which they all aspired to.

On the eighth day of Joseph's captivity in the dry well, it was Asher and Dan's turn to wear the royal robe of many colors. Asher wore the coat for the morning meal. He lowered the morning meal down to him and watched Joseph start eating.

"Behold the dreamer eats his breakfast," Gad said with a loud mocking voice as he lowered a vessel of water to him. "Eat well, my lord, my prince and rejoice as I bow myself to thee." Gad laughed with an evil tone that came from the gates of hell.

The eighth day was unusual because all ten brothers actually went out to work in the fields to check up on the sheep and their servants keeping watch over the flocks.

Why is this happening to me? Why must I suffer like this? What good does all this suffering do me? What will become of me? Will I die? What will happen to me if I do not die? In the heat of the late afternoon Joseph slipped off into sleep and a subsequent dream. He dreamed that there was a giant sheaf of grain in a bundle. It was bulging at its bindings. It gave life to all that were around him. Then

The Dreamer

eleven withered sheaves approached him begging for relief. They were brown and wilted. After a few moments of reflecting and thinking the golden giant sheaf provided relief to the eleven withering sheaves and then they received their brightness and ceased to be bent any longer.

When Joseph gazed on the eleven sheaves, he felt their sorrow and despair. When he gazed on the giant golden sheaf he felt hope, strength and power. He woke up feeling warm and content and for a few moments he didn't feel the constant pain that racked his entire body. He finally felt enough physical strength to try and stand up. He managed to get on his feet, but the effort winded him, forcing him to breathe hard against his pain filled ribs.

Day nine came and went much like the other days. Day ten was marked like every other day being mocked by his brethren as they disrespected the coat of many colors. Day eleven came and while eating his dirt filled morning meal Joseph heard Judah cry out to his brothers, "Look out to the east. Isn't that an Ishmeelites caravan?"

"It looks like it, at least as far as I can tell from this far off," said Naphtali.

They watched it slowly and steadily move closer. The caravan was coming straight for them, but when they were three miles from the main camp, they would turn to the south as they went to the final destination, Egypt.

Judah had an idea. "What if we were to take Joseph and sell him to the Ishmeelites from Gilead and maybe we could earn a few dollars and perhaps some spice for this bland food we are eating?"

"That would solve our Joseph problem," added Gad.

"Yes, we could sell him" confirmed Dan

"Then we could tear up the coat of many colors and

The Dreamer

dip it in goats' blood, and tell father that a wild beast devoured him," added Issachar.

"We would tell father that all we found were the tattered remains of his coat," said Levi.

"It has been eleven days and since we threw that venomous viper into the pit, why not be rid of him and be a little richer for it," said Asher.

"At least this way we will not be killing him. That should make Reuben happy," said Naphtali.

They all quickly agreed to the idea. They rounded up their camels and lit out after the approaching caravan.

Joseph overheard everything they said. He had been abused and beaten by his brothers, but he couldn't imagine they would want him permanently out of their lives. Without him around they would have no one to mistreat and they seemed to enjoy torturing him. He hadn't heard Reuben's voice and wondered where he was. Reuben seemed to be the only voice of reason among his ten oldest bothers. Of course, there was a lot of talk about killing him, yet they hadn't done it yet. There were times he thought they just might let him live and eventually take him back to Canaan.

A while later he heard some nearby sheep bleating. Soon he heard the reason for the noisy sheep. He heard the guttural sounds of camels approaching. The bellowing of the camels grew louder. It seemed a little soon for his brothers to be back. He heard men talking in a language Joseph didn't recognize. One man ordered another man to draw water from the well so they could freshen their water supply and water their animals.

He heard a bucket bounce off the side of the dry well as it came tumbling down the well. When it got down to his

The Dreamer

level, Joseph yanked hard on the bucket. He was hoping he had the strength to call for help once someone bent over the well. He didn't want to waste effort until he could see someone. He was still weak and in a lot of pain from the trauma he had been through.

"Something is down there," cried the man with a rope in his hand. He knelt down by the side of the well and looked down. He heard a faint voice. "Help me. Please help me."

"By the stars above, there is someone down in the well," exclaimed Ezra, the man with the rope.

"Ezra, throw a rope down there and pull him up," said Micah, the leader of the group.

While Ezra was looking for a bigger rope, he heard another man in the company say, "What makes you think it's a man? Maybe, if we're smiled upon by the god of Hathor, we might bring up a woman."

"Sounded like a man," said Ezra. He yelled down the pit, "Tie the rope around your shoulders and we will pull you up."

Joseph's ribs were still broken and painful. *Are these men the ones taking me away from my brothers? I wonder how much they paid for me?* With a great deal of painful effort he tied the roped around his shoulders and gave the rope a tug. A moment later a severe pain exploded in Joseph as the rope grew taut as they pulled him up. Soon his body was hanging mid air with the rope slowly and surely pulling him up. Joseph fainted from the pain.

They pulled him up and onto the hard valley floor. He was unresponsive. The leader of the Midianites walked over to a slump of a body and kicked him in the head. The pile of a body showed little signs of life, but the force of being kicked in the head caused a faint groan to escape Joseph's

The Dreamer

mouth.

"Well, at least he's alive. Throw him on top of the wagon. Let's get out of here," said the leader in a gruff voice.

"What will we do with this pathetic Hebrew?" asked the number two guy.

"We can sell him, if we get the chance, if he is worth anything. He looks pretty beat up. If not, he can be our slave."

The small group of Midianites kept on going as they gave up their quest for fresh water. Soon they were climbing up the hill on their way out of the land of Dothan when they came upon a large caravan of people headed toward Egypt.

"Hey boss, maybe we can sell that pile of flesh to these Ishmeelites?" the number two guy asked his boss.

"I think so. They're merchantmen to be sure. They just might be interested in a trade."

"How do you know they are merchantmen?"

"Can you not smell the spices from here? There is a small breeze carrying the smell of spices from their wagon. Do you smell it?"

"Mmm, yes I do."

Soon the two caravans met in the middle of the road. Mica and Ezra approached the larger caravan.

"We have a slave for sale. Are you interested?"

"Always interested in doing business. Let's see what you have."

"Go get the slave, said Micah."

Then Ezra went back to the wagon carrying the slave and tried to wake Joseph. He didn't move. He got out a water vessel and doused Joseph's face. After the second dousing Joseph opened his eyes and wiped his face. He looked around confused and wondering where his brothers

The Dreamer

were. Then he realized he had been sold into slavery.

"Get on your feet boy."

Dazed and in a state of confusion Joseph looked around to get his bearings. He slowly responded to the threats of the angry Midianite and finally got on his feet. He was unsteady, and he was bent over holding his ribs on each side.

"Get going. Go on. Get over there. Move it," said Ezra.

The number two guy gave young Joseph a shove with the heel of his foot. Joseph nearly fell to the ground, but managed only to stumble. Within a long two minutes Joseph was standing in front of the Ishmeelites leader.

"What have you done to this poor soul? He's half-broken up."

"We found him that way. He'll heal up. He's young and you can tell he's strong. Give him a week and he'll be good as new."

Shaking his head like he wasn't interested, the Ishmeelite said, "I'll give you a pound of spice for this boy."

"We'll gladly take the spices, but we want some silver for him. You know he's worth at least forty pieces of silver being young and strong as he is."

"Ten pieces of silver and a half pound of spice."

"Thirty pieces of silver and one pound of spice."

"Twenty pieces of silver and no spice," said the Ishmeelites.

"We'll take the twenty pieces of silver, but we want a half pound of spice."

"All right. It is a deal."

As soon as they made the transaction the Midianites made way for the Ishmeelites to pass on their way to Egypt.

The Dreamer

They had ten slaves in their caravan in addition to Joseph. They threw Joseph on an unused wagon in hopes that he would heal faster and command a better price if he rested on their way to Egypt.

The Dreamer

Chapter 9: Joseph's Coat

And he that searcheth the hearts knoweth what is the mind of the Spirit, because he maketh intercession for the saints according to the will of God. Romans 8:27

The brilliant blue sky and the crisp horizon contradicted the terrible scene of anguish that was occurring as Judah and his nine brothers returned to the main camp and saw Reuben with his clothes rent. Reuben was livid and screaming at his servants since he didn't have anyone else to scream at. Reuben was waiting for Simeon and Levi to dismount from their camels, when they did, he lit into them as soon as they secured their mounts.

"What have you done with Joseph? Do not tell me he is dead. Do not tell me some wild beast devoured him. I want to know exactly what happened to the boy!" demanded Reuben.

Simeon wasn't prepared to respond since none of this was his idea. He looked nervously to Levi, who in turn looked at Judah. "It was your idea. You tell him."

"When we left, Joseph was alive and well. We do not know what has happened to the lad. We left to visit the Ishmeelites to inquire if they would buy Joseph as a slave. After they agreed, we rushed back to get the boy and that is where we ran into you." Judah walked past Reuben to the pit and looked down to see the pit empty other than the remains of eleven days worth of living.

"What has happened to Joseph?" asked Judah to himself as much as to anyone else. "He was down there when we left." Judah was shaking his head is disbelief.

The Dreamer

"Look at this rope. This was not here when we left. It is not our kind of rope," said Levi. Reuben and Judah also examined the rope.

"What have you done to Joseph?" Demand an angry Reuben.

"I have told you already. We do not know what has become of him."

"Could it be someone came along and took the boy?" asked Judah. As he was speaking, two servants came riding hard into camp.

"Master," said one of the servants. "We saw a small caravan of Midianites come into camp. As soon as they left, we got on our camels and made our way back to camp."

"Did you see what happened while they were in our camp?"

"No master, they were not here for long and we were too far away to see anything other than their wagons and the camels."

"If I may, master," said the other servant. "I cannot be sure, but it is possible they pulled master Joseph out of the well. This is a clear day and we saw a lot of haze rise up from the camp. I think it came from something more than getting off their camels and walking around."

"Did you see which way they went?" asked Judah.

Both servants pointed in the same direction. Judah and Reuben climbed back on their camels and went in that direction. In a few miles they were on a ridge which allowed them a view of the next valley. There they saw the Midianite caravan. They ran after it and caught up with it in two miles. They were informed that Joseph was sold to the Ishmeelites, and showed them the direction of their caravan.

"Beware, they have a large caravan and they have

The Dreamer

many in their group. They are mean and they will put up a good fight."

Reuben and Judah rushed back to camp in an attempt to gather their brothers and servants for a fight. By the time they arrived at their camp and gathered everyone together the sun was nearly gone over the western horizon. The air over the camp was filled with a dirty haze and the temperature was still scorching. They had no idea just how far the Ishmeelites were and Reuben was concerned about their manpower. They couldn't leave that night. They didn't dare leave the sheep unattended at night when the wolves came out. Reuben called off the quest for Joseph.

"You fools. You are all fools. Do you not understand our situation now?"

They all shook their heads. They didn't understand what Reuben meant.

"We all have our personal inheritance of Father Jacob. Now his favorite son is gone, who knows what will become of our personal inheritance? We will be held responsible for the loss of Joseph. He is as good as gone forever. You fools!"

"What do you mean by that? What are you getting at?" asked Judah.

"I lost the birthright for my transgression and no one was dead as a result of my foolish behavior. Imagine what Father Jacob will do to us all when he thinks Joseph is dead? We all could well lose our personal inheritance. For that matter, we could all be excommunicated from the family and be reduced to servants."

"Why would father do that to us?"

"Because he could hold us responsible for losing Joseph."

The Dreamer

"But he has given the birthright to Joseph. That makes him our ruler. How can we be held responsible for our ruler's demise? He is better than us, should he not be held responsible for his own actions?" asked Gad defensively.

"One would think so, but father considers Joseph to be his favorite and Joseph is only seventeen years old. If Father Jacob holds us responsible, it won't bode well for us."

"Maybe we should tell Father Jacob the truth that Joseph was kidnapped by Ishmeelites," suggested Asher.

"It could get complicated," suggested Judah. "It will be best to make up a story that will explain it all and be easy for us to confirm. That would be showing him the coat of many colors covered in blood. It may be harsh, but it will be the easiest story to explain."

"I do not like it, but I agree with Judah. Let us follow your evil plan and cover the coat in the blood of a goat," said Reuben. "I will return to Father Jacob with the coat. I will tell him this story and when you all arrive with the flocks and herds you will repeat the same story."

All the ten brothers agreed with that idea. They killed a goat and dipped the torn coat of many colors in the blood. The next morning Reuben and his company left for the land of Canaan. They took with them fresh mounts so they could ride hard to reach Israel as fast as they could. All the servants that knew the evil report were sworn to silence under the penalty of death.

Reuben arrived at the house of Jacob, and he went in to see his father.

"Father. I have bad news to report." He held out the coat of many colors and Father Jacob saw it was ragged, torn and bloody.

The Dreamer

"What is this? What has happened to my dear Joseph?"

"We came back to the main camp and saw his coat and a messy scene of blood and gore. We buried what was left of him and brought the coat of many colors as a testament as to what happened. I am sorry father to have to show this to you. I hurried back to bring word as quickly as possible."

Father Jacob had already rent his clothes in mourning the passing of his Father Isaac, upon hearing these words he cried out all the more in anguish. Soon thereafter, Israel clothed himself in sackcloth to mourn the unsettling loss of his dear Joseph. Days turned to weeks and Father Jacob could not be comforted by Reuben, Dinah or any of his daughters or grandchildren. The weeks turned into a month and the mournful weeks continued on. Israel could not find comfort.

"I will go down into the grave mourning my son. How can I ever find comfort again?" said Father Jacob as he continued to weep. Almost two months later the rest of his sons returned from Dothan and told Israel the same story. They tried unsuccessfully to comfort their father. Some of the sons actually felt a degree of sorrow for their father and his terrible mourning.

The Dreamer

Chapter 10: Egyptian Slave

Many are the afflictions of the righteous: but the Lord delivereth him out of them all. Psalms 34:19

The day Joseph was bought by the Ishmeelites, he became sick in addition to his severe injuries. The slave traders kept him in a wagon to rest and heal, hoping they could sell him for more if he appeared healthy and strong. A fellow slave was assigned to tend to Joseph while they made their long trip to Egypt. The fever that overtook Joseph plagued him for a week.

During that time the slave who was taking care of Joseph maintained a bucket of water and would soak a rag and wipe Joseph's face in an attempt to bring the fever down. He also tried cleaning and tending to the myriad of other wounds young Joseph had.

The eighth day of Joseph's new captivity was hot and dry without a cloud in the sky. His fever started to break. On the ninth day he regained consciousness, but was too weak to speak. He noticed a familiar face tending to him.

All he could think to do was try and say a prayer. *Dear God, I am so sick and I feel terrible. Please help me feel better.*

He didn't understand where he was or what was going on around him. He was laying flat on the back of the wagon, sick with a headache and in pain, creaking and bouncing over a rough and bouncy road. He wondered, who that familiar and friendly face was that kept helping him?

He remembered being sold to the Ishmeelites. He remembered getting beaten by his brothers and having his

The Dreamer

coat of many colors ripped off of him. He was confused because he recognized the kindly older man who was taking care of him as they plodded along the dry, dusty road toward Egypt. He didn't understand how he knew this man or why this man was helping him. Why was he so familiar?

As Joseph started to realize what his circumstances were, he expected to be surrounded by unfamiliar people, yet there was this kindly looking older man who he recognized. Joseph found it was hard to focus on reality, but then the familiar stranger started to feed him some cold broth. Slowly Joseph regained enough strength to speak.

"Thank you old man for your kindly help. I know your face, but I do not know why it is familiar to me. Who are you?"

"My name is Mordecai. Do you not remember me from the land of Shechem? We ate dinner together and shared the same camp before you went on your way to Dothan."

"Oh yes. I do remember you. My ten older brothers stole your flock of sheep."

"That is correct."

"What are you doing here? For that matter, what am I doing here? Where are we?" Joseph was about to go on when Mordecai grabbed his hand.

"Easy my boy. Relax and allow yourself to get better. I will gladly answer your questions. Just take it easy all right?"

"All right," Joseph responded weakly.

"I was kidnapped by these Ishmeelites. Several of the slaves here have been kidnapped by these slave traders on their way to Egypt. We will all be sold when we arrive in Egypt. You were sold by some Midianites as a slave to these Ishmeelites. You were all broken, bloodied, and unconscious

The Dreamer

when they bought you. I do not know why you were in such bad shape."

Joseph furrowed his forehead and asked, "Where are we going?"

"To Egypt to be sold as slaves."

"Oh yes, Egypt . . . You said that already. Why are you so kind to me after my brothers stole your sheep?"

"Since we are both captives of the Ishmeelites, we can use all the friends we can get. Also, while it was true that your brothers did indeed wrong me, you did not. You offered me your protection if I wanted to go on to Dothan with you. I can see by the condition you are in that you would not have been able to protect me."

"Thank you for your kindness. How long have I been delirious and unconscious?"

"About a week. Do you not remember the first couple of days in this wagon before you slipped away from us?"

"No. The last fuzzy memory was being kidnapped by the Midianites, I think."

"I better get off this wagon before the guards see me talking to you. They do not want me on this wagon any more than is needed. I will bring you water later on. Rest and get your strength back. Sip as much water as you can tolerate. I will see you get fed as soon as we make camp for the night."

Joseph lay back on the bottom of the wagon and tried to rest his head, but the wagon was bouncing too much which made it impossible to rest. His head kept bouncing up and down as the wagon jostled over bumps.

How did I not wake up sooner? How could I have slept through this terrible wagon ride? I would rather be walking if I had the strength. He tried to turn on his side and put his arms under his head, but the pain in his ribs was too

The Dreamer

severe. He did manage to slip one arm under his head, which didn't hurt as bad and allowed his head to rest more comfortably.

Why is this happening to me? How can this be happening to me? I am the bearer of the birthright and I can do nothing with that blessing if I am away from my family. I cannot preside over the flocks and herds of Father Jacob. I cannot execute the spiritual blessings of the birthright if I am a slave somewhere far from home. Why did my brothers do this to me?

Joseph raised his shoulders and head just barely high enough to look around at the landscape. He had no idea where he was or where he had been for the last week. He was lost with no orientation to figure out where he might be. *What will become of me? Where is my father? What have I got to live for? Maybe I will die.*

Joseph felt like giving up. If he didn't know where he was then his father would never know where he was and couldn't look for him. For that matter, his father probably still thought that Joseph was with his brothers in Dothan. Joseph felt conflicted, on the one hand, he wanted to just give up, but he also loved God and wanted to please him. God wouldn't want him to give up. *Dear God, please help me . . . Strengthen me and deliver me. Help me understand why this is happening?*

Joseph was entirely unsure what his future held for him. Would he die in slavery? Would he make it to Egypt?

As he was contemplating his fate, his memories went back in time to when he was a young boy of seven or eight years old, just before his mother died. His mother Racheal was pregnant with Benjamin. He imagined sitting in her lap, feeling her arms around him. He felt warm and safe. He

The Dreamer

heard her voice in his mind. "Wherever you are, no matter what the circumstances, you are never lost. You will always have the God of your Fathers to lead you and guide you and deliver you. As long as God is with you, you are truly blessed."

Is God with me? Is the God of my fathers aware of this terrible ordeal, I am going through? How can he help me? Can he come down and smite these Ishmeelites to the ground allowing me to escape? Sure, he can. God can do anything, but why has he not helped me?

A strange feeling of calm came over Joseph. He felt relaxed and he no longer felt afraid of his circumstances and his unknown future. He didn't like where he was and he hated his circumstances, but somehow he felt calm. He was able to breathe better. It still hurt to breathe deeply, but he could still breathe better than a week ago. He laid himself down on the hard floor boards of the wagon and drifted off to sleep.

The ever familiar dreams of the sheaves and the eleven stars coursed through Joseph's mind. Then a new dream came to him. In this dream he saw a hand holding a tiny mustard seed. It was very small. The hand prepared the ground for planting and then put the small seeds into the ground. The ground was watered by the hand. The sun shone down on the ground and soon the mustard seed sprouted. Then it grew and grew. The goodly hand kept taking care of the new sprout and the seed grew into a tall plant. That plant, by the ever present care of the hand, continued to grow into a large and beautiful mustard tree.

He marveled at the strong and beautiful tree he saw before him, where only moments ago was a tiny round mustard seed. Then it seemed as though it had started to

The Dreamer

rain on the mighty mustard tree.

He woke up to Mordecai wiping his face with a wet cloth. Joseph no longer felt jostled by the wagon. He realized he was on the ground and he felt much more comfortable.

"I must have fallen to sleep," said Joseph.

"Yes, you did," Mordecai wiped his forehead with the damp rag.

"Thank you for your kind help," replied Joseph.

"What happened to you before we picked you up in Dothan?"

"My brothers did this to me. They beat me and caged me in a dry well"

"Would that be the same brothers who stole my sheep?"

"Yes, the very same . . . Terrible brothers," Joseph shook his head.

"How is it you turned out so much better than all of your brothers?"

"That is a good question. We are all from the same father and we were all taught the same teachings of the Hebrew God." Joseph reached for a water vessel and sipped a little water. "I think the main difference between them and me is that I have chosen to follow the teachings of my father, and I choose to worship the God of Abraham, Isaac and Jacob. They do not."

"Why would your God let you be taken as a slave?"

"I feel like I should know the answer to that question, but I do not. I have asked that same question many times since my brothers turned on me and beat and kidnapped me. I have faith that in time I can answer that question. I just can't answer it right now."

The Dreamer

"You are a truly gifted young man to have so much faith and trust in a God you cannot see," said Mordecai.

Mordecai helped Joseph eat his evening meal. Every day thereafter Joseph made remarkable strides in healing. When they arrived in Egypt, he looked strong and vigorous with only a few light bruises and pink scars remaining.

~

Potiphar was a powerful officer of the Pharaoh's court. He was as wealthy as he was powerful. His wife was renown for her beauty. Potiphar was in need of some new slaves so he came to the midweek slave auction. The Ishmeelites were at the same auction to sell the eleven slaves they had procured on their journey toward Egypt. Among the slaves for sale were Mordecai and Joseph.

"Beware of a man they call Potiphar, he is well known as a powerful and evil man. He is a captain of the Pharaohs' guard and the Pharaoh's chief butcher. He has a license to kill for the king and he kills at will for his own pleasure. No one has the power to stop him except for the Pharaoh," said Mordecai.

"Why are you telling me this? Do I have a choice who buys me as a slave?" asked Joseph.

"You are a perceptive young man. Of course, you have no choice, but if he purchases you beware. Stay as far away from him as you can."

The auction started with Mordecai. There was a flurry of beginning bids until Potiphar jumped into the bidding. As soon as he did the other bids stopped abruptly. No one

The Dreamer

wanted to run up the price against Potiphar who had the reputation of getting what he wanted at any cost.

Joseph saw his friend Mordecai being bought by the man they called Potiphar. He was sad for Mordecai and sad for himself. He had been hoping that he would stay with Mordecai. As soon as the Mordecai transaction was done, Joseph was put up for bid. Joseph was a very handsome young man with a scruffy beard and deep brown hair. He looked good and strong. No one knew he was still tender in his ribs, but he could now breathe easier.

Because he was young and in apparently good health he was examined by interested buyers. Some people forced open his mouth and looked at his teeth like they would a horse. People grabbed at him and poked at him like he was livestock, as a slave, that's all he would ever be.

Joseph was numb inside as he witnesses all these evil people violate him. *I am not an animal, get your hands off of me.* He thrashed himself around as much as he could. He was restricted by being tied at his ankles and wrists. Some of those examining him were impressed by his spirit. A few slapped him, to try and calm him down. As soon as everyone was satisfied with Joseph's health and strength they started the bidding. There was a flurry of bidding just like with Mordecai and just like Mordecai, the bidding stopped just as fast when Potiphar joined in the bidding.

Mordecai and Joseph were in a holding cell while Potiphar finished his bidding and bought three more slaves. The three additional slaves were put in the same holding cell as Joseph and Mordecai. The holding cell was designed to hold up to three slaves at a time. Potiphar was called away before he could arrange for his slaves to be transported back to his estate. He sent word to his wife Zeleakia, who was at the nearby market to make arrangements for transporting the slaves to their estate.

Zeleakia was, by virtue of her marriage to Potiphar, one of the primary socialites of the city. She was as beautiful as she was popular and she had drawn many friends to her over the years.

When she came to the slave auction, she had the slaves parade before her. She examined them all personally. "There, that young one, bring him before me." One of her servants grabbed Joseph by the arm and brought him to stand before her. "He is filthy, clean him up," she commanded.

The servants dowsed him with water and scrubbed him clean as if he were an animal going to be judged before some livestock auction. This was humiliating to Joseph. He was tempted to beat these servants who mindlessly did as they were told. *No one treats a man of the birthright like this and gets away with it*, he thought. Joseph's mind was flashing between being confused and shocked at the proceedings as well as being humiliated and defiled at the same time. These conflicting emotions paralyzed him into submission.

Once he was clean, he was barely covered with enough cloth to be modest and no more. He was presented to Zeleakia one more time. During these public proceedings the slaves and those gathered at the auctions were viewing Joseph's humiliation. She checked him over one more time.

"Much better. I thought I saw a nice looking young man underneath that filth. I will make of him a houseboy. The rest will be placed in the field as Potiphar intended." She instructed her senior servant to go to the market for fabric from which to make Joseph clothes suitable for being

The Dreamer

in her house.

   When Joseph realized what was going on his heart sank. Not only was he property of the most feared man in Egypt, he would now be working in his house. He would be separated from Mordecai, the only friend he had in the world. Life was going from terrible to worse. It was as if he was falling down a well with no bottom to reach. How could it get any worse?

Chapter 11: Houseboy

Behold, I have refined thee, but not with silver; I have chosen thee in the furnace of affliction. Isaiah 48:10

As the slaves were walking under a strong guard to Potiphar's house, Joseph found himself in deep anguish. He was still reeling from the public humiliation of being stripped down and cleaned like a horse in front of total strangers. He felt shamed and violated. For the first time in his life, he felt helpless.

While it was stifling hot, there were dark clouds hanging over the path Joseph was on. They seemed to foretell the growing doom and darkness that were filling Joseph's life.

Joseph felt beaten down. He stood there, in public while strangers stripped him and washed him like livestock and he did nothing to stop it. He didn't even lift a finger to fight back. He had fought against his brothers, why didn't he fight back against the servants of Potiphar? His confidence was damaged. He now knew what it felt like to have no hope. What did he have to look forward to? He couldn't imagine any hope for a bright future. This was the worst despair he had ever been in.

As Joseph grew nearer to Potiphar's estate, he tried desperately to find a reason for hope. He had never been in such a depressing situation and he was desperate to find hope. As a slave, what was there to hope for? As long as he remained a slave, he would not have the power of the birthright. He couldn't achieve his goals he had set out for his young life. He would never see his father, his brother Benjamin or his sister Dinah ever again.

The Dreamer

Even when he was beaten, bloodied and in the pit, he didn't know despair like this. In the pit, he still had hope.

As they entered the yard of the estate, they passed through an entrance that was heavily guarded by four armed guards. Just inside the gate were two one-man chariots ready to chase down any prisoners who managed to get through sword-wielding guards.

The supervising guard that was taking Joseph and his fellow slaves into Potiphar's estate said, "Every entry and exit of Potiphar's land is guarded the same as this gate. Trying to escape will result in death. There is no way to escape so do not try it."

As they made their way through the estate, they dropped off slaves at various locations along the way. Mordecai was one of the first slaves assigned a spot in the far away fields. They didn't have a chance to say goodbye. At the beginning of the day they were friends on a journey to Egypt, now they may never see each other again. By the time they started their approach to the main house, Joseph was the last slave. He was shown his quarters in the out-building next to the main house. He was instructed to go the slave's bath and clean himself up properly, which meant that he would need to shave his head. This time he would have some degree of privacy and he would be free from his bindings, but not free to choose what to do, not free to voluntarily shave his head and face. The house servants were required to shave and bathe daily. After his bath, he would be fitted for a household uniform.

He was escorted down a cobblestone pathway to a rather elegant pool that was used by all servants and slaves of the master's household. The bath was lined with

The Dreamer

white and turquoise patterned tiles. Palm trees surround the bath. Even though he was the only one in the bath, he still had two guards watching him so he wouldn't run off. As he washed and was allowed a few minutes to soak in the water, he thought about how dramatically his life had changed. He grew up with servants that tended to many of his needs. Father Jacob did not maintain slaves, but hired scores of servants for their household and to work their fields, flocks, and herds. Joseph worked alongside the servants in the fields and flocks, but there was an unwritten rule that you didn't interact with the servants. Now he was less than a servant.

Why would Father Jacob give me the birthright only for me to become a slave in far off Egypt? What good does the birthright do me now? As a slave, I have no freedom. I am not in a position to do anything on my own. Was Father wrong to give me the birthright? Why has God not delivered me from this ordeal? He was perplexed at how he could hold the birthright and be so far away from his family and his Hebrew people. Having the birthright was no good to him now.

He was told to finish his bath. When the guards spoke roughly to him, he was reminded that he was now a slave. This was his life. No privacy, no freedom, no hope, and no future. He could do nothing without his owner's consent. How is it now, that I am someone's property?" Joseph shook his head at the thought.

As he was escorted back to the slave quarters, he was reminded how futile trying to escape would be. "If you decide you are tired of being a slave, then try and escape. You will be granted an escape in the ground after you are killed. If the guards decide not to kill you, Potiphar will gladly do it himself," said one of the guards escorting him back to his slave quarters. They sure seemed to enjoy threatening me.

Since Potiphar commanded the Pharaoh's guards and was the chief executioner, his slaves had more to fear. It was against Egyptian law to kill a slave. You could work them as hard as you wanted, you could work them to death, but you could not kill them outright. This was a rule that Potiphar and his guards overlooked. Potiphar could afford to do things his way due to his high rank in Pharaoh Sesostris's court.

After being fitted for his uniform he was also told of his duties as a houseboy. He would be awakened one hour before sunup to prepare the dining table for the morning meal and other subsequent housework until it was time to serve the morning meal.

Joseph was never more grateful to go to sleep than he was that night. Perhaps sleep would afford him some freedom from being a slave, if only for a few precious moments. Sleep would become his only escape. While asleep, he dreamed again of the mustard tree.

The mustard seed was planted in a fenced off area away from anyone or anything. The mustard seed grew and grew until it matured into a mighty mustard tree giving beneficial shade to everything around. As Joseph looked around at the benefits of the shade and how far-reaching it was, he could see that the shade-covered Potiphar's estate and even Fathers Jacobs far off fields. He was amazed at how far reaching the benefits of the mighty mustard tree were.

Suddenly Joseph heard a loud, raucous noise and then his name was shouted, "Joseph, get up!" he was

The Dreamer

quickly roused from his peaceful and engaging sleep. Apparently, that was the sign that his first full day of slave labor was beginning. He had to get out of bed immediately. There wasn't time to reflect on the dream. He had to get dressed and get busy. He reported himself to Aaron the chief servant over the entire main house. Aaron assigned him to work with Sarin. He was to follow in Sarin's steps and observe all that Sarin did. He was instructed not to look anyone in the eye. He was to bow to Potiphar, Zeleakia and any other family when serving them. He was not to speak unless spoken to for any reason. The rules were strict. Breaking the rules resulted in severe punishment.

    Sarin was holding a wine vessel, Joseph was holding a plate of freshly made bread. Behind him stood three other servants with platters of other food such as melons, dates, figs, stewed pork, and pomegranates. Joseph considered the unique circumstances. He was probably the only servant used to eating like this. Whereas the other servants or slaves were probably born into slavery or came from the lower classes. Joseph felt a little pride creep into his heart as he considered all of this only to have the pride ripped violently from him as the breakfast bell rang and he was brought out of his thoughts to reality which was him dressed in a servant uniform serving hot bread to Zeleakia, Potiphar, their four children and two adult guests.

    As he hovered over Potiphar while he helped himself to the fresh bread, Joseph could sense the evil within that man. It made the hair on his arms and neck stand on end. As he bent over Zeleakia to serve her morning bread Joseph sensed a lonely and unhappy

The Dreamer

woman, who looked beautiful on the outside and seemed empty on the inside. Joseph was surrounded by beautiful women back home in Canaan, but there was something different about this woman.

As he walked to the first adult guest, he heard Zeleakia say under her breath, "What a handsome and strong young man. He should grow nicely into my plaything by and by." He blushed and looked side to side and glanced at the guests in the eye. He quickly looked down. *What did she just say? Was that about me?*

While bowing and serving bread to everyone, he noticed Potiphar placing honey on his bread. He hoped that he would have a chance to eat some honey and bread. Honey was a special treat in Canaan. His father's house wanted for nothing, but many of the finer things had to be traded for and imported to their land.

Once he was serving bread, he went to the kitchen and placed more fresh warm bread on the serving tray and stood at attention waiting for someone to call out for more bread.

When breakfast was over and the breakfast servants were dismissed, they went into a back room adjacent to the kitchen where they were served barley and left-over fruit. To Joseph's dismay, there was no honey.

While the Hyksos were now ruling Egypt and it wasn't considered breaking the law to eat next to a common sheep-herder, Hebrew or other lower class citizens. This was a much older house that was built previous to the Hyksos invasion. It was designed to separate the lower class people from the ruling class Egyptians while they ate. They designed the house with a kitchen that divided the servant dining area from the

The Dreamer

Master's household dining area. The servants and slaves were only allowed to pass through the kitchen or to stand in the kitchen. They were not allowed to sit or eat in the kitchen or the families dining area.

While Joseph was eating his disappointing breakfast, he refused to eat picked over fruit. He was the man of the birthright and he deserved better food. He didn't mind the barely. While this work was beneath him, it wasn't hard work he noted to himself. He wondered about his new friend Mordecai and what his life was like working in Potiphar's fields. He was still nervous working so close to where Potiphar was, and he wished he were in the fields with Mordecai, much further away from the man of the house.

A week later Joseph had been fully trained in the art of serving breakfast to the family of the house. It wasn't hard work, in fact, he felt he could do it in his sleep. He was also trained in serving the midday and evening meals. Sarin was impressed and a little jealous that Joseph picked up on everything so fast. Joseph was unimpressed with the work. The only bright spot, if there was a bright spot, was that he ate well for a slave. He was adjusting to the reality of being a slave. He did not have a single minute to himself. Everything he did every day was scheduled to the minute. He bathed and shaved at a precise time. He went to bed or woke up at a precise time. The only thing he had that he could possibly control was his thoughts during the day and dreams at night.

He longed for his freedom, even after one short week. During his first full week, he was fully trained in his in between meal duties. None of it was hard or complicated work, just work that was beneath him.

The Dreamer

Joseph was doing his afternoon work when he found himself caught up in his thoughts. He was thinking about a dream he had the night before. In his dream, he was in the number two position serving the family breakfast. Only when he came to the table, the table was actually a plot of land behind a fence. In the middle of the plot was a small mustard plant. He served the mustard plant bread and other servants provided stewed pork, fruit, and other breakfast food. He noted the mustard plant helped itself to plenty of honey on the warm bread. He wondered, having dreams of the mustard tree so many times, what the tree symbolized.

While it was normal for the house slaves to be trained in all aspects of housework, they would be permanently assigned to a specific area. Once Sarin was done training Joseph as a meal server for all three meals of the day, he was assigned to clean the public areas of the first floor when he was not serving the meals.

Not much time had passed when Aaron made some new assignments as other new slaves came to serve in the house. Joseph noticed that many of these new slaves were handsome young men. As Aaron saw the potential in Joseph, he took him under his wing to train him in other areas of the household.

Much time had passed and Joseph still frequently wondered why he was in this position as a slave in a far off land so far away from his father and family.   Time passed by and Joseph continued to be trained in all the affairs of Potiphar's house. He found these various tasks to lack any challenge. His only challenge was to show a proper subservient attitude to the evil chief butcher and his family. He found it hard to bow to people he had no

The Dreamer

respect for.

It wasn't the work Joseph minded as much as the fact that he had no choice in the matter. He compared it to working back at home on Fathers Jacobs estate. He had responsibilities he alone was responsible for. He had challenging work to do, but above all, he could choose to do the work or not do the work. There were consequences if the work didn't get done, but the consequences did not include getting severely beaten or killed. Joseph saw Seth, a slave just a little older than Joseph, come out of Zeleakia's bedchambers. No one was allowed in Zeleakia's chambers other than her personal chambermaid. That was strange indeed. In fact, it was a very dangerous thing. Something that Joseph would never be caught doing for fear of the penalty of looking at the ruler's family in the eyes and that it was wrong. Being in private chambers was something that didn't show a subservient attitude and showed a familiar lack of respect. He could fathom what a man slave would be doing in a woman's chamber.

Joseph spoke of the situation with Aaron without mentioning any names. Aaron smiled as Joseph related the story. Aaron replied there would be times when some of the slave men were called upon to serve Zeleakia in a private and special way. He was instructed that because Joseph was a handsome young man to expect to be called upon by Zeleakia and to not refuse her. He was told to do exactly as she instructed.

"However, do not, under any circumstances, let Potiphar catch you doing special servant work for Zeleakia, as the consequence will be death," said Aaron.

"How can Potiphar penalize someone with their life

The Dreamer

if they are doing a service for the lady of the house?" asked Joseph naively.

Aaron knew Joseph to be well educated and a hard worker, and was surprised at the question. He wasn't sure if Joseph was acting stupid or if he really didn't know.

"I think you can figure out what kind of service the menservants are providing the lady of the manor," Aaron said with a grin.

Joseph furrowed his eyebrows and he thought about it. "No, I am sorry. I do not understand. It makes no sense and seems arbitrary. . ." Then Joseph thought back to his eldest brother Reuben and how he had laid with one of his fathers' wives.

"Are you saying that the lady of the house expects menservants to be intimate with her?"

"You are correct and never speak of it. It is something that must be done. If you refuse her, she can make your life miserable, she can even make up stories that she will tell her husband and have you put to death. That has only happened once. But it has happened, but mostly, no manswervant refuses her advances."

The Dreamer

Chapter 12: Mustard Tree

And the Lord, he it is that doth go before thee; he will be with thee, he will not fail thee, neither forsake thee: fear not, neither be dismayed. Deuteronomy 31:8

As Joseph's one year anniversary of being a slave came around, Aaron was promoted to an overseer of the manor and the estate grounds which included all the slaves in the outside gardens. Aaron was expected to manage it all by himself, but Joseph was a willing friend who helped Aaron by managing the affairs of the home, including the kitchen, all the meal service and household cleaning responsibilities, It was unofficial, but in Aaron's eyes, Joseph surpassed Sarin in working and getting things done. He was a reliable friend to have.

Joseph still had recurring dreams of the sheaves and the eleven stars which frustrated him since he could see no way that he could preside over the birthright as a slave in a far away country. Who would bow to a slave? He also had a recurring dream of the mustard tree. He still didn't understand the symbolism of that fascinating tree.

Joseph frequently felt that his life was pointless. As a slave the most he could hope for was to stay alive and have enough to eat. There were countless slaves who feared for both.

Prior to being beaten, kidnapped and sold into slavery, he had the whole world open to him with the birthright. Even if he hadn't been given the birthright, he had an exciting future to look forward to. When he contemplated these things, he would easily get depressed.

There were times when he wondered, "Why live if

The Dreamer

my future is based on getting enough to eat and avoiding getting beaten?" He wasn't afraid of death, he just didn't want to get beaten. He knew from his relationship with his Lord and the teachings of his mother and father that death wasn't anything to be feared if you lived a good and righteous life. He had lived a good life as a slave as far as that was possible. He wasn't in a position to serve God, all he really could do was to pray and be honest. If he were to die, and with the grace of God, he should have a good future waiting for him in the afterlife.

In this life, all he had was the past. His future was laid out for him with nothing to look forward to except a merciful death. With his past, he had wonderful memories of his father and mother. He also had great memories of his sister Dinah and limited memories of his younger brother Benjamin. He also had many spiritual experiences that he enjoyed reliving.

He was coming to terms with the idea that he would have to rely on himself if he wanted to maintain a relationship with God. He could no longer fall back on his father. He would have to learn to interpret his own dreams and he would have to learn how to commune with God if he wanted to learn more about the gospel life he should live.

Was there a reason to live the gospel he had been taught if he was going to spend his life as a slave in Potiphar's house? These thoughts and question had been weighing heavily on his mind for quite some time. After all, who could he serve and who could he influence. His every move was dictated by virtue of him being a slave. He had no freedom to do anything but think and in the night time, dream. Although of late, some of his dreams were

The Dreamer

nightmares brought on by the past years' life of a slave.

Joseph was trying to make sense of his life. It wasn't easy because he wasn't used to relying on himself and not being able to turn to his father for guidance and clarification. One day, as he was pondering his dilemma when the thought occurred to him that one of the recurring pieces of advice his father gave him was to pray and ask the Lord for guidance. He had been good at praying before going to sleep and many times through the day as time and circumstances allowed. But this was a different type of prayer and it would require a different approach. He wasn't sure how to approach the Lord, he just knew that he was on the right track. He was getting tired and he knew whatever that new approach was, it required more effort than he had left in him for the day.

Joseph had another night full of dreams. That night in his dreams he had the usual birthright dreams followed by the mustard plant dream with a twist. This time the mustard seed was planted in the desert near the mighty Nile. The plot of land where the seed was planted was then covered by a mighty estate and the primary building of that estate rested on top of where the seed had been planted.

The seed was nourished and watered and cared for with the mighty hand. The seed sprouted and soon the leaves and vines grew out of the doorways and windows and soon grew into a mighty tree. The base of the tree where the roots grew into the ground was covered by an estate that seemed somehow familiar.

The dream ended and Joseph woke up for another day of slave labor. He could perform any slave task in Potiphar's house without thinking because he knew them

The Dreamer

all so well. This morning he went about those tasks with an air of confidence that was so strong that it startled Joseph. He was so efficient in all his duties that he was allowed some time to ponder the dream of the mustard seed.

He slipped away to a garden near the kitchen that was surrounded by tall Date trees. In this small garden he could have a few moments alone. He found it curious that the small mustard plant had such humble beginnings and then grew into such a magnificent shade tree that served the surrounding land. Even unfamiliar, far away land was blessed by the mighty mustard tree. He was amazed at how far and wide the shade of that tree went.

As he came to realize this, he felt a warm, easy sensation overtake his body. It was a warm, pleasant sensation and something he couldn't deny. It was a very physical experience.

He thought about how that dream was different. He thought of an estate being placed on the surrounding area of where the seed was planted. Then he thought of the main house that was directly over the seed. It came to him as he pondered that the main house was the building he worked in. It was Potiphar's house and the rest of the lands and buildings were Potiphar's estate. As he worked over those thoughts, he felt a great calm and warm sensation flood his soul.

Then he felt extremely confused because he knew that Potiphar was an evil man. Not only did he preside over the Pharaoh's executions, he committed murder when it suited his purposes. His evil knew no bounds. He was rewarded by the Pharaoh for his evil deeds. His slaves lived in constant fear of punishment by death.

Why would a huge mustard tree that benefitted so

The Dreamer

many people come from Potiphar's home? A rule of nature is that a good tree cannot bring forth bad fruit, and a bad tree cannot produce good fruit. So how then could this mustard seed come from Potiphar and serve so many people for good?

Joseph knew he was onto something as he pondered over these thoughts. He felt like he was very close to figuring it out, but he seemed to come up just short of fully understanding the dream. Weeks turned into months and the new found confidence that came from Joseph did not go unnoticed.

Joseph's friend Aaron was caught in Zeleakia's room. He was following the commands of Zeleakia, but he was caught by Potiphar and then quickly put to death by Potiphar's own hand.

Potiphar called for Joseph to come to his office. Joseph was frightened because this was the first time he had been called on by the master of the house. Aaron was dead and Joseph just might be next. It was no secret that Joseph and Aaron were friends. On his way down the last long hallway to Potiphar's office, Joseph had a deep and overwhelming feeling of peace and comfort came over him. So much so that he feared nothing. Not even Potiphar.

"Aaron betrayed me, by sleeping with my wife. That is unforgivable. His punishment was just. Now he sleeps with the worms. I am appointing you to be the overseer of all of my household and estate. In matters of my household and estate you report to me and me alone. Do you understand?"

Joseph bowed to Potiphar as he answered, "Yes, my lord."

The Dreamer

"Among your many new duties is to keep a watchful eye on my wife and see that no one goes in unto her. Do you understand?"

"Yes, my lord."

"With these new responsibilities come new quarters. You will move your belongings to Aaron's old room. Take as your own anything of his that you like and you may distribute anything that remains to your fellow slaves as you see fit."

Bowing again, Joseph said, "Yes, my lord."

"You will be held accountable for any infraction of the slaves of this household and on my estate. Therefore, you may use any force you deem necessary to keep the slaves in line and serving me to my satisfaction."

"Yes, my lord."

"Do you have anything else to say?"

"Yes, my lord," Joseph bowed again. "Thank you, my lord, for your trust and faith me, your lowly servant."

"Very well then, see to it. You are dismissed."

Bowing again, "Thank you, my lord." Joseph turned and exited Potiphar's room.

While Joseph was doing the needed work to change his living quarters, he thought of the mustard plant. Suddenly he knew what it all meant. It was related to his birthright. Even though he was no longer living under his father's roof, he was still destined for greatness under the Lord. The mustard seed was him. He was the mustard plant and somehow, he would serve far and wide, at least that is what he thought it meant.

It didn't seem possible, and he wondered how that could ever happen. The only thing he knew for sure was the marvelous and strong spiritual feeling he had been

The Dreamer

blessed with. He didn't know how he would become that mighty mustard tree, but he knew he would.

The Dreamer

Chapter 13: Overseer

That ye may be the children of your Father which is in heaven: for he maketh his sun to rise on the evil and on the good, and sendeth rain on the just and on the unjust. Matthew 5:45

Joseph was lonely as a slave. He had been lonely since he was sold into Egyptian slavery and had never felt anything as bad as loneliness. His days were long, but he quickly grew adept to the new requirements that were associated with his job. Joseph was on his way to check on the field servants when the idea came to him to transfer Mordecai to the house. By doing that, he would have a friend. He sent a messenger ahead of him to gather all the slaves and servants together in front of the slave quarters.

Potiphar's estate was well manicured with endless flowers and greenery. The roads and walkways were lined with cobblestones. In spite of such close proximity to the vast, dry, sandy desert, the estate was lush and verdant. Joseph was coming to enjoy these visits he needed to make to various groups of fields slaves. The scenery was engaging. He was learning to appreciate the small things. When he arrived, he spoke to all that were gathered.

"I have been appointed by Potiphar to oversee all of his household and his estate," said Joseph as he stood tall commanding respect. "As your actions reflect on me, by edict from Potiphar you will report directly to me. I do not want to be punished by Potiphar and so I will hold you all accountable for the job you do. If you please me and I please Potiphar then we will all get along together. I will do all in my power to make your lives as enjoyable as possible, but so long as we are all slaves to the master of this estate, we will all have to live accordingly. I will remain here to answer any questions or concerns you have, but remember, you still have your days work to do so be wise with your questions. Before I dismiss all of you, Mordecai, wherever you are, please come forward."

There was a small disturbance in the middle of the crowd of slaves as Mordecai made his way to the front of the group of servants. Joseph reached out his hand. Mordecai walked up to young Joseph and reached for Joseph's hand and shook it.

"It is good to see you, Joseph. I wondered if our paths would ever cross again."

"I have wondered the same thing. It occurred to me on my way out to the fields, with this new assignment, I have the power to reassign you. I am taking you back with me to serve in the main house. Why don't you gather your things while I answer a few questions," said Joseph as he noticed a line forming to talk to him.

"All I have is a plate and a cup."

"You don't even have a change of clothes?"

"No. I have what I am wearing and the plate and cup."

"Never mind getting your things. I have several items of clothing we can make to fit you and some other items you might like from Aaron. Since he is dead, I have been distributing his things to those who need them. Say your goodbyes and we will leave shortly."

Joseph turned to the small line and went through everyone's questions. Shortly he was on his way back to the main house, only this time he had someone he knew from before he was a slave.

The Dreamer

"I have been living the lonely life of a slave. It is good to see you again Mordecai."

"It is indeed good to see you, Joseph. How have things been working so close to Potiphar?"

"I was afraid at first because of your warning to stay as far away from him as I could. I still follow that advice."

"From the look of things, I doubt you need to follow anyone's advice. You seem to be doing exceptionally well."

"The Lord has truly blessed me, that is for sure."

"Why would your God bless you in your service to a wicked man? I know you are not doing anything wicked, but blessing you is blessing Potiphar."

"If I had not had a recurring dream to explain it, I do not think I could answer that question. I still do not know exactly how it will work out. What I do know for now is, in the long run, these blessings will be for the greater good. In the meantime, Potiphar will be greatly blessed."

"I have thought countless times of the long conversation we had that night in Shechem, and I have pondered over it. I have always struggled with having faith in our Hebrew God. Since being in Egypt and being a little exposed to all this idol worship and all these pagan gods, I feel like our Hebrew God makes sense. I feel like I am on the verge of believing in the God of our Fathers. I hope we can discuss my faith and I hope you will teach me more about our God."

"I will be happy to tell you anything you want to know and explain everything I can about our God. I am very glad to hear you talk like that. Our God not only is a jealous God as far as not wanting us to worship pagan Gods, but he only wants us to worship him and him alone."

"How long until we will be at the main building?"

The Dreamer

asked Mordecai as he scratched his beard.

"We have a few minutes."

"I was hoping we could start our conversation now about our Hebrew God."

"I frequently take walks around the fields and estates to oversee what is going on. We can take one of those walks now and be out as long as we want," replied Joseph.

"That is amazing freedom for a slave," observed Mordecai.

"It is, but in the end, I am still just a slave like everyone else around here," said Joseph as he waved his hand toward the southern horizon where there were scores of slaves working in a large corn field.

Joseph had an epiphany as he made that comment about being a slave. "Mordecai, like I said, I will answer all your questions the best I can and teach you all I know, but you need to know that in the end, I am no better than you. None of us are any better than anyone else. In God's eyes any King of any kingdom, including the Pharaoh are not valued any higher than any slave of any race or nationality."

"I like that lesson," said Mordecai. "When you think about it, it all makes sense, after all, we are all cousins when you consider we all come from Adam and Eve."

"It is more than just that. To me, it is a new revelation. You see, I was raised by, Israel and we were very wealthy and my Father was very prosperous. I was raised with servants. True, I worked the fields and the flocks alongside the servants, but growing up I always thought that because they were hired hands and from a lower class, I was better than them."

The Dreamer

"Really? That surprises me a little," responded Mordecai.

"It saddens me that I have behaved that way and felt that way for so long. I really need to repent of those feelings. I feel terrible. Being a slave, lower than servants I still felt that way until just now."

"If you have room for repentance, then that gives me hope. I know that the more I learn of God, I will have need to repent and change my ways," said Mordecai.

"Repentance is a wonderful blessing. It is with the grace of God that we can repent and be forgiven of our sins. God is ready and waiting to forgive us, if and when we come to him," said Joseph.

"That sounds so kind and nice, a real blessing from God."

"Our God is truly a God of love, grace, and forgiveness, that is for certain."

"I have only been away from the backbreaking work of the fields for less than an hour and I feel so much better. It is like my feet are barely touching the ground. Thank you for coming to get me."

"You are welcome, but I wonder if it is being away from the fields that is making you feel so good or could it be because of the sweet spirit that we are feeling as we learn and talk about our Lord?"

As Joseph made that comment, something profound and deep came over Mordecai. It was like a pleasant warm feeling radiating in his chest. His soul felt so peaceful and calm.

"I am feeling something so wonderful and profound right now and I know it has something to do with what we are talking about," said Mordecai.

The Dreamer

"The Lord blesses us with gifts of his spirit to help us find and understand truth. I think that is what you are experiencing."

"It makes perfect sense. I know I am feeling something and whatever it is . . . The Spirit of God. . . It is wonderful."

"I am certain that I am feeling it too. The words you are using to describe the feelings make perfect sense to me. Your job is twofold. One is to work in and eventually supervise the household slaves. The second aspect of your job will be acting as my assistant. We will spend a lot of time together. We will be able to talk and learn together, even pray together."

"I am truly looking forward to it," said Mordecai.

"I am hoping that the work in the household will be physically easier on you." They finished the tour of that section of Potiphar's estate and turned toward the main house. Once they got there, Joseph had Mordecai rummage through Aaron's clothing and belongings and pick out whatever suited him. He was also measured for his housework clothes to match what the other slaves wore.

Joseph escorted Mordecai to the beautiful pool where he could clean himself off.

"I am sorry to inform you," said Joseph, "but you will be required to be clean shaven, and that includes your head." Joseph made sure that this bathing experience was much better for Mordecai than it was for Joseph. He gave Mordecai full privacy and a sharp razor.

Mordecai quickly learned his personal duties of the household and advanced quickly to supervisor of the entire household. He was a quick study in the various tasks he

The Dreamer

worked on with Joseph. He was proving to be well-favored of the Lord, like his friend Joseph.

As they would take trips around the sprawling estate, they would talk often about the Hebrew God and Mordecai's heart was on fire. He was anxious to learn and to apply the teaching in his everyday life.

Time passed, first one year, then another. There had been harmony in the household and in the fields. Mordecai and Joseph developed a deep and abiding friendship that was the highlight of their day.

Then one day Joseph was summoned into Potiphar's office.

"Yes, my lord, what can I do for you?" asked Joseph with a distinct air of confidence in his voice.

"I have been going over the annual reports and I have noticed in the two years you have been the overseer of my household and the slaves of the fields, my profits have increased threefold. That is very impressive. Also, I have noticed the harmony among the slaves in my home and throughout my estate. Other than that nasty mess with Aaron, things have not been better."

Joseph disapproved of the way Potiphar handled Aaron by killing him because of getting caught with Zeleakia, he was not in a position, he felt, to say anything about that matter.

"I am going to make you overseer of everything I own. I want to see if you can do with my herds and crops in the farmland near the Nile that you have done on my Estate."

"Your confidence in me is humbling my Lord"

"Just do whatever it is you have been doing and I am sure it will all work out as I hope it will. You will oversee the slaves and servants, even the paid servants. I will send an edict around all of my holdings telling everyone of this change. They will report directly to you."

"May I ask a question, my lord?"

"Indeed."

"If I am to be responsible for all of your wealth, does that give me control over the slaves and servants as far as when to acquire more slaves and when to retire them?"

"My boy, slaves do not retire. But yes indeed. You will oversee the accounting and every conceivable thing that I own, including nannies' and tutors for my children. Your authority is full and complete. The only thing not in your control is my wife Zeleakia. Am I clear?"

"Pardon my slowness in catching on to what you are telling me my lord, but I am a slave and you are giving me such power and control even over-paid servants– "

"Like I said," Potiphar interrupted, "You are in charge of everything I own. Your responsibility is to make them as profitable as you have done with my estate."

"Are you concerned about my loyalty?"

"I have watched you from afar. I know that you assemble my servants and slaves and teach them of your Hebrew God. I know you teach integrity and honesty which is no small thing to teach to the slaves whose only desire is freedom. In the two years, you have been in charge, we have had untold harmony with no attempted escapes and no serious punishment. For all I know, your teachings to my servants and slaves may be what has made my profits soar.

However, since you are in charge of everything I own, I will assign guards from the Pharaoh's army that I command, to watch you and protect you on your comings

The Dreamer

and goings. A slave with as much power as you now have, it may be disconcerting to the average Egyptian. Your duties will take you away from time to time and they will go with you wherever you need to go."

Joseph knew that while Potiphar may be telling the truth for the need for guards, they were also there to ensure that Joseph did not escape. Joseph wondered about the lack of directness coming from Potiphar.

"Thank you, my lord. Is there anything else you wish to say to me?" asked Joseph.

"Your first assignment will be to deliver a notice of the new changes with you in charge. Create a document that will explain everything to my slaves and servants and after I approve it, I will attach my seal to it and you will deliver it as soon as possible. I am anxious to employ your methods and increase my wealth."

"Very well. I will have a document ready for you within the hour."

"Tomorrow morning will be soon enough."

"Thank you, my lord. . . As you wish."

Joseph left Potiphar's office and went to his own office where Mordecai was waiting for him to arrive. Joseph told Mordecai every detail of his conversation with Potiphar.

"You know Joseph," Mordecai said, "I have wondered why you work so hard and so efficiently for a man you hate and for a man who keeps you as a slave. Now I see why."

"What might that be?" asked Joseph.

"It is no secret that the Hebrew God you worship is with you. The Hebrew God is not like the Egyptian Gods or other idles that are worshiped around this country, but

The Dreamer

rather your God is a living God who is with you. He inspires you and blesses you. Now you have a chance to make life better for all these poor slaves and servants with no place to go."

"I have told you the dream of the tares of wheat and I've told you the dream about the eleven stars, but I have kept one important dream from you because while I thought I understood it I still had doubts. Now I am fairly certain of the interpretation.

"You are known in private circles as the Dreamer," said Mordecai. "You have also shared many other dreams and even interpreted a few dreams for fellow slaves. I am curious to this other dream you're talking about. I would be grateful to hear it."

"I call it the dream of the mustard plant . . ." Joseph proceeded to tell Mordecai the details of the dream of the mustard tree.

After hearing about that dream Mordecai spoke up and said, "While I do not have the gift of dreams like you do, I think it is obvious that one aspect of that dream is you now have the power to make things a little more tolerable for all your fellow slaves and all of Potiphar's servants. Our work conditions, well at least the conditions for the slaves in the fields are rough, and maybe some of the shade of that mustard tree is symbolic of what you can do for all the slaves. The size of the tree might be the increase in wealth you are creating for Potiphar."

"Isn't that wonderful," said Joseph. "All that hard work we provide for Potiphar gives us better conditions, but creates untold wealth for that evil man." Joseph shook his head in disbelief.

"Every little bit of hope for the slaves is more than

The Dreamer

they had the day before," said a wise Mordecai.

The Dreamer

Chapter 14: Zeleakia

Blessed are they which are persecuted for righteousness' sake: for theirs is the kingdom of heaven. Matthew 5:10

The burning sun was overhead in the midst of a bright blue sky as Joseph and Mordecai walked together, with the guards giving them a degree of privacy by walking ahead and behind them. The road was long and dusty, but Joseph and Mordecai were well provided for with cool, clear water to drink, and plenty of food to eat.

Mordecai now served as Joseph's personal assistant. Along with their guards, they were on their way to some of Potiphar's fields near the Nile. They were deep in conversation. Many of their conversations were about work and managing resources, but they found plenty of time to talk about God and personal things.

"I've been thinking," said Mordecai, "about how things work in the main house. I've noticed that there are a number of strong young slaves who could be better used in the fields and get more work done than the very young and very old slaves that now work hard in the crop lands. Replace the young, strong house servants with the old and young and you increase productivity by using slaves where they can do the best.

The younger and older slaves could easily do the housework and be equally productive. It would be somewhat fair, at least as fair as slave labor can be," said Mordecai as he rubbed his bald head.

"That is a terrific idea," declared Joseph. "I have been looking for ways to take care of the elderly slaves and this could well be the way to do it."

The Dreamer

Joseph was thinking about the idea when he said, "There is one serious problem with that idea."

"What is that?" asked Mordecai, who was sipping from the water vessel.

"One of the reasons why we have young, strong slaves working in the main house is because of Zeleakia. Many of them have been hand picked by her."

"Are you not responsible for them?" asked Mordecai thoughtfully.

"Yes, yes I am. According to what Potiphar said, I am responsible for every slave and servant who works for Potiphar."

"What do you suppose Zeleakia would say if you transferred some of them into the fields?"

"I do not know, but I could try it. Just two or three at a time and get a feel for things, to see how she might react. I can always transfer them back to the way they were if I am told to."

"What have you got to lose?" replied Mordecai.

"That is true. There are worse things in life than death," said Joseph as he smiled. "Your ideas of letting the weaker slaves work in the house is similar to my idea about retiring the older slaves. If we had enough slaves to put those stronger ones to work in the field, then rotate the weaker ones into the house and eventually let the oldest retire and just do the odd's jobs that crop up . . . But I would have to show Potiphar that he is still gaining wealth. All he cares about are his profits," said Joseph.

"Do you have to tell him what you are doing ahead of time or could you make the changes and show him the end of year production results?" asked Mordecai.

"He made it sound like he would be content with

The Dreamer

year-end profits, especially if they showed an increase."

Ideas were flowing into Joseph's head as he was talking with Mordecai. "I can hire new strong slaves, especially to replace the oldest slaves. Between that and rotating the strong house slaves out to the field, the older ones work in the house and the oldest ones retire . . . It will take some time to implement, but if I can ease the burden of the slaves it would be worth the effort," Joseph was nodding his head.

While Joseph knew he was doing right by easing the burden of the slaves as much as possible, he was not content to remain a slave. He had great faith and knew that with God all things are possible. He just wondered why Almighty God had not seen fit to deliver him from bondage. Joseph and Mordecai started to implement the new plans. They bought new salves to help. They didn't like buying slaves, but they figured that all the places these slaves could work, working under Joseph was better than working for other slave owners.

Joseph was on a brisk walk alone to check on some of the slaves in the distant farmlands and he got lost in his mind. He was filled with wonderful memories of his mother and father. One of the topics his Mother and father, loved to talk about was the doctrine of charity, which was the pure love of God. He mentally reviewed the attributes of charity the best that he could remember, being long-suffering, not being puffed up, not easily provoked, not behaving unseemly and enduring all things.

He had tried to endure all things and had taught his servants the importance of enduring along with the other aspects of the Lords love. He taught them as they learned about God and his teachings they would grow to love the

The Dreamer

Lord, and as they did, they would want to live like him and that is where charity came in.

It was easy to see these aspects of love from God's perspective, like being long-suffering to his children on earth as they went around doing good sometimes and evil other times. God did not give up on his children. To apply the concept of long-suffering, Joseph was determined he would not give up on God. Therefore, he needed to be long-suffering to God while he was waiting on him for deliverance or some other type of blessing.

Joseph and Mordecai strived to teach the benefits of loving God with all one's heart, might, mind and strength because when someone loves so completely it becomes a natural desire to want to please that person.

He was glad Mordecai wasn't with him this time because as he thought these things he felt tender-hearted. He thought about his mother and the profound impact she had on him when he was young. The impact was so great in spite of having only a few years with her, her influence continued throughout Joseph's life.

Joseph's heart was full of tenderness and of longing for his mother. In that moment, time seemed to stop. It was almost as if she was there with him in that moment, holding his hand and sharing his burdens. Why cannot life be like this all the time? Joseph lamented.

That idea of easing the burdens of the slaves was what kept Joseph going for the next five years. For those years there was harmony among the slaves and the oldest and youngest slaves were able to have much more rest than ever before. Joseph was judged successful at the end of every year by Potiphar. Every year there was a twofold or threefold increase in wealth which was

The Dreamer

miraculous because Potiphar still had the same acreage. But with each harvest, there was more grain. More corn and more calves. It was as if his increase of wealth came from out of nowhere. Although Potiphar didn't believe in the Hebrew God, he acknowledged that Joseph's God may be the reason for the dramatic increase, even if it didn't make sense.

Potiphar always gave Zeleakia what she wanted, until now. When she complained that many of her hand-picked young servants were being rotated to the fields, Potiphar let it stand and didn't bother Joseph with the complaints. Potiphar was content to let Joseph do whatever he wanted so long as the profits soared every year.

~

The beautiful and worldly Zeleakia was out with many of her socialite friends, shopping at the market as much for fun and entertainment as for anything else since she had servants do her shopping.

"Zeleakia, how are your man-servants serving you lately?" giggled Amense.

"Stop that. That is none of your business," replied Zeleakia with a smile.

"Oh, come on, tell us about your latest conquest," teased Hotep as she grinned at Zeleakia, "or are there not enough menservants for you?"

"Well, all right. I will tell you all. Joseph, that young Hebrew you have teased me about. He is older now and

The Dreamer

his good looks have gotten even better if you can believe that. He is the prettiest man I have ever seen which is why I talk about him so much."

"That young Hebrew is all that you have been talking about for the last six or seven years," said Hasina.

"Well, I do not know for certain," replied Amense. "She has had her eyes on a few of the other slaves recently.

"And her hands," giggled Cabar.

"You ladies would not give me such a hard time if you knew just how handsome Joseph is. I declare, the older that man gets the better looking he is," explained Zeleakia. "He is filling out quite nicely."

"Why do you not invite us all over for a peek at your harem?" asked Cabar.

"If I do, then you must all promise me you will keep your hands to yourself. Joseph is all mine."

They all agreed to Zeleakia's request and they were all given invitations for an afternoon garden party. The day of the party arrived along with several of Zeleakia's society friends. They were all given a small bowl of fruit and a knife to slice the fruit.

"Come this way, ladies. We will adjourn to the courtyard where were we will eat our fruit and drink our wine," said Zeleakia as she led them through her mansion.

Zeleakia worked out a plan that while all her friends were in the middle of cutting their fruit she would summon Joseph. Everything went as planned. Her friends were cutting and preparing their fruit when Zeleakia called Joseph. A few moments later in walked Joseph. He walked from one side of the courtyard to the other where Zeleakia was. He spoke with Zeleakia and she issued some

The Dreamer

frivolous orders. As they were engaged in a made up conversation, Zeleakia heard small cries of pain from a few of the ladies in the room.

Ever the loyal servant, Joseph went to the women in distress asking what their trouble was. Each of them had been carried away looking at the gorgeous Joseph and stopped concentrating on their fruit, in the process cutting their fingers. They had cut their finger, leaving blood on some of the fruit and cutting block. Joseph called some of the servants to help bind the wounds. He was oblivious to Zeleakia's scheme. While the servants scurried to resolve the trouble caused by Zeleakia, she watched the women with a big smile on her face. Maybe now they wouldn't be so quick to judge.

From that time forward her friends refrained from teasing Zeleakia. They acknowledged Joseph was the prettiest man alive. Their new concern was how had Zeleakia kept her hands off of him for so long.

~

Joseph was celebrating his twenty-sixth birthday by reminiscing about his life. A third of his young life had been spent as a slave to the evilest man in Egypt. He had worked hard and as a result of his efforts and the many blessings of the Lord he had greatly expanded Potiphar's wealth. As a result of Joseph's efforts, the slave conditions improved as much as they could for the slaves and when Potiphar finally found out what Joseph was doing, he let it slide since his wealth was so vast and continued to

The Dreamer

increase. He didn't want to interfere with whatever was working to make him so wealthy. He was wealthy before Joseph, but now it was rumored that he was the wealthiest man in all of Egypt other than King Sesostris.

Mordecai happened upon Joseph as he was pondering his life. He could see Joseph was deep in thought.

"Is everything all right Joseph?"

"Well, no. Not at all. I am a slave and that is as far from all right as you can get."

"Is it any comfort to know all you have accomplished for your fellow slaves?"

"I am grateful for that, but in all honesty, I would much rather not be a slave. I sometimes think I would prefer my brother's company over being a slave and they all hated me."

"I have often wondered why you were such a hard worker when you first became a slave. You did not seem to let things get to you. You had lost everything and yet you were diligent."

"I think I did it out of self-preservation," said Joseph.

"That does not make any sense to me," sighed Mordecai. "You can still work with a bad attitude."

"That is what I did for a while. I did my job and nothing more. I let life get to me. I let life beat me up. Somehow I figured out I should try working harder and better and not dwell on the past or on things that I cannot change. When I did all that, I felt the blessings of God come upon me, the greatest blessing was feeling good about the work I had done. It seemed to me when I chose to not let life get to me, I felt better."

"I know your story and I know what you have been

The Dreamer

through being kidnapped and being sold into slavery. Life hit you hard."

"Do not forget Mordecai, you got hit hard as well."

"Yes, my flocks were stolen by your brothers and my new flock was scattered by the Ishmeelites, and I was kidnapped and sold into slavery, but at least it was not my own kindred doing it to me, and I did not have the good attitude that you did."

"I guess not having your freedom is hard no matter your circumstances," said Joseph.

The conversation between Joseph and Mordecai was interrupted when Potiphar rode up in his chariot and gave the reigns to Mordecai. Potiphar's feet were covered in blood and the cuffs of his sleeves were crimson with blood. There was some blood splatter on his tunic. The smell of death came from him.

Deliberately and most carefully Mordecai kept his distance as much as was possible as he gathered the reigns and lead the two horses and chariot into the barn.

"Good afternoon, my lord," said Joseph with a distasteful lump in his throat. He loathed Potiphar and times like this reminded Joseph just how evil this man was. You never knew if the blood on Potiphar came from his job as chief executioner for the Pharaoh or if it was his personal rage that lead him to end someone's precious life.

The Dreamer

Chapter 15: Still A Slave

And we know that all things work together for good to them that love God, to them who are the called according to his purpose. Romans 8:28

Potiphar killed Aaron for being caught with Zeleakia. After that, Joseph assigned most of the young, strong, and robust men to the fields and brought in young slaves along with older slaves to work in the main house. This made it impossible for Zeleakia to find any men who suited her taste.

She had to look outside the home for her trysts. In spite of that, she had been known to flirt with Joseph from time to time. Every time she did, she was rebuffed by Joseph in the most polite and tactful manner possible. Even though Joseph had virtually full power over the estate, he still had to flatter Zeleakia and answer to her and Potiphar. After all, he was still a slave.

To Joseph's annoyance, she had been coming onto him more frequently. In an effort to thwart her advances, Joseph made sure that wherever he was, there would be at least two or three people with him. She was less inclined to flirt with him in front of others. She was well known for her beautiful looks as well as her appetites of the flesh.

It seemed as if everyone knew what she did with men, including Potiphar, yet her inappropriate behavior continued. This confused Joseph. If the men were killed who were caught with her, then why would any man even respond to her advances. Joseph was a devoted man of God and everyone knew it. He lived in such a way as to command everyone's respect. He was well aware of worldly ways, especially after living in Egypt for so long. He knew Zeleakia was a stunning woman, but he honestly had no physical interest in her in the least. He understood why so many men did, he was just not one of them. He appreciated gorgeous women, but he conducted himself so as to not let himself be tempted by them. Lately, it seemed a constant battle, avoiding Zeleakia.

Mordecai asked him how he withstood her advances, and his response was the same answer as how he dealt with his other trials and tribulations that he encountered as a slave. He put his trust and worries in the Lord. So far it worked and Joseph had been able to avoid or overcome Zeleakia's flirtations.

Joseph was working in the main room using the big dining table to placed countless papyri in a particular order. He was preparing year-end reports for Potiphar and he needed the room. He had Mordecai and three other men with him to work on the reports. He felt confident that he was well protected against Zeleakia if she should return home early. He left nothing to chance. He was more concerned about not offending his God than he was about Potiphar's wrath. Although if he let the Lord down, he might appreciate Potiphar's wrath.

Joseph, Mordecai and their assistants had been working most of the day and it was getting late. These assistants who were helping Joseph had other responsibilities they needed to attend to so Joseph dismissed them. He figured he and Mordecai would be wrapping up shortly. They had worked pass dinner and so Mordecai went into the kitchen to ask the cook to prepare something for Joseph and him.

The Dreamer

Zeleakia came barging through the doors of the main house while Joseph was hunched over the papyri. He was deep in thought and didn't hear Zeleakia's entrance. Then he felt a hand softly touch the small of his back as it slid up to his neck. As her hand was sliding, he was startled and jumped. He turned to see Zeleakia standing so close to him he flinched again. He had been so careful to keep his distance from her that he was bewildered at how she managed to get so close to him.

"My, my Joseph. Why are you so jittery? What is wrong with my handsome slave?" said Zeleakia in a controlling and seductive tone.

"Nothing is wrong now that I have my wits about me," said Joseph. "Is there something I can help you with my lady?" Joseph was discretely stepping away from her as he spoke.

As he quickly took small, steady steps away from her, she followed him, which flustered him and he picked up the pace. She responded accordingly. "What is wrong my handsome fellow? Why are you avoiding me? Do you not find me desirable?"

She had never been this blunt. He couldn't respond without being blunt as well. Taking courage from his trust in God, he replied, "I do not look upon you in a worldly sense and I have no desire to be familiar with you."

"Hmm, that is courageous talk from a slave. You know, I can make up whatever story I want to tell my husband and he would only be too happy to kill you."

She was about to say more when Mordecai entered the room. "I have been observing your conversation and I am only too glad to testify on Joseph's behalf. I think he is safe from you." Mordecai swallowed hard after he realized

The Dreamer

what he had just said and who he said it too.

"How dare you speak to me that way Mordecai. I will have your head." Zeleakia turned toward the stairs and left the main room in a huff.

"Joseph, did I just sign my death warrant?" asked a visibly upset Mordecai.

"No, I doubt it. That was taking a chance though, speaking that way. If Potiphar says anything, I will clear it up. He knows how I rely on you." Joseph started to collect all the forms and charts as he went on to say, "Thank you for your entrance. I was running out of things to say to Zeleakia. You could have made a quicker entrance, though."

"I am sorry about that. I heard what she was saying and I just listened for a minute. I was kind of startled at how brazen she was toward you. I will not let that happen again."

They both cleaned off the table in time for their food to be served to them. Since Joseph had been so successful for Potiphar, he relaxed the rules regarding Joseph and Mordecai's use of the main house. They didn't eat often in the main dining hall, but tonight it made sense.

~

A week had passed since that terrible ordeal with Zeleakia. Joseph and Mordecai had finished all the reports and Joseph presented them to Potiphar. The past year had seen a fourfold increase in profits. Potiphar was exceedingly pleased with Joseph. After they were done with the official portion of the meeting, Potiphar mentioned that Zeleakia had told him a terrible story of how Mordecai had come onto her and propositioned her. He asked Joseph if he knew anything about it.

Joseph knew that an honest answer could potentially put his own standing with Potiphar in jeopardy, but he knew he had to be honest, both for his desire to please his God and because he told Mordecai he would handle it.

"My Lord," Joseph started off weakly, "Mordecai and I were working late on the reports in the dining hall. He left for a few minutes to the kitchen and your wife came into the hall and started talking to me. With all due respect, my Lord," Joseph coughed to clear his throat, "she was flirting with me and I was refusing her advances. Mordecai saw the whole thing and when she threatened me, he stood up for me by telling her he saw what really happened. Mordecai is not guilty of anything except for standing up to her and that was only in my defense."

Shaking his head, Potiphar said, "I suspected as much. I highly doubted that Mordecai would do something so brazen as what she claimed. I was hoping you would verify my assumptions and you did. That is all that needs to be said. The situation need not be worried about any longer. You are dismissed."

Joseph bowed to Potiphar and left the room and went off to find Mordecai and tell him what had just happened.

~

Joseph was out in the middle of Potiphar's estate on his way to pay a visit to some of the slaves working in the fields. He was taking a route that involved going over a

The Dreamer

hill. At the top of that hill, he could see over the walls that surrounded Potiphar's vast estate. He was able to see the mighty Nile river.

As Joseph scanned his surroundings, he marveled at the mighty Nile. All around him was the desert, but wherever the river and its tributaries touched land out came abundant life. A tributary reached far from the appointed course of the Nile, it reached far enough inland that it created wonderful farm land for Potiphar's estate. Joseph was surrounded on both sides of the hill with beautiful and peaceful gardens. This location was one of Joseph's favorite spots.

It served as a place of private worship for Joseph. He found a large rock, big enough to sit on and still see the Nile. Joseph first started thinking about various things and slowly he started daydreaming about his beloved father and mother. He reflected on various memories of both of his parents. As he wiped a tear away, he started thinking just about his father. He longed for an opportunity to hug his father and be held in his arms. As he reflected on some of the momentous memories that included hugging his father, he got caught up in what he thought was another daydream.

"Father, why did you give me the birthright? I have spent all of my adult life in captivity as a slave. How can I exercise the gifts of the birthright while in captivity?" asked an emotional Joseph.

"I did not give you the birthright. It was not mine to give. The birthright came from the God of Abraham. I was instructed by the Lord to place the birthright on you."

"What good is it for me to have the birthright when I will spend the rest of my life as a slave for a murderous

The Dreamer

Egyptian?"

"Mans ways are not Gods ways and God's ways are not man's ways. The God of our fathers wanted you to have the birthright which is a blessing you will have for the rest of your life, so long as you are worthy of it. Always live so that you can bear up the responsibilities of the birthright."

"What does that mean father?"

"God knows everything. He can see the beginning from the end. We are limited as to what we can see in our earthly mind. He will tell us to do things when there does not appear to be anyway to accomplish it, but that is only because we cannot see what Jehovah can see. Often we just have to be patient and wait to see how all things work together for the good of man from the blessings of God."

"I have been a slave for so long now . . . I hate the word 'patience', I do not want to be patience any longer," said Joseph with angst.

"When Jehovah tells us to do something we must do it with faith knowing he knows how it will turn out. And it will turn out for our good. But we need to have faith, be patient and desire to submit our self to the will of God."

"Are you saying it is the will of God that I am a slave?" asked Joseph.

"I cannot answer that. What I can answer is that all things work out for the good of those who love their God, and are willing to be humble and obedient to him. He will always provide a way for us to accomplish whatever he requires from us," said Father Jacob.

Joseph just shook his head in disbelief. He wasn't sure what to think. He could see the vision of his father starting to fade. "Father, do not go, please do not leave

The Dreamer

me."

"Do not question the ways of the Lord, my son. Have faith and hope in Jehovah, and you will live a wonderful life that you can be proud of," said Father Jacob as he faded away.

Joseph was left alone with his thoughts. What did I just experience? Was it a dream or a vision? Was it even real? Joseph knew it was real because of the overwhelming feelings inside of him. The things he learned were true even if it was only a daytime dream and not really his father. He wished he would have thought to try and hug his father.

Another year passed for Joseph in slavery as Potiphar's wealth continued to grow. The conditions of the slaves improved steadily due to the changes he and Mordecai had implemented. As time progressed, Zeleakia's advances became more brazen, but Joseph was able to withstand them.

He worked hard living up to his birthright blessing. So far as he understood, he still carried the blessing. He hung onto the many dreams that he had received over the years. He would receive various new dreams from time to time to help educate him and strengthen him. He still had periods of despair, but he was able to acknowledge that even though he was a slave, Jehovah was with him and blessing him. He just couldn't understand the direction he was in, only that he was being watched over by his God.

Time went on and as Potiphar's wealth increased, Joseph and Mordecai's responsibilities increased. They were having to divide themselves up to oversee all that was going on. They were not able to enjoy each other's friendship as much as they would like. Time passed slowly

The Dreamer

for Joseph because he was still, at the end of the day a slave. His conditions were as good as they possibly could be for him, but he was still just a slave.

Joseph had his ups and downs. One day while he was down at the pool bathing himself he felt overwhelmed. The feeling was so great he quickly looked around to see if anyone was present. He was alone. The feeling of being overwhelmed was crippling. It affected him emotionally and physically. As he mourned his loss of freedom he felt anger and rage at being a slave. He felt out of control, like his life was crumbling down around him. Joseph was in deep despair sobbing out of control. It was as if a darkness was overcoming him.

As he felt he was about to lose all hope of life and breathing, an overwhelming feeling of hope came over him telling him that he could just call upon the God of his fathers and find help.

He was already on his knees in the middle of the pool. He cried out to Almighty God, "Please help me. I know death is not to be feared, but I still have a desire to live. Please strengthen me and give me the power to overcome whatever it is that has control over me." As he was thus calling upon Jehovah, he felt a tremendous spirit of peace, hope, and love. It was the peace that comes from God alone. It was the hope that comes from knowing that your God has all power, and a love that is so strong it can only come from him.

The Dreamer

Chapter 16: Falsely Accused

When thou art in tribulation, and all these things are come upon thee . . . if thou turn to the Lord thy God, and shalt be obedient unto his voice. For the Lord thy God is a merciful God; he will not forsake thee, neither destroy thee, nor forget the covenant of thy fathers which he sware unto them. Deuteronomy 4:30-31

     Everyday seemed to pass by slowly for Joseph, yet the year as a whole seemed to have passed by quickly. Ever since he had the dream with his Father Jacob, he had pursued his life, such as it was, with a renewed strength and a new, improved attitude. People around him noticed something new and different about him, even Potiphar mentioned to Joseph that he seemed different. Yet Potiphar still had two royal guards go with Joseph whenever he left the estate.

     Zeleakia had come on to Joseph many times over the past year and he had been able to slip out from under her influence. Of late, her advancements had come more frequently and more urgent in spite of his best efforts.

     It seemed whenever he went into the main house, Zeleakia was waiting for him. Joseph tried the best he could to send Mordecai into the main house with the authority to do whatever he needed to get done. He had managed for an entire month to avoid her, but he could not completely avoid her with his many responsibilities.

     He had to go into the main house so he waited until he heard that she was gone to the market. He was in the house taking care of his business. It was quiet because no one was around. Joseph was getting a good deal of work

The Dreamer

done when he heard some commotion he thought was coming from the kitchen.

It was only a moment later when he felt a hand on his shoulder. As he turned around to see who it was, Zeleakia grabbed him by the coat he was wearing. She whispered close to his ear, "We are all alone. Come with me to my private room and lie with me. There is no one around. You do not need to worry about being caught. Of course, you do not need to worry about what my husband will do to you. He loves his wealth more than anything else. You have nothing to lose." She gave Joseph a seductive look.

Zeleakia smiled at Joseph with unusual confidence thinking he would give in to her demands finally. Instinctively Joseph pulled away from her, but she had a good grip on his coat.

"Let go of me this instant. I have been entrusted with everything in this house, except for you. You are my Master's wife and you are not a Hebrew. I cannot be with you. I will not be with you!" As he said that he bent over and slipped out of his coat leaving it limp in her hands. He then took his papers and ran into the main room to be in someone's company, which had in the past, tamed Zeleakia advances. The only ones in the main room were Zeleakia's personal assistants and slaves.

Seeing there were not any friendly slaves or servants around, he ran out of the main room, down the hall and out the front door where there were many fellow slaves milling around.

Seeing that Joseph left his coat in her hands, Zeleakia ripped her clothes and picked up Joseph's familiar robe and ran screaming into the main room where

The Dreamer

her servants were.

"Look at me, look and see what that filthy Hebrew has done to me. He tried to rape me, but I was able to fight him off. Go, send word to Potiphar to come home immediately." Two senior slaves immediately left the house to do as their master requested.

~

Joseph went to his quarters where he sat down in his chair still breathing hard. He was grateful he was able to get away from Zeleakia. After he regained control of himself, he pondered on what may yet happen. Since he had been brought into Potiphar's home as a houseboy eleven years ago, he had seen several slaves executed personally by Potiphar, Aaron being the last one. How could he expect anything else? It had to be a matter of pride with Potiphar.

But then he realized he had done nothing to Zeleakia. He had been loyal to the murderous Potiphar and most importantly, he had been loyal to Jehovah. Joseph was nervous as to what Zeleakia might tell Potiphar. He knew he had no control over what would happen next. He kneeled down and prayed to seek the Lords' guidance. When he was done with his prayer, he sat back on his chair and felt a great peace settle over him. He didn't know what to expect, but he felt confidence in the Lord to take care of him. He had learned over the years he could trust the Lord. He was reminded by the spirit of his dream about Father Jacob.

The Dreamer

~

Zeleakia held on tight to Joseph's robe. She did not let it out of her sight. This was her evidence she would give Potiphar when he arrived home. Indisputable evidence. Eventually, Potiphar arrived and went swiftly to Zeleakia.

"What is happening that I had to hurry home so fast?"

"That filthy Hebrew of yours, the one you love so much has tried to rape me."

"Oh come on, I know your tricks. You know what happens when you try to seduce the slaves. I have killed each one and Joseph knows this and would not be caught with you."

"Are you taking the side of a slave over your wife? Look at this," she said as she threw Joseph's coat to Potiphar. "This is the evidence that he was here. What more do you need to believe me?"

"Do you realize what will happen if I believe you? Do you realize that you will be affected as well as me? Every year our wealth has increased two or three fold under his management. His Hebrew God is with him. He would not do this to you, or to me or to his God."

"But I have his robe. He was here trying to rape me."

"If I go through the motions and treat Joseph according to what you are accusing him of, it will greatly affect our future wealth."

"He tried to rape me and I fought him off. Do not let

him be a mockery to our house and to me. Deal with him as you know how to do."

"Very well, I will have to deal with it one way or another, even though I know he is innocent of your accusations. Where did he go?"

"He ran out of the house, that is all I know," replied Zeleakia with an evil grin on her face.

Potiphar easily found Joseph in his quarters. Normally Potiphar would bind the servant and execute him with his bare hands and a sword and let the buzzards devour the servant leaving the body on the ground for everyone to see. He felt he couldn't kill Joseph, but he knew he had to do something decisive so long as Zeleakia was going to make a stink out of the false accusations.

"Joseph!"

"Yes, my Lord."

"Zeleakia, has accused you of trying to rape her."

"I have done no such thing. I have refused her advances, many times, why would I try to rape her?"

"She had your coat in her hand. She claims she pulled it off you in the struggle. That evidence is damning. How do you explain it?"

"She tore it off me when I was trying to get away from her. She was coming on to me and she had her hand on my shoulder. I left and got away from her as fast as I could. I did not want to stop, even to retrieve my coat. I would never do anything to her out of loyalty to my God and out of loyalty to you my Lord." Joseph declared with confidence.

"I am terribly sorry to you and to my profits, but with the evidence against you and the fact that almost the entire estate knows about this, I have to do something or I

The Dreamer

could lose control of the entire estate. Normally I would kill you where you stand, but I do not feel like that would be just. That only leaves putting you in prison, which may not be just either, but at least you would still be alive."

He bound Joseph and took him into the city to King Sesostris's prison. Potiphar and other leaders in Pharaoh's circle were allowed to use it as well.

The Dreamer

Chapter 17: Prison

And not only so, but we glory in tribulations also: knowing that tribulation worketh patience; And patience, experience; and experience, hope: And hope maketh not ashamed; because the love of God is shed abroad in our hearts by the Holy Ghost which is given unto us. Romans 5:3-5

Joseph woke up on the floor in a dark and dusty prison cell. Three walls were made of rock and the fourth wall was covered by bars. There were no windows and the only light was faint, and it came from the far end of the main hallway.

He could hear snoring in the dark somewhere past his cell. He had no idea how long he had been asleep, or what time it was. All he knew was he was alive and that wasn't anything to be excited about. Joseph knew there were worse things than death. He didn't know what to do.

He was given the birthright by Father Jacob after taking it away from Reuben. A few years later he was kidnapped and sold into slavery. Then he had dreams bringing comfort and some instruction about his future. At least then he had a future, no matter how bleak. Now he was in prison. Whatever future, he thought he had was now gone. He hadn't been through any sort of court or hearing. He hadn't been given any sort of sentence. He was placed in prison by the second most powerful man in Egypt, Potiphar the captain of Pharaoh's guard and his chief executioner. There were other more powerful officers in Pharaoh's court, but none had a license to kill like Potiphar.

The Dreamer

There would be no trial and no one would dare to question Potiphar. Joseph was doomed to spend an indefinite amount of time, perhaps life, behind bars. He felt like he came close to losing hope when he was sold into slavery. The only thing worse than slavery was being locked up in a deep dark prison cell. Things couldn't get any worse for him.

He stretched out and tried to get comfortable. He was cold and without a blanket. No fire, no light, just despair. Not being so hot might actually be a blessing. He wasn't sure how to feel. He thought he had felt as bad as anyone could, he thought he was as low as a person could get and now here he was in prison. *Can it get any worse than this?* By now, the only thing worse would be death. His freedom could not be restricted any more than in this small dusty, dirty prison cell.

Not knowing how to feel, Joseph thought he had experienced the roughest of emotions, but now he wasn't so sure how to feel. He had been through a lot of bad situations in his life, was this worse than all of them? Was there anything he could look forward to now that he was in a hopeless situation?

As he tried to find something to occupy his mind there was some noise in the hall on the other side of his cell. It turned out to be one of the guards bringing him his morning meal. He took the cup of water and the plate of food and found himself thanking the guard. He looked at the food and saw that it wasn't anything to be thankful for.

Why did I thank the guard for this putrid slop? As he picked through his food finding the eatable pieces, his thoughts jumped on their own to his loving, kind and beautiful mother, Racheal. He thought about how she

The Dreamer

taught him about love, the kind of love Jehovah has for us and the kind of love we should have for him. As he reminisced about his mother and her kind teachings, he felt a degree of joy as he imagined himself being young and in her loving arms. Two thoughts worked their way to the top, one was love suffers long and the other, love bears all things. It was as if his mother was talking to him from her grave. He mentally reviewed these thoughts, suffering long and bearing all things. If that is God's love for us, we should love God the same way. He is long-suffering toward us, his children, putting up with our sins and shortcomings. We should be long-suffering with God as we wait for him to bless and help us. That makes sense for a loving, caring Jehovah.

The phrase that God suffers long made Joseph think of patience. How could Joseph be patient in prison? He was probably in for life and then he would be released from a life of captivity to the joy of being reunited with God. Was that what he was to be patient for?

He couldn't get comfortable, so he got up on his feet and walked around his cell trying to get his blood flowing so he wouldn't be so stiff and cold.

He had stopped wondering what his father and brothers were doing after so many years apart from them. Now he was wondering what Mordecai was doing? Who was taking his place? He wondered what time it was. Then he noticed the light at the end of the hall seemed to grow just a little brighter. Was the light coming from a fire or from the outside? How far down was he? He assumed he was in the dungeon part of the prison because of the rocky walls, but then again, he could be in a cell in the middle of the prison where the light had a hard time reaching.

The Dreamer

Shouldn't there be a jailer or someone who worked in the prison? He didn't know why, but he needed to know what time it was. Maybe knowing what time it was would help him get himself oriented. As he walked around the jail cell, he looked for anything left from the last prisoner. Could there be a stool to sit on or could there be a blanket? A candle would be nice. He found nothing but a rusty cup and a stained plate. The more he moved the less cold he was. He was far from warm, but being less cold was a blessing.

He had nothing to do and it was still mostly dark. Joseph decided to lie down and see if he could drift off to sleep. He was restless and couldn't fall asleep. He wasn't tired enough to sleep and he had nothing to do.

He thought about the dream of the mustard plant and the growth coming out of the house that he lived in while he was a slave to Potiphar. He had never doubted his dreams until now. It was one thing to have birthright dreams like the sheaves and the eleven stars, but then he had the dream of the mustard plant to let him know he still had a great future ahead of him. Now he was disoriented and in prison with no hope.

Let us see me have a dream of the mustard seed in prison, he thought to himself with sarcasm. *I would like to see that happen.* His thoughts went on.

Then just as suddenly as he thought those thoughts a feeling of guilt came over him as a very clear invisible voice said to him, "The Lord thy God, the creator of the heavens and the earth can plant a mustard seed in the very waters of the Nile and it would grow up to be a floating mustard tree if the Lord willed it so."

As Joseph pondered that thought, he struggled

The Dreamer

between feelings of despair and feelings of hope and confidence in the Lord. The thoughts were as profound as his night time dreams. For all he knew, he could have been dreaming when he had that thought.

As he started to accept that maybe he still had a purpose, even in prison, he wondered how long he would have to be patient while he waited on the Lord. During this experience, he felt something stir inside of him and soon he felt warm and light from the inside out. He felt his confidence growing. Then he had an experience he had never had before. He heard the prisoner stir and he started to come awake in the cell next to Joseph. He felt some of the love the Lord had for that prisoner. He somehow knew it was only a portion of God's love for him, but even that small portion was enough to overwhelm Joseph which took of all his energy. Joseph sunk back down on the ground since he no longer had the strength to stand.

That experience was overwhelming and profound. If the Lord could love a sinner in prison that much, then how much more would he love someone who had not sinned so grievously? That thought was quickly corrected. A strong feeling made him understand God loves all his children the same and the love he had is immeasurable by men's capacity. That experience changed Joseph in ways he couldn't understand, but he was anxious to.

Normally Joseph would think himself above the prisoner, but if he, an innocent man could be put in prison, then it was possible that some of the other prisoners were innocent or at the least, not such bad people. No doubt there were some very bad men in the prison, but Joseph was much more open-minded than he normally would be.

The Dreamer

He returned to his thoughts while trying to regain his strength.

"Oh my Father in heaven, is this thy will, that I am in prison at this time in my life?"

Joseph's prayer was answered not by words or by a dream, but by a feeling that overwhelmed him. He had never been this overwhelmed by anything in his life, good or bad. He wasn't sure what to make of it. All he knew for sure was the place where upon he stood was holy ground.

Joseph felt like he was in heaven in spite of the smelly, dusty and drab conditions he found himself in. He was startled back to the reality of his conditions when he heard talking at the end of the hall. Steadily that sound got closer until Joseph could tell it was someone bringing food to the prisoners. When the man got to Joseph he yelled at him to have his plate and cup ready. Joseph quickly complied and asked the guard what time of the day it was. The guard replied that it was high noon. Joseph hoped this information would give him an anchor for his disorientation.

The days were long and they slowly evolved into weeks then slowly turned into months. Joseph made friends of all the prisoners within talking distance and he earned the respect of the guard who delivered food by the kindness that Joseph showed him every time they interacted. This guard talked to the main guard of the prison and he often mentioned how kind Joseph was. The guard also mentioned how the prisoners in the cells near Joseph had seemed to change into more likable people. With each report about the Hebrew man, the head guard was growing in curiosity. He finally decided to make the long walk down the dark hall and visit this popular prisoner and see the cause of the good report.

The Dreamer

The lead guard was impressed by Joseph and his kindness. Joseph came across as an intelligent, confident man secure in the knowledge that he was innocent of the charges against him. Seth, the chief guard was impressed by this man and how his disposition had rubbed off on his nearby fellow prisoners. Anyone who could contribute to a better running prison was a good man, thought Seth. He was so impressed that he was also moved to compassion toward the Hebrew. He brought Joseph two blankets, a sturdy stool, a clean plate and a new cup from which to drink.

"I want you to be more comfortable. I wish you could feel as good as you have made me feel, but this will have to do for now," said Seth.

Joseph noticed from that time forward his food was better and there was more of it. He had water to drink more often through the day. A few days later Seth came by and unlocked Joseph's cell door inviting him to come out into the hall. "Come with me, I will take you upstairs to look out and see the sunshine. That might make you feel better."

Joseph eagerly followed Seth out of his cell and down the long dirt hall. "Several of us have noticed a change in the prisoners near your cell. It happened a few weeks after your arrival to the prison. Do you have any idea why, after all these years their behavior would change?" asked Seth.

"We have spent many hours everyday talking. I have told them about my Hebrew God and how we can be happy in whatever circumstance we find ourselves. They seem to respond well to those teachings. I do not know if that answers your question, but that is all I can say."

The Dreamer

They arrived to the stairs and Seth warned Joseph that the sudden brightness might be hard on his eyes at first. "You might want to close your eyes and once you are upstairs open them slowly, allowing your eyes to adjust to the bright light."

"I will try to do as you suggest, but I am very anxious and excited to see the sunlight after these many months." He closed his eyes and held onto Seth while they scaled the stairs.

Joseph could see the dark under his eyelids grow less dark and more bright as they got closer to the top of the stairs. Once they were upstairs, Seth told him to slowly open his eyes. Joseph tried, but once he opened his eyelids a little he was impatient and opened them all the way. All he could see for several moments was a blinding brightness. He rubbed his light and started to chuckle followed by some tearing up. Joseph never appreciated, until that moment, how he had taken for granted the beauty of the sun and the life-giving light that radiated from its brightness.

Soon Joseph's vision returned to him and he was able to look out on the city. He looked around without saying anything. He noticed in the far off distance the date and palm trees of Potiphar's estate. His stomach flopped a little as anger flooded his peaceful frame of mind. *All those years of hard work ruined because of Zeleakia and now, because of her, I am in prison for the rest of my life.*

After a while it became difficult for Joseph to look out to enjoy the sunlight, because in addition to seeing the sunlight, he saw people walking around enjoying their freedom. Even the slaves who were going back and forth had a degree of freedom and even though it was just a

The Dreamer

little, it was more than Joseph had. It reminded him of his incarceration. He asked Seth to return him to his jail cell. On the way down, Seth asked Joseph, "What would you say if I asked you to teach all the prisoners the way you have taught your cell mates?"

"I would never say no to the opportunity of teaching others about the God of my fathers, but would that get me out of my cell more and allow me to come and go within the prison?" Joseph felt he would go crazy being constantly confined to a small prison cell.

A few days later, Seth came to visit Joseph. He took him out of his cell and up to the ground floor where he could enjoy the sunlight and the sights of people coming and going.

"What will you teach the prisoners?" asked Seth.

"There are a lot of different things I will teach them. They will mostly be the teaching of my Hebrew God like faith, repentance, the grace of God and more."

"Only a few days later, Joseph started his first class of all the prisoners who wanted to come. Seth originally said he would send all the prisoners to Joseph for instruction. He told him to only send the prisoners who wanted to come because only the interested men would be receptive to whatever he taught them.

When many of the prisoners were gathered together for the first lesson, Joseph told them they would start out with questions first then get into a prepared lesson.

The first question was from a prisoner who was next to Joseph's cell. "How can you be in such good spirits even though you are locked away in a prison cell and probably will be for the rest of your life?"

The Dreamer

"I have faith in my God that he will help me along the way. If I did not have faith in God, I think I would go crazy being locked away and restricted to this prison forever."

"How does faith make each long day go by?" asked another prisoner.

"My faith helps me believe in my God and my God is loving. I believe he will help each day go by without much stress. I do not know how he does it, I just know that I will make it until the end of the day. Maybe he makes the day go by faster or maybe he blesses my mind to seem like the day is going by faster than it really is. I cannot say for sure how it is done, only that it is done. That bothers a lot of people because they want to know how that works. For me it is enough to know it works, I do not have to know how," said Joseph.

The first meeting was full of additional questions and answers. After all questions were answered, Joseph felt like they had covered enough ground to inspire hope in most of those that were in attendance.

Every day there were classes. Seth and Joseph soon noticed more men starting to attend. Men were talking among themselves and to their cellmates and that created interest among more prisoners. Some men progressed faster than others, but after a few months, Seth noticed a change in the prison as more and more prisoners were exposed to this Hebrews teachings.

The Dreamer

Chapter 18: Butler and Baker

The Lord is far from the wicked: but he heareth the prayer of the righteous.
Proverbs 15:29

Dear God, I am frustrated. It is hard to see an end in sight. I appreciate thy help, but I am really frustrated. Why is all this happening to me? I really need thy spirit to be with me, to strengthen me and help me overcome the feeling of despair that seems to be overcoming me right now. Every time I feel like I am about to give up, thou has helped me and I need that same help now. . . Joseph drifted off to sleep.

He had been blessed greatly since being in prison, yet he was feeling down trodden. When his brothers were a trial, he had hope, even when he was a slave, he had hope, thanks to the dream of the mustard tree. But since being in prison, he hadn't had the same kinds of dreams. He had a few of the old dreams, but then they seemed vague and lacked impact on his life. He was striving hard to say his prayers and reach out to the Lord.

He seemed fully aware he was asleep, but the darkness of night opened slowly to reveal a building. It was made known to him that the building he was seeing was the prison he was in. He saw the gardener's hand appear and plant a tiny mustard seed. Everything about this dream of the mustard seed growing into a vast mustard tree was familiar to Joseph. Except for the fact that he took this dream to mean that since the seed was planted in the prison he was in, the hope of the mustard tree still applied to him. He didn't know how, only that this dream was a

The Dreamer

message from Jehovah telling him that he was still a chosen vessel with a specific mission.

The dream repeated itself over and over again until Joseph awoke to another morning in prison. This time, when Joseph got up off of the floor where he had been sleeping, he was filled with joy and profound hope.

It only took a few weeks of Joseph's prison-wide teaching for Seth to notice a difference in the prison. As a result of the positive differences, Seth gave Joseph more responsibilities and deferred much of the decision making to him. He was amazed at how well Joseph responded to the responsibilities of dealing with the prisoners. It was like Joseph was born to lead.

Seth was doing less work and finding things were running much better. Joseph found great favor in Seth's eyes.

Prisoners came and went from the prison. Some would be released back into the public, others would be executed. Joseph kept track of the prisoners among his new responsibilities. As his influence was felt throughout the prison, the guards also noticed greater peace in the prison and the prisoners were able to have more freedom and were allowed on occasion, to go upstairs and enjoy the sun. Everyone was happy with Joseph and the way he managed his new responsibilities.

One day two new prisoners were brought to the prison. They were both prisoners from King Sesostris. One was the Chief of Pharaoh's Butlers, Tutten and the other was the Chief of Pharaoh's Bakers, Sarin. Joseph brought them in like any other prisoner and soon they were assimilated into prison life. They joined in the gatherings taught by Joseph about his Hebrew God.

The Dreamer

In spite of Joseph's best efforts, life was still difficult for the prisoners with their freedom taken from them. Some deserved prison while others were placed there by the King Sesostris out of rage. Others were put in prison, like Joseph was, by people in Pharaoh court.

Three of the things Joseph tried to teach the prisoners above all else was first repentance. Repentance for whatever crimes they may have committed on the outside and repentance for those who desired to worship the God of Abraham, Isaac, and Jacob.

The second thing was to teach these prisoners, while their bodies may be captive, their spirits and their minds can be free if they chose to live their life with faith in the Almighty God. Their minds could be freed to believe and exercise faith in the power of redemption through the coming Messiah. This brought joy and happiness to many.

The third item Joseph tried teaching these captive men was the attributes of Godlike love, and he emphasized different attributes depending on the individual's needs, but most often long-suffering and enduring all things was the top of the list.

There were times when the men in prison would get unruly in spite of his best efforts to teach and influence them to peaceful resolutions. Sometimes Joseph had to use his size and strength to resolve issues. He was in the course of his prison duties when he started to wonder whatever happened to Mordecai? Did he take Joseph's position or did Potiphar organize things the way they were before Joseph? He said a prayer for his dear friend that whatever happens, it would be good for Mordecai.

One day, as life in the prison droned on and on, Joseph came across Tutten the butler of the Pharaoh.

The Dreamer

Tutten was downcast and unhappy.

"Why do you look so unsettled Tutten?" asked Joseph.

"I am frustrated by a dream I had. It was so vivid and real that even though it was just a dream, it still bothers me because certain aspects of the dream are still in my mind and I do not understand what it all means, if it means anything at all."

"Maybe I can help you. I have experience with dreams. Many people in my past have called me the Dreamer. If you'll tell me what you remember, I'll help if I can."

"I remember a small plant grew fast and magically into a big vine with three large branches with buds on each branch. Then the buds burst into clusters of small grapes. Very soon the grapes were ripe and ready to pick. I picked off all the grapes and pressed them and prepared them for the Pharaoh's cup. Once the juice was ready, I gave the cup to Pharaoh to enjoy. That is all that I can remember."

Let me pray and I will do my best to interpret the dream for you. So Joseph left Tutten for a while so he could pray and commune with his creator. He returned with an interpretation.

"I believe I have an appropriate interpretation of your dream. The three branches on the vine represent three days. In three days the King of Egypt will take you out of this prison and restore you to your position knowing that you were not guilty of the offense that put you here. You will indeed serve Pharaoh, placing plates of food and cups of wine before him. Since I have given you this interpretation, please do me a favor when you are released from prison and brought before the King. Please

The Dreamer

tell him what I have done for you, how I interpreted your dream. Like you, I have unjustly been put in prison and only Potiphar or the King can release me." The Butler thanked Joseph warmly and agreed to tell the Pharaoh of Joseph.

Sarin the Pharaohs baker was there and saw how Joseph interpreted Tutten's dream. He asked Joseph if he could do the same for him and interpret his dream. Joseph agreed. Sarin then related his dream unto Joseph.

"In my dream, I remember having a basket placed upon my head and then another basket and finally a third basket was placed on my head. The top basket was filled with all kinds of warm and delicious baked foods, but the birds kept eating the food from that top basket. No matter how much food was in the basket the bird kept eating it," said Sarin.

"Is that all of the dream?" asked Joseph.

"Yes, that is all I remember," said Sarin.

Joseph left like he did before and went to pray and ponder over the baker's dream. He didn't return as fast as he did with the first dream. In fact, he stalled. He didn't like the answer to this dream. Joseph was not anxious to deliver bad news. If his interpretation was right, and he knew that it was, Sarin didn't have much time to live. He finally worked up the nerve to return with the interpretation.

"Here is what you dream means. The three baskets represent three days. In three days you will be brought out of prison, where the Pharaoh will have Potiphar behead you. Your head will be lifted up to hang from a tall tree where the birds will eat the flesh from off your head."

"Why is my dream so different from Tutten's dream? Why cannot my dream have a good meaning like

The Dreamer

Tutten's?"

"The interpretation of the dream is not mine. The interpretation of dreams is a gift from God and it comes from inspiration from the most High. I am sorry and sad to give you such bad news, but I can only tell you what your dream means from the inspiration of the Lord. If I were to tell you anything else it would not come true. Only what I have said will happen, nothing else."

There was a dark cloud of despair and uncertainty over the prison for the next three long days. The word had spread about the two dreams and Joseph's interpretation. No one doubted the interpretations.

Three days later Tutten the baker was released from prison and restored to his previous post as Butler just as Joseph prophesied. And Just as Joseph prophesied, Sarin the baker was also removed from prison whereupon he was beheaded and his head was hung from a tall tree where the birds pecked at his flesh until there was nothing left.

Joseph was told by the prison warden what happened to the baker and the butler. Joseph, trusting the butler, expected to be released from prison. He figured it might take some time for things to work out, but after two months of waiting, he gave up hope that Tutten had said anything to the King.

Life went on as it had with Joseph striving to serve the Lord in the prison. He had some of his familiar dreams and he had a few new ones. He was able to make the most of his time in the dungeon by teaching and inspiring many of the prisoners to repent and turn their hearts over to the great God of Creation.

The Dreamer

Chapter 19: Pharaohs Dream

But if from thence thou shalt seek the Lord thy God, thou shalt find him, if thou seek him with all thy heart and with all thy soul. Deuteronomy 4:29

    King Sesostris had been troubled for a week, ever since he had two vivid and dramatic dreams that he did not understand. They seemed plain on the surface, yet they were troubling because he couldn't put the symbols together to make sense of the dreams. The Pharaoh wasn't known to have many night visions, let alone anything so distinct and striking.
    He pondered over them. Two of the main symbols were a cow and the Nile river. The cow was known as a common symbol that could represent a symbol of the god Isis, the all-sustaining earth or agriculture. The Nile river typically represented the fertility of the land. The King, with the help of some of his scribes, researched the emblems in the royal library to come up empty-handed. He was growing frustrated. If the dreams were not so vivid and if they had not left such an indelible mark on the Pharaoh's mind, he might have been tempted to let it go, but he couldn't.
    One of the Kings scribes suggested King Sesostris call a conference of all of his Magicians, priests, astrologers, fortune tellers, and wise men, along with his full royal court to see if any of them could determine what the Kings dreams meant. Liking that idea, the Pharaoh issued a decree to gather them all together in one weeks time. One by one they all arrived at the royal court. Once they all had arrived, they were assembled together where

The Dreamer

the King could speak with them. He shared the first dream with those assembled.

"I was standing on the shore of the Nile river near where all the farmland was. I saw seven fat cows. I have never seen such fat cows so robust and healthy. These seven cows grazed in the meadow getting even larger.

I blinked my eyes and then out of the Nile came seven lean cows. These skinny cows stood near the fat cows in the meadow. Soon the lean cows started feasting on the fat cows until there was nothing left. It was horrifying. I then abruptly woke up with those images seared into my mind."

The King looked at his assemblage to see if any of their faces showed any signs of recognition or understanding. All he saw were blank looks. Truly they were all interested, but none showed any signs of understanding. He went on with the second dream.

"I had another dream, just as vivid and real as the first dream. I looked to the farmland where a large tract of corn was supposed to be located only to see seven ears of corn on a single stalk. They were plump and good to the taste. After that came seven ears of corn on one stalk, only these ears of corn were thin and blasted by the east wind. After a short time, the thin and ill-favored ears of corn devoured the seven plump ears of corn."

The Pharaoh cast his eyes round about the wise men and magicians, the astrologers and the fortune tellers and they all had a look of interest, but with blank stares. Soon they turned to each other and started talking to see if they could help each other come up with a meaning for the dreams.

The King allowed them time to talk among

themselves, but their conversations didn't last long as they were all stumped. After they grew silent the King spoke and said, surely these common signs of the cow and the Nile river should mean something to you all. These dreams have troubled me a great deal and I need to know the meaning of these things. Are these dreams a warning? Do they mean anything or are they just nonsense?

Since they remained silent, the king told them he would give them the rest of the day to figure something out. "You have until the evening dinner bell to figure these things out. Upon hearing the bell you will send a delegation of three among you to tell me what you have determined about these two dreams of mine."

The King got up off of his throne and went to his private quarters where his family resided. Speaking to his wife, he said. "they had better figure out what my dreams mean. They have got to mean something. Even to this day, I can recall every element of these distinct dreams. That has got to mean something. Normally, when I wake up having had a dream, I quickly forget it"

As King Sesostris went on speaking to his wife, Tutten the Butler poured the King and Queen a glass of wine. He then went to the edge of the room and stood at attention with his back to the wall as they went on speaking.

"What will you do if they cannot come up with an acceptable interpretation of the dream?" asked the Queen.

"I had not thought of that possibility. I assumed if they were all together they could come up with something," said the Pharaoh. "Maybe I will need to give them more time. I am anxious to know what the meaning of the dreams are."

The Dreamer

The dinner bell rang and within a few moments Tutten, the Butler announced to the King that the delegation from earlier that day had arrived.

"We have considered all that we had time for and cannot come up with a plausible explanation my Lord, please forgive your humble servants. It could mean that the dream has no meaning, but we cannot, at this time be sure."

The King took a deep breath and then said, "Very well then. I will give you all just one week to consider the dream and come up with an answer. You will return to me by the dinner bell in seven days." The King rubbed his bald head and furrowed his eyebrows in distress as he dismissed the delegation.

Tutten, all of the sudden remembered about Joseph in prison who correctly interpreted his dream and the dream of the baker. His interpretation was very accurate. *Should I tell the King about Joseph? I did tell Joseph, I would mention him to the King, but what if the King is not happy with me involving myself in his business? I do not want to do anything to anger the King. I do not want to end up in jail again.*

The following week sailed by for the wise men, but it dragged by for the King. It was a very long and painful week for Tutten as well. Every day he debated within himself whether or not he should involve himself in the Pharaoh's business.

The dinner bell rang and within moments the delegation of wise men arrived in the King's chambers to report on their efforts for the past week. They came up with a long and painful speech about all the efforts they had made to interpret the dream, but in the end, they could

The Dreamer

not make sense of the dream, but they stopped short of saying the King's dream was nonsense.

In anger, the King dismissed the delegation for the evening, but he didn't dismiss the group yet. Tutten was there watching everything unfold. He felt a strong impression that he should mention Joseph to the King, but he also experienced a great deal of fear at the possible reaction of the King. Later that evening he worked up the courage to talk to the Pharaoh.

"Excuse me, my Lord."

"What is it?

"While I was in prison, I had a dream that was vivid and confusing. The baker also had a dream at the same time. There was a man by the name of Joseph, who interpreted both of our dreams and what he said about our dreams came true, just as he said it would."

"Did I not execute the Baker?"

"Yes, you did my Lord, just as this man, Joseph said you would."

"This man, Joseph, he works in the prison?"

"No, my Lord. He is a prisoner."

"Do you think he could interpret my dreams?"

"I hope so, my Lord. I know him to have accurately interpreted two dreams."

"That is more than I have gotten from my delegation. Send for the warden of the prison immediately. I want him here within the hour." The hour flew by.

"Yes, my Lord?" said the warden.

"I understand you have in prison a Hebrew who interprets dreams?"

"Yes, my Lord, the man's name is Joseph."

"I would like him brought before me tomorrow

The Dreamer

morning after my morning meal."

"Yes, my Lord, it will be done as you wish," said the warden.

The warden was quickly ushered out of the Pharaoh's reception hall and he rushed to the prison. He went straight to Joseph.

"Tutten the Butler has finally told the Pharaoh about you and your ability to interpret dreams. The King wants to see you tomorrow morning. This may be your opportunity to get out of prison," said the warden.

"I should shave and clean myself up before I go see the King," said Joseph.

"I agree." said the Warden, "you should also have some clean clothes. You get yourself cleaned up and I will go see what I can find for you to wear." The warden was glad to have a chance to help Joseph get out of prison since he never believed he should have been put in prison.

Joseph shaved his head and beard and was well cleaned by the time the warden brought him fresh clothes. All he needed to do now was try and sleep. He was excited for the opportunity to serve the King in an effort to free himself from prison. Sleep was hard to come by, but it did finally come. To Joseph's surprise, by the time he woke up, he had no recollection of any dreams.

Tutten was also tasked with assembling all the magicians, fortune tellers, and various other wise men. The morning meal was done and the King went into his courtyard and took the throne, this time with his Queen.

Tutten presented Joseph to the King.

The King was anxious to test this Hebrew man to see if he could tell him what his dreams meant. He told him exactly what he told the magicians and wise men.

The Dreamer

"Thank you, my Lord, for this chance to serve you. Now that I know what your dreams are, I will need to be alone where I can ponder and pray to my God that I might be able to give you a proper interpretation."

"I gave my magicians and wise men a week. I will also give you a week. Tutten, my butler will tend to your needs while you are thus occupied." Tutten took Joseph to a very nice room with all the comforts a room in the palace could afford. This brought back memories to Joseph on his days when he was assistant to Potiphar. He felt like he needed a little time to get his head cleared and get his heart into the right frame of mind. This was his chance to prove himself to the King and he wanted to give the interpretation everything he had. He had Tutten bring him some food. The butler brought him large quantities of fine food and wine.

"Joseph, I am sorry for not mentioning you sooner to the King. I was afraid of what the King might do or say if I told him about you with you being a prisoner. I wish you well."

"Thank you Tutten. I was unhappy and thought you had forgotten me. But in the end you came through for me."

Then next day Joseph was still pondering over the two dreams the Pharaoh had, one with the cows and the other of the corn. He felt impressed by the spirit to approach the Lord in prayer for understanding of these dreams. He did and after his prayer, Joseph was convinced on the correct interpretation. He thought about what he should do. It didn't matter how correct the interpretation was, if the King didn't like it, he would be put back into the dungeon.

The Dreamer

Joseph thought it might be wise to wait for the full week so he could live it up and enjoy his lodging, a nice bed and fine food to eat. After he thought about it more, he felt a sense of urgency to tell the Pharaoh the interpretation.

Joseph sent word for Tutten. Tutten told the King that Joseph was ready to give the King an interpretation. The King told him to assemble all the wise men and then bring Joseph to the royal court. Tutten brought Joseph to the Pharaoh and Joseph bowed himself before the King and started to explain to the Pharaoh and the assembled wise men, the interpretations to the dreams the King had.

"The two dreams are really one dream. This dream is God showing the Pharaoh what he is about to do. The seven fat cows and the seven good ears of corn represent seven years of plenty. The seven thin cows and the blighted seven ears of corn, together they represent seven years of famine."

What this all means is that there will be seven years of plenty in Egypt, followed by seven years of famine in the land. The famine will be catastrophic. The seven years of plenty will be forgotten and famine will consume all of the land of Egypt and the lands round about. The starvation will be truly grievous. You were given the dream in two parts to emphasize how important the next fourteen years will be. The seven years of plenty will be forthcoming very soon. This is a warning from God to you my Lord."

The King was thrilled to hear the interpretation. He felt in his heart an undeniable feeling that what this Hebrew man told him was true.

"I discern that you are wise and inspired. Tell me then Hebrew, what shall I do about this dream and your

The Dreamer

interpretations?"

"Seek out a man who is discreet and wise who you can trust and put him in charge over all the land of Egypt. Have him oversee all the crops and herds and cattle and save one-fifth of the increase each year during the seven years of plenty, setting it aside for use during the seven years of famine."

King Sesostris dismissed Joseph back to the room he was staying in. The butler still served Joseph all that he desired. Joseph took advantage of the hospitality and enjoyed his favorite foods in abundance.

The King spoke to the group of wise men asking them who they thought should oversee Egypt during the next fourteen years. Some of those that were present volunteered for the post while others argued the interpretation of the dreams. After three days of this, the Pharaoh sent them away seeing that they didn't have Egypt's future in their hearts. He called Joseph to him. When the butler presented Joseph to the King, he bowed himself before the Pharaoh as a sign of respect for the king's position.

"What more can I do to serve the King of all Egypt?"

"I have consulted my wise men, magicians, and officers and found no one equal to the task of managing Egypt for the next fourteen years. You have the gift and the wisdom to interpret my dreams correctly, surely you have the spirit of your God with you and I believe you are the one to manage Egypt and implement the advice you have given me. I would like to appoint you to be Governor of all of Egypt."

At that moment time stood still as Joseph thought

The Dreamer

back on his life of struggle and countless trials. He was given the birthright, yet very little time to exercise the birthright blessings and now he was going to be Governor over all Egypt. His father told him he was destined to be someone great spiritually and temporally. Then a series of terrible events unfolded, including being kidnapped by wicked brothers and sold into slavery. He was falsely accused of raping Zeleakia and put in prison. Now he was standing before the most powerful man in the world being given a position that would rival the temporal birthright from his father Israel.

He was stunned and completely unsure of what to do. Would it be wrong to work for the Pharaoh as Governor? Will I still be a slave or will I be a free man?

"My Lord, my King. I truly am flattered by your offer. I would like some time to consider it and time to pray to my God. Would it be all right if I gave you my answer tomorrow?"

This response stunned the Pharaoh, but he also could sense something great in Joseph who stood before him. This man had the presence of mind to shave and clean himself up from the grime and filth of prison. He didn't rush to interpret the Kings dreams. He was a thoughtful and deliberate man who seemed to be spiritually gifted.

"Very well then. I will give you until tomorrow to give me word. I will say this one thing to you. While you may be a mighty man of your God, I am the King of all Egypt and I want you to take this position. If for some reason you should refuse me, I will demand that you provide me with a name of someone I can trust to be my Governor. You are dismissed."

The Dreamer

Chapter 20: Zaphnath-paaneah

For I am persuaded, that neither death, nor life, nor angels, nor principalities, nor powers, nor things present, nor things to come, nor height, nor depth, nor any other creature, shall be able to separate us from the love of God, which is in Christ Jesus our Lord. Romans 8:38-39

Joseph's head was swimming in a sea of confusion as he was as escorted back to his room. For those last several minutes since King Sesostris offered Joseph the position of Governor, Joseph was overwhelmed by the possibilities. Here he was, a slave who was currently a prisoner in the Kings' prison, being offered the second highest position in all the land. There would be no one higher than him. He would report directly to the Pharaoh.

Joseph poured himself a glass of clear, cool water and sipped on it as he sat on the chair in his room. *What am I to make of all of this? If I accept the Pharaoh's offer, I become the second most powerful man in Egypt. But I want to go home and see my father and Benjamin, Dinah and some other family members. I want to be with my people and finely exercise the birthright after all these years.*

He thought about his family and his brothers and their hatred toward him? *Do they still hate me after these all these years? Have the years tamed their evil desires? How would I serve as Governor of Egypt? Why would King Sesostris want me to serve as his number two?*

Joseph was still beside himself in shock over the offer. He didn't know what to do. He thought back to his parents and wondered what it would be like to still have his

The Dreamer

mother around to give him advice. He missed her so much that it hurt. He missed the wise and comforting guidance of his father as well. He would know exactly what Joseph should do.

What would Father Jacob tell me? What about the birthright he gave me? Will King Sesostris let me leave for Canaan if I ask him? Joseph had more questions than answers. He wanted to talk to the King more to find out about his options and if he was free to leave Egypt? Surely he wouldn't want a slave to act as Governor. *So if I am not a slave then I should be free to go. I wish I knew what the King was thinking.*

The thought came to him out of nowhere. What would Jehovah want me to do? After all, pleasing him is more important than what my father would say or even what my mother would say.

Joseph got up off the chair and placed the glass on the ledge. He then got down on his knees and prayed. He prayed long and hard. Longer and harder than he had ever prayed. He realized that more than anything he wanted to be right with his Maker. Nothing else mattered if he wasn't seeking to do the will of his God.

He had a spiritual experience praying that was so deep and profound he couldn't possibly describe it to anyone even if he wanted to. Somehow he knew after his prayer was over that a big part of the spiritual side of his birthright was still before him in the matter of temporally saving Egypt from the coming seven years of famine. He could bless more peoples lives right now than he could for the rest of his life living with his people. After all, a big part of the birthright was serving others. He knew he was being called out of his afflictions to serve God and man as

The Dreamer

Governor of all of Egypt. He knew that he had to answer yes to King Sesostris. Not for the Kings benefit, but for the benefit of Egypt and surrounding lands. He wondered if that included Canaan?

After making up his mind to do the will of God, he heard some words through a still small voice that said, "Be strong and of a good courage; be not afraid, neither be thou dismayed: for the Lord thy God is with thee whithersoever thou goest."

Joseph was still nervous concerning the task at hand, but he had a profound sense of calm and peace fill his heart and mind. He rested comfortably in his room as he pondered over what he would do as Governor. A few hours later one of the Kings servants came to him to issue an invitation for Joseph to eat his evening meal with the Pharaoh. He gladly accepted the invitation.

He was sitting at the Kings dining table when the Pharaoh entered the dining room. Joseph and the others surrounding the table stood. The Pharaoh took his seat and then motioned for everyone to sit. Joseph remained standing.

He bowed before the Pharaoh and said, "My lord, I am pleased to accept your offer to serve you as Governor for the purpose of dealing with the next fourteen years of plenty and famine."

The king motioned for him to be seated. "You do me a great honor by accepting the appointment. Thank you." Then the king motioned for his attending steward to come forward. "Please assemble my court and wise men for an evening assembly in two hours."

The king went on to tell Joseph more of what he expected from him as he served as Governor telling him

The Dreamer

that he had all the authority to command anyone and everyone in regards to the infrastructure and economy, essentially everything except control over the army. He could get whatever military help he needed through the king or the prince. Otherwise, Joseph had complete authority over the laws of the land, over the royal court and everything else imaginable. In many ways, he was even more powerful than the prince.

After King Sesostris finished, Joseph told him that there were certain conditions of his that needed to be mentioned. He told the Pharaoh that he would run his stewardship based on the laws of Jehovah, and if that interfered with the laws of the land then the laws of God would override the Kings' laws.

"I prayed long and hard to my God before deciding to accept this position," Joseph told the King, "and I pledge my loyalty to you, however, my primary loyalty is and will always be to my God." The Pharaoh nodded his assent to Joseph. "Lastly," Joseph went on to say, "I was sold into slavery against my will and I will not do anything if I am in any way considered a slave–"

"No, no, you are no longer a slave," said the King. "When I say you are second only to me, I mean it. You are nobody's slave. You belong to no one except your God. You are a free man."

"That brings up an interesting issue," said Joseph. "If I am no longer a slave and since slavery is an abomination to the Lord, I want to use my power to free all the slaves in Egypt and turn them into paid servants, if they wish to still work for their former masters. Otherwise, they are free to strike out on their own."

"Mmm . . . I am not sure what to say to that. I know I

emphasized that you have virtually all power, but I do not know if that would be wise or even possible to decree any end to slavery."

"Why not?"

"Because there are certain areas that are part of my rule that is more of a coalition that direct rule. Where I have direct rule, it might be easier, but in those areas where they pay tribute and are only a coalition with us, they may reject the attempt to end slavery. Why is this such an issue with you now that you are free?"

"For a few reasons, one being that slavery is wrong and a sin. Secondly, slave labor may seem efficient, but a well-managed approach of servants that are paid is more productive. When I was a slave for Potiphar, we had a working model that was similar to what I am suggesting, although, in that case, it was done primarily with slaves, slaves with improved conditions."

"Would you consider taking a different approach to ending slavery and slowly implementing it and documenting the results so we can show the success to those who are not directly under my rule? Taking that approach might, in the long run, be better than a decree. If I simply decreed it and they did not obey I would have to rescind the decree or go to war with them. I cannot show weakness to them and I do not want to go to war over the issue."

Joseph felt an impression to let the slave issue rest for a while, at least for now. "All right. I will work out a program and give it some time and then when I demonstrate the great results will you support my efforts to abolish slavery?"

"I will strongly consider everything you show me."

The Dreamer

Shortly all the magicians, fortune tellers, wise men, sorcerers, astrologers and the rest of the Kings court were all assembled in the great hall. The King brought Joseph into that room and made a spectacle out of elevating him to Governor.

The King reviewed the dreams and told how Joseph interpreted them, then he called Joseph to stand before him. Joseph came up to the podium where the King stood. Joseph was arrayed in fine colorful linens, similar to the coat of many colors. The Pharaoh took a royal signet ring off of his finger and gave it to Joseph to wear on his finger. Then the King placed a solid gold necklace around Joseph's neck, both symbols of Joseph's new found authority.

"I give unto you the royal name of Zaphnath-paaneah, one who reveals mysteries. Before my royal court, I appoint you Governor and ruler over all Egypt. You report to no man save me alone. All kneel before Joseph the Governor," commanded the Pharaoh.

Everyone present kneeled before the Pharaoh and Joseph. After the ceremony was over the Pharaoh had his second chariot brought in with some of the finest horses in kings stable and it was presented to the new Governor.

Following the ceremony, the King had all of his officer's parade before Joseph and bow before him and introduce themselves to Joseph. The Pharaoh brought a smaller throne in for Joseph to sit on as the officers lined up to greet the Governor.

As the officials were lining up Joseph saw Potiphar in the line. He wondered what he would say to the man that put him in prison for more than two years? He also wondered what Potiphar might say to him? Should I

The Dreamer

forgive him by letting go of the past and look to a brighter future? Should I punish Potiphar to get even with him and test my newfound power and authority? According to the Pharaoh, Joseph reported to no one save the King. He could do what he wanted and dealing with Potiphar might be a good test of his power. He looked again at Potiphar who was getting closer to him. He appeared not to be his confident self. He looked almost frightened to approach Joseph.

The line continued to move and Joseph spoke to each of the officers as they came through the line. Soon Potiphar was next in line. Joseph wasn't sure what his approach to Potiphar would be.

Potiphar stood before Joseph and he made a show of bowing before Joseph. "My lord," he said, "it is good to see you so well after these past years."

Time seemed to stand still again for Joseph as a moment of truth came to him. His first test of authority. Would he get even with Potiphar or would he let things stay the way they were?

He motioned for Potiphar to come closer to him. Joseph bent forward and said, "I want Mordecai sent to me immediately. I order you to no longer kill or punish any man who sleeps with your wife. You need to deal with her, not those who are manipulated into her unlawful service."

"Thank you, my Lord. Indeed, Mordecai will be at your service before the sun goes down. Thank you for your instruction concerning my wayward wife my Lord. It shall be done as you say."

Joseph nodded his head toward Potiphar and waved him on. He felt good inside after he dismissed Potiphar. He felt like he passed his first temptation in

The Dreamer

power. Here he was, thirty years old and he sat on a throne of power, second only to the King of Egypt. Thirteen years ago he was checking on his brothers and they beat him, kidnapped him and threw him into a dry well. His brothers talked about selling him into slavery and shortly after that he was lifted out of the well and kidnapped by a traveling group of merchants and sold to Potiphar as a slave.

He was in a position of power undreamt of, before in his years of being a slave and his years being a prisoner in the dungeon. He knew from his dreams and his father's teachings that he was destined for greatness. Was this it? Was being a Governor in Egypt his crowning glory? Was this how he was meant to serve his fellow man?

He was different now than when he was seventeen and hated by his brothers. He was more serious and he was more thoughtful, after all, he had all those years of reflection and growth. He knew he had some opportunities ahead of him that would make a difference in the lives of others.

The Pharaoh told him he could have any woman in his kingdom for a wife, all he had to do was find one. Joseph was also given the choice to have a wife given to him but he chose to find his own. Joseph knew there were many Hebrew slaves in the kingdom and he would have to look hard to find them as they would generally be kept within the house and gardens and they would likely not be in public much. The day was nearly done and there was no sign of Mordecai. If he is not delivered by nightfall there would be serious consequences for Potiphar. Joseph needed to start building a staff so that he could operate as Governor. The Pharaoh had promised him everything he

The Dreamer

needed. Tomorrow he would start talking to people in the Kings court and starting there to build up his staff.

There was some commotion at one of the entryways near where Joseph was. Potiphar made his way through the throng of people and came before Governor and bowed himself before Joseph.

"My Lord, Mordecai was returned to his previous duties as a slave when you were, um, when I placed you in prison." Potiphar cleared his throat and swallowed his pride. "Forgive me, my Lord, for ever putting you in prison when I knew you were innocent– "

"Get on with it. Where is Mordecai?"

"He is in a wagon outside of the entrance down on the street."

"Why is he not standing here before me?"

"He is physically unable. He is recuperating from some discipline his taskmasters give him. That is why I am running late. I drove the wagon slowly to make his travels as easy as possible," said Potiphar.

"Whose authority was he punished by?" Joseph knew the answer, but he wanted to see Potiphar squirm under this pressure and his authority.

"Under my authority, my Lord."

"Find out where my quarters will be and place him in my bed, and summon the physician immediately to see to his wounds and pray to your Gods that he does not die."

The Dreamer

Chapter 21: Governor

Who comforteth us in all our tribulation, that we may be able to comfort them which are in any trouble, by the comfort wherewith we ourselves are comforted of God.
2 Corinthians 1:4

    Aseneth, a daughter of the Egyptian Priest of On, grew up in opulence and surrounded by idol gods made with the finest craftsmanship and material. She ate the best food and learned from the best teachers and scribes. She was raised with the best nannies and had all the best opportunities possible. She was well versed in the sciences and the many Egyptian gods.

    The older she got, the more beautiful she became with long flowing black hair and dark eyes with perfectly symmetrical facial features. She was the epitome of Egyptian beauty.

    She had countless suitors from well-placed families in the Pharaohs' royal court of astrologers, magicians, wise men, and priests. The Pharaoh's own son had tried to court her before being called by his father to lead a military expedition to a far away country. Aseneth was not attracted to any of her suitors. Everyone, including her own parents, complained that she was too picky. No one seemed to measure up to her standards.

    She would say she was saving herself to worship the many gods which adorned their house or sometimes she would say the closest suitor she might possibly like was the Pharaoh's son who was gone and would be for a long time. The years went by and she seemed to be pickier. She didn't seem to have a care in the world,

The Dreamer

especially when it came to men.

Aseneth was devout to the Egyptian gods and a well-behaved child who loved her parents and family a great deal. Not wanting to disappoint her parents she didn't want to marry just for the sake of getting married. She was fiercely independent. It was a high honor to have a priest in the family, it was even a higher honor to have one's child follow in the parents' footsteps and become a priest or priestess. That's what Aseneth wanted to achieve. However, her father placed more value on having her marry well, which would provide greater power and security if she married the son of someone in a higher status. That was what motivated her parents. Aseneth was torn between her desire to be a priestess and to live up to the expectations of her parents.

~

Joseph had personally tended to Mordecai for the past week. While Mordecai was convalescing, Joseph kept an eye on the doctors to see which he liked the best. His staff would need his own doctors. Mordecai was attended by three doctors each day to do all within their power to help him heal as fast as possible. They all had their specialty with various herbs and magic.

One night Joseph was sleeping near where Mordecai was sleeping. He had a dream where he saw Mordecai dying on his bed. There were hundreds of doctors lined up to take their turn attending to him. Each time a new doctor stood next to him to administer their

The Dreamer

herbs and balms Mordecai grew sicker and weaker.

Mordecai was suffering, and in spite of the best efforts of the physician's he grew closer to death. Then Joseph saw a man dressed in a coat of many colors standing at the head of Mordecai. That man had his hands on the head of Mordecai and he was bowing his head and praying. When the prayer was done, Mordecai seemed to revive.

The dream started over again and Joseph witnessed the same dream as before. It replayed itself several times, nothing changed except Joseph grew closer to the bed that Mordecai was in, every time the dream played in his mind. The closer Joseph got, the more he heard.

The last time the dream played in Joseph's mind, he heard the entire prayer and saw the face of the man in the coat of many colors. It was himself. He had witnessed himself praying over Mordecai with his hands on his head.

This time the end of the dream was so powerful that it woke Joseph from his dream. He got up and walked over to check on his friend. His friend was awake and groaning in a soft whisper like voice. Joseph told him about the dream he had and Mordecai asked him to put his hands on his head and pray.

"I no longer have the coat of many colors," replied Joseph

"Was the power of the birthright on the coat or on the wearer of the coat?" asked Mordecai wisely. After thinking about it Joseph concluded that power would be on the person, not the coat. Joseph was hesitant.

"I am dying. Try and do what you saw in the dream and if I revive then wonderful, if I die, well then, I was

The Dreamer

going to die anyway," urged Mordecai. He was feeling desperate.

Joseph spoke to the Lord earnestly in the quiet of his mind as he stood up straight and cleared his throat and placed his hands on the head of Mordecai. He was asking for help and grace from the Lord to do this correctly.

Joseph bowed his head and repeated the words of the prayer from the dream. After the prayer, Mordecai was breathing easily and he was fast asleep. *That is not quite what I had in mind, I thought he would rise up like in the dream. At least he is finally really sleeping and he seems to be restful and calm.*

Joseph went back to sleep and slept well and peacefully. He woke up hearing someone in the room, moving around. He opened his eyes to see the rays of the sun glaring down on his face. He turned his head and blinked his eyes hard. He got up out of his bed and then when his eyes finally adjusted to the bright light, he saw that Mordecai was up and moving around tidying up the room.

"What are you doing?" asked a startled Joseph. "How are you feeling?"

"I have not felt this good in a long time. I fell to sleep after your prayer. I slept better than ever. I woke a few minutes ago and decided to tidy your messy room."

"Turn around, I would like to see your back," said Joseph.

Mordecai's back was raw with gaping wounds, red with infection when Potiphar brought him to Joseph more than a week ago. Now Mordecai's back looked fine, other than numerous scars from the many whippings Mordecai had received. There was no redness or swelling. Just

The Dreamer

scars. Mordecai was whole. Joseph was grateful for the miracle. He wondered if maybe he didn't need a physician on his staff, just faithful men who could pray. As they ate their morning meal, they both expressed gratitude for Mordecai's healing.

Joseph took Mordecai for a walk. He explained what was going on and about Joseph's new role as governor. He told his friend what he needed from him. The opulence and vastness of the grounds were intimidating to both of them. While they had both been free men before being kidnapped and sold into slavery, they had tasted the good life. Joseph came from vast wealth from Father Jacob's holdings, but it did not compare to what was before them. They climbed a high tower that overlooked in all directions, countless miles of the Nile river and the vast pastures and crop land. They also saw many stately monuments and a pyramid being constructed for King Sesostris.

As they gazed over the lush prosperity of Egypt, Mordecai observed, "Like you brother Joseph, everything the Nile touches blossoms like a rose. It is too bad the Pharaoh's armies are otherwise engaged. Securing more shoreline to the mighty Nile would certainly help grow more crops."

"That is a good observation," Joseph sighed.

Mordecai observed a golden glow about Joseph's face as he appeared to be caught in some trance-like state.

"Joseph? Are you with me?" asked Mordecai.

There was no response from Joseph. He was looking to some far off place and yet looking at nothing in particular. Mordecai could sense something important was

The Dreamer

happening, but wasn't sure what. Waiting patiently, he reflected on his life and what a difference Joseph had made. He thought back to the time before they were sold into slavery when they first met. Joseph was looking for his brothers who had stolen Mordecai's flocks. Joseph was impressive back then as a young man. Now he was on a tower in the middle of the most powerful kingdom in the world. He couldn't help but think that something big was happening, and he had a front row seat to observe it all.

Joseph blinked and wiped the beads of sweat forming on his forehead.

"Mordecai, you have inspired me to think of something great. There are thousands of slaves building monuments to the King and thousands of men constructing a pyramid. We can take those thousands of men and build tributaries from the Nile into Egyptian land and create much more land suitable for farming that we may extend the life-giving properties of the Nile. We can dramatically increase the crops, flocks, and herds. It could make all the difference in putting aside all that is needed for the coming seven years of famine."

"That is a wonderful, powerful idea. Do you think the King will allow it?"

"Even though I have all power in the kingdom second only to him I should get his blessing," said Joseph with a little hesitation. "If he does not give it to me then I will explain how unlikely it will be that we can put enough in storage to last seven years."

"What do you have in mind for me to do? Will I be alongside you, acting as your personal servant?"

"No. I will create a royal seal for you so you can represent me. It would be the same as if I were there.

The Dreamer

What you will do is implementing the same system for the slave labor that we did in Potiphar's court. You will make sure the slaves are assigned according to their abilities and make sure the workload is not too much for anyone slave. We will also work on eliminating slavery by freeing the slaves and if they want, they can work as paid servants." Joseph went on to tell Mordecai the conversation he had with the Pharaoh regarding slavery.

"I will work on reassigning the builders of the monuments and the pyramid to building canals from off of the Nile to create more floodplains."

They climbed down from off the tower and made their way back to Joseph's quarters. Joseph had established quarters for Mordecai once he was healed. While Mordecai was recuperating from his near death experience, Joseph made living arrangements for this staff once he started to build one. He also realized that Mordecai would need a staff as well.

As they ate their midday meal, they were engaged in conversation. Joseph asked, "Who whipped you so badly, just before you were brought to me?"

"It was the supervisor over the section of crop land I was working in," answered Mordecai matter-of-factly.

"I saw other scars on your back that were healed, who gave those wounds to you?"

"That would be Potiphar."

"Potiphar himself whipped you after he saw how successful you were working with me?" Asked Joseph.

"I think it was more out of rage. After he put you in prison, he needed to hurt someone. He chose me and two other household slaves to whip."

"Was it just the one time or did you get whipped by

any others?"

"No just the two times," responded Mordecai.

When Mordecai heard Joseph say, "I hate Potiphar," he looked at him with raised eyebrows. He was surprised that such a godly man would hate anyone.

"I hate him for what he did to me and I hate him for what he did you," Joseph went on, "I know that we are supposed to forgive our enemies and move on with our lives, but when people are so wicked and hurtful to others . . ." Joseph's voice trailed off as he shook his head.

"He's a killer and we are both alive, I guess that is something," added Mordecai. "We are in a position to ruin Potiphar if we choose to do so."

"I have been thinking of that very thing and as much as I want to, I also want to learn to forgive him and get on with my life. I do not want to give him any more of my thoughts or energy. He has had enough of that already. I want to get on with my life once and for all."

"You are a better man than me," said Mordecai, "I just as soon ruin him and leave him nothing. It would be the answer to many prayers I am sure. When you were put in prison Potiphar's house fell apart. Everything you touched seemed to turn to gold. Once you were gone, nothing seemed to work out for Potiphar. His crops all but failed. His flocks and herds stop multiplying. All the profit you made for him is all but gone now. His wealth is back to the level before you were put in charge. He is one miserable man."

"I guess it is time to get back to our work. We have a great responsibility before us to protect so many thousands from famine, let us focus on that and not on Potiphar."

The Dreamer

"I will do whatever you wish of me," responded Mordecai.

"Now that you know what our individual responsibilities are, do you know of any slaves or servants, we can start with?" asked Joseph.

"The only slaves I know of are from Potiphar's estate."

"Let us start there," said Joseph. "While you were recuperating, I had my gold ring and necklace replicated for you to show your new status and authority. This also means that you are legally no longer a slave, but an equal and in many cases a superior to those you will come across," said Joseph as he slid the signet ring onto Mordecai's finger. This gold chain and ring must never be taken off as it is a sign of your authority and will serve as a protection to you wherever you go."

"I am no longer a slave?"

"You are a free man."

"To do whatever I please?"

"That is correct." Joseph was suddenly worried, "you will be paid very well for your work. You can come and go as you wish."

"If I am free . . . That means I am free to refuse this offer?"

"Yes, that is true," said Joseph, his fears seemed to be coming true. "I just assumed you would join me . . . At least I hoped you would."

"Oh, I will work for you– "

"No, no, work with me, not for me," interrupted Joseph.

"I wanted to know just how free I really am. I will be happy to work with you, Joseph."

The Dreamer

"Thank you. I guess I should have asked you rather than assume you would want to work with me. Thank you for agreeing to work with me."

"I believe, if I may have two wagons, I could go to Potiphar's household and recruit the slaves, I think that would be helpful," said Mordecai.

"Let me write a note of explanation on this papyri to give Potiphar, and take a dozen guards as a show of force," said Joseph as he handed him the small scroll.

"I must confess, it is not becoming of me, but I am gladdened by the knowledge Potiphar has been punished for what he did to me. I guess I have not yet truly forgiven him."

"When you figure it out please tell me. I do not know if forgiveness is even possible for someone who abuses slaves like he does. He is an evil man," said Mordecai.

The Dreamer

Chapter 22: Hebrew God

Be strong and of a good courage, fear not, nor be afraid of them: for the Lord thy God, he it is that doth go with thee; he will not fail thee, nor forsake thee. Deuteronomy 31:6

Potipherah, the Priest of On, came home from a meeting with the Pharaoh. His wife greeted him and saw that he was angry and carrying a burden.

"What is wrong to make you so angry?" asked Hasina.

After taking in a deep breath, Potipherah let it out slow and steady. "It is that Hebrew slave that the King promoted to Governor. He is free to do whatever he wants. He has taken to teaching all the Hebrew slaves about his Hebrew God."

"What is so wrong with that?" asked Hasina. "We do not care about the slaves or what they believe in. Right?"

"You are correct. However, others are listening to these teachings and the message is falling on receptive ears."

"Others? What others, Egyptians?" asked Hasina.

"Yes. That is exactly the problem."

"Can we not just add the Hebrew God icon to the pantheon of Gods we worship and acknowledge one more God?"

"It is not that easy," said Potipherah. "Among the teachings of the Hebrew God are that he is the one and only true and living God. There should be no other Gods before him or after him. Furthermore, the teachings say that men are children of this one and only God. We cannot have a God like that in our pantheon. It would demote all our Gods to nothing."

"And that would take away our position as Priest and Priestess of On. Other Priests and Priestesses would also lose their standing in our society. That would reduce us to nothing more than wise men or magicians or whatever we can get," said Hasina.

"Exactly. That is my grave concern! If Joseph is permitted to continue teaching his religion, it could seriously jeopardize our livelihood."

~

"Good morning Joseph," said Mordecai as Joseph entered their shared office.

"Good morning Mordecai."

"Here is a note that the Pharaoh's Page left just a few moments ago," Mordecai said as he handed the papyri to Joseph.

"The Pharaoh wants to see me immediately?"

"Would you like me to go with you?" asked Mordecai.

"Yes. I do not know what the King wants. Come with me in case I do not have an answer for him. You can assist me."

They left for the five-minute walk to the Pharaoh's court. On their way, they spoke to each other about the things that they had accomplished over the past two months. It had been a very busy two months, especially on the side of reassigning the builders and craftsmen from the pyramid and monuments. Joseph was pleased with

The Dreamer

Mordecai on the effort being made by teaching the Hebrews about the one true God.

They arrived at the Kings court and notified the attendant that they were there in response to a summons from the Pharaoh. They were promptly announced and those who were in the middle of an audience with the King were summarily dismissed as Joseph's presence was deemed far more important.

"Joseph, Mordecai. I have heard good things about your recent efforts. However, I was just informed this morning by my building superintendent that all work on the Pyramid has come to a complete standstill by your orders. Is that true?" asked the King.

"Yes, your majesty. It is true. I stopped construction by your authority more than a month ago. The same is true for the monument projects as well."

"Why is that?"

"I have come up with a building project to construct eight canals from the Nile into dry land to create more farmable land in order to raise more grain and create more pasture land."

"Do we not have enough land to achieve our goals of taxing one-fifth part of everything grown for the coming famine?"

"I do not think so. But we will most assuredly need more pasture land for the increase in flocks and herds. Not only will we set aside one-fifth every year, but the sheep and cows will reproduce as well and by the end of the first seven years we will have massive flocks and herds."

"I am pleased with your foresight on pasture land. What about storage facilities with the grain and other produce?"

The Dreamer

"That is a good question, my Lord. Once the canals are fully constructed and the farmland and pasture land are underway, the royal builders will go to work constructing silos and other facilities to store the produce. Once that work is done, they will be free to resume their work on the pyramid and monuments."

"That all makes good sense, but I am unsure how I feel about my monuments and my final resting place being stalled for so many years," said the King.

"Did I not give you an accurate interpretation of your dream your majesty?"

"Yes, you did."

"Did you not appoint me to this position with all the authority in all of Egypt second only to you?"

"Yes, I did."

"Then will thou please let me tend to the responsibility that you appointed me to? I cannot go about my business wondering if you are second guessing me? I need to know I have your full confidence," said Joseph with an air of authority in his voice.

"Very well then. You are dismissed."

Potipherah and his wife were outside the courtyard, but within hearing distance and overheard the conversation between Joseph and the King.

"I cannot believe the power Joseph has. He speaks to the Pharaoh with such confidence. I am worried that our complaints may fall on deaf ears."

"We came this far. We may as well say what we need to say. After all, he has to be concerned for his power base like we are. We support him through the many gods we promote. I think the Hebrew God is a threat to him as well as to us."

The Dreamer

Potipherah and his priestess wife were announced to the Pharaoh. "Your majesty. We are here seeking an audience with you to discuss the worrisome problem of the Hebrew God that is being taught among the Hebrew slaves," said the Priest of On.

"What difference does one more god make among our pantheon of gods?" asked the King.

"The teachings associated with the Hebrew God are that he is the one true and living God and not having any other gods before him. To them, you cannot believe in the Hebrew God and all the Gods we worship."

"That does seem like a potential problem. What would you suggest we do?" asked the Pharaoh.

Potipherah was surprised at the apparent openness of the King to their complaint. He took courage and continued his plea before the King. "Take away the power of Joseph. Return him to prison or to a slave in Potiphar's household, that would stop the whole thing right in its tracks," suggested Potipherah.

"Do you have another interpretation of my dreams?"

"No my Lord."

"No one does. Joseph was the only one who gave me an interpretation. His interpretation makes so much sense. I cannot have someone preside over all that needs to be done who does not have the gift of seership that he does. I gave him all the power he could possibly need to get things done. I even let him transfer my workers on my monuments and pyramid to work for him. Why does it matter what god the Hebrew slaves believe in?"

"It does not matter about the slaves, but many Egyptian guards hear the message and many are believing in it and turning from our pantheon to this one

The Dreamer

Hebrew God."

"The citizens are also sharing these teachings with others Egyptians. The message seems to be spreading," added Hasina.

"Are we in any eminent danger?" asked the King.

"No, but it is a threat we need to monitor and prevent from becoming a serious problem. Your throne could be in danger as well as our position as priests," said Potipherah.

"The question we need to consider is what is the biggest threat to our society? A seven-year famine or the risk of the Hebrew God? Right now I am going to concern myself with the famine. When the seven years of hunger are upon us, it will not matter about which god is right when everyone is starving. We can consolidate any power that may be lost."

"The Pharaoh is wise," said Potipherah with Hasina nodding in agreement.

"We will convene an assembly with all the priests and priestesses. There we will discuss what we can do to promote our gods over the Hebrew god. We will see if there are ways to make our gods more palatable to those who prefer the Hebrew God," the king declared. "We will convene it two weeks from today."

On the way out of the courtyard, Hasina said, "I understand the Pharaoh's concerns, but I fear that seven years is a long time to compete with the Hebrew God. We need to talk to all the priests and priestesses and see if we can pressure them to urge the King to do something against the spread of that Hebrew's religious views."

"I agree. We can start with Aseneth, our own daughter. She will soon be a priestess and she has a

The Dreamer

strong will. We can test our arguments on her," said Potipherah. We will teach her to hate Joseph and his Hebrew God.

Chapter 23: The Joseph Canal

And said, I cried by reason of mine affliction unto the Lord, and he heard me; out of the belly of hell cried I, and thou heardest my voice. Jonah 2:2

Like the mighty Nile's life-giving powers, everything Joseph touched turned to gold. The first canal was built in time for the Nile floods, leaving behind the life-sustaining silt to create fertile farmland. The Pharaoh held a ceremony where he named the first canal after Joseph. Attending the ceremony were all of the Kings Court, including the priests and priestesses.

Aseneth was a strong-willed woman who thought for herself. She had turned down every suitor who had come her way. She was not impressed with any of them. She went with her parents, the Priest and Priestess of On to the ceremony where they would honor the Hebrew slave who was miraculously promoted to Governor over all Egypt. Potipherah and Hasina had success turning their strong-willed daughter against Joseph and they had some success with other Priests and Priestesses. They were hoping for a chance at this three-day ceremony to turn other Priests against Joseph.

While everyone was impressed with the number of granaries and other storage facilities there were still many in the ruling class, who resented Joseph's promotion to such a powerful position. Others were impressed and believed in his interpretations of Pharaoh's dreams and supported him. Now that he had constructed the first of many canals and the floods had rendered the land farmable, Joseph gained more supporters.

The Dreamer

Potipherah, Hasina, Aseneth were all seated in the second row behind the King and Queen, the Governor and Mordecai. Sitting close the Potipherah was Potiphar. He was on the side of those opposed to Joseph's promotion. He knew first hand of Joseph's gifts, but he resented his promotion. More than anything he resented the fact that Joseph was no longer his slave looking out for his household. He mourned the wealth that had been lost since he put Joseph in prison. He also resented losing so many good slaves to Joseph who had given them all their freedom and paid them for their service.

Word was getting out that Joseph did not employ slaves, but took slaves from everyone else, freed them and paid them. Hebrew slaves, in particular, were interested in this talk. There was a degree of fear among the ruling class that things might be changing in regards to the use of slaves.

The King took the stand at the appointed time and called the ceremony to order. He related to all those present the story behind his dreams and how Joseph interpreted them. Then he rehearsed how things had been over the last growing season and now they were at the beginning of the next growing season they had thousands of acres of additional farmland to grow corn, wheat, and other grains. The Pharaoh also explained about the vast network of granaries and other storage facilities. Then lastly he reminded everyone that Joseph and his servants would be coming around with their wagons to collect the first tax of one-fifth of all the grain and others would come to collect one-fifth of all the flocks, herds and other increases in livestock. All were commanded to comply this season and for the next six years.

The Dreamer

The king went on to explain what would transpire over the next three days of festivities. All of the most important attendees would be treated to an excursion on the king's boat to the Canal of Joseph to see the progress being made.

The first trip down the Nile to the canal of Joseph would leave within the hour. Potiphar, Zeleakia, Potipherah, Hasina, Aseneth and three other dignitaries would accompany the King, the Governor, and Mordecai. Mordecai was with Joseph wherever he went unless he was on assignment.

On their way to the dock, Hasina spoke just loud enough so Potipherah could hear, "This should be very interesting to see Potiphar, Zeleakia, and Joseph on the same boat for the afternoon. Do you not agree?"

"I was thinking the same thing," added Potipherah. "We may be in for a treat. At least we will have an interesting story to tell."

Palace intrigue had managed to spread the story of Zeleakia accusing Joseph of rape, though most knew she was to blame. They all mostly wondered about Potiphar not putting Joseph to death rather than put him in prison. The Priest of On, not sold on the interpretation of the dreams, much less the seven years of plenty and seven years of famine wished Joseph would have been executed. Then there would not be a problem of the Hebrew God.

Aseneth was walking alone behind her parents. She was troubled. She knew Joseph to be an evil man with his one true Hebrew God, at least that's what her parents said. She knew of the concern of the Hebrew God and she also understood the issues with the Hebrew slaves being

The Dreamer

given their freedom. Joseph was turning everything upside down. This was all bad, but the first time she laid eyes on him a mere two hours ago she felt something in her stomach she had never felt before. It was a quivering, fluttering feeling. Her heart seemed to agree as it skipped a beat. He was a very handsome man with wavy dark hair, a rugged looking face with a strong jawline. He moved in a way that commanded respect and dignity.

Her heart and her mind seemed to be at odds with each other. This had never happened before. It was the first time she could remember being physically attracted to a man this strongly. There was the Pharaoh's son, but the attraction was nothing compared to this. This was a new experience for her and a strong one. She knew in the end that her mind would win the war of emotions at least that's how she hoped it would work out. There was too much riding on the hate her parents had for Joseph, for it to turn out any other way. Lastly, she knew a Priestess wouldn't marry a Hebrew.

They were on the boat when the reality of the situation dawned upon Joseph. Here he was with both Potiphar and Zeleakia. He had interacted with Potiphar a few times, but he had never seen Zeleakia since that fateful day almost three years ago when she falsely accused him of trying to rape her. Mordecai was busy answering questions about the construction of the canal.

He had not had much time to think about Zeleakia and now that he was, the animosity toward her was rising to the surface and he wasn't sure how he should feel. After all, it was because of her that he went from slavery to prison for two years. Joseph thought about his life since he was first made a slave at seventeen years old. He had

The Dreamer

struggled with the twists and turns of his life, but he also it. Things were going well for him. Should he waste time and effort holding a grudge against Zeleakia or should he let go of the grudge and keep moving forward?

Many good things had happened to him since he last interacted with her, but she still victimized him and he had suffered as a result of her actions. He thought about how he had dealt with the victimization of his last thirteen years of slavery and being denied his freedom and the society of his family.

He had long practiced the concept of letting go of the bad and unhappy aspects of his life and rather than let those terrible circumstances define him or control him, he let go of them and focused on being as happy as he could be. There were many people who had caused him such agony in life. They had robbed him of so many things. He wasn't going to let them rob him of basic daily happiness. He focused on being faithful to his God and serving Him in every way he could. As a result, he did have good moments in time of slavery. He was blessed by the Lord. He had decided not to let anything get in the way of him and his Lord. After all, all he really had was his God. His God the creator of all was his one constant.

The question was, could he apply that philosophy toward Zeleakia? He decided he didn't want to take the time to nurse a grudge. He had too much to concern himself with and decided to let go of the hard feelings he had of her. She would never again be in a position to hurt him and that was something. He would not let her victimize him a second time by letting her destroy his peace again. He closed the door on her influence on him. Now if he could just figure out how to feel toward his ten hateful

The Dreamer

brothers.

Joseph was called back to the present by a question from Potipherah. "Why do you feel inclined to teach the Hebrew slaves about the Hebrew God? Would they not be better served by not knowing a God that cannot deliver them from their slavery?"

"Why do you teach the Egyptians about the many gods in your faith?" Without letting him answer, Joseph, followed up with another question. "How does it serve them?" asked Joseph with an air of resolute confidence.

After an empty pause, Joseph went on to say, "It is all about faith right?"

"Mm, indeed," replied Potipherah. He was disappointed by Joseph's response and thought it would be easier to snag Joseph and make him look bad. He had to let it drop since he didn't have another avenue to pursue in putting Joseph down. He was beginning to wonder if he would ever be able to.

One of the other guests asked them about why he was organizing the slaves like he was, trying to match them up with so-called better-matched jobs. After all, slave labor is free and what did it matter who did the work as long as the work got done?

"Everything I do is designed to optimize every effort toward storing food supplies for the next seven years. Is it optimal to have a young, strong worker serve bread for a meal and have an older weaker man work digging a canal? We can always make slave labor more productive. Let the weaker, older man serve bread and the younger strong man dig a canal."

"Also, the slaves will be happier and thus more productive if they serve in a well-thought-out assignment."

The Dreamer

"Who cares about how a slave feels. Slaves have no feelings we care about?" said Potipherah.

"Remember, we do not employ slave labor, they are all paid servants," Joseph reminded them. "Let us get another opinion on this discussion," said Joseph with a teasing smile. "Potiphar, was I not your slave for many years?"

Everyone, including King Sesostris, turned quickly to see Potiphar's expression and to hear his answer.

"Indeed, you were my Lord."

"Did I not increase your wealth every year that I served you?"

"Indeed, my Lord. You were very successful." Potiphar's face showed both worry and embarrassment at the same time.

"Did you ever change the way I managed your estate?"

"No. Your efforts at managing my estate were worthy of my respect. Everything you touched turned to gold."

"Did I not reassign many slaves and servants to different assignments even retiring some along the way?"

"Yes, you did."

"So my managerial methods allowed slaves to retire and give you increased profits every year?" asked Joseph.

Potiphar felt small and very insecure at this continued line of questioning, but was powerless to stop it. His eyes begged for mercy.

"Yes. Your managerial methods were beyond reproach. They were inspired," said Potiphar hoping the questions would soon end.

"Do you feel the methods used to grant you such

The Dreamer

growth and success would apply to the entire land of Egypt?"

Potipherah hoped Potiphar would answer "No," but could see he was in a corner and could only answer affirmatively.

"I do. King Sesostris is blessed to have you serve him."

Aseneth was very impressed with the way he handled himself with all these older men asking him questions intended to put him down. She was very impressed with what this Hebrew had accomplished. He was a handsome man, but she knew she could never allow herself to be attracted to him.

Chapter 24: Attraction

For thou, Lord, art good, and ready to forgive; and plenteous in mercy unto all them that call upon thee. Psalm 86:5

Months had passed since the celebration and each month a canal was opening. Even though they would need to wait for the Nile to flood at the beginning of the growing season, they were able to irrigate and prepare some land to house the growing flocks, herds and other livestock. The granaries were being filled, except some that were already full and Joseph had to rotate some builders to those areas and build more and larger silo's.

As he toured the land and interacted with people in various cities he kept his eye open for a lovely Hebrew woman with whom he could consider marrying. On the few occasions where a woman caught his eye, she was already married. He had lost a lot by being a slave for thirteen years, but now he had the freedom to marry whoever he wanted and he was anxious about looking for that special someone. He may, after all, be able to marry and have children, he could raise up to the God of Abraham, Isaac, and Jacob.

Joseph was happy he could look for a wife and in spite of all that had happened to him, he wasn't poisoned by all the terrible things that had occurred. He may never achieve all that he planned in life, but he was, at least, in a position to marry and have children.

Joseph and Mordecai were at the market sitting on a bench watching people pass by as they spoke to each other. They were taking a much-needed rest from their

The Dreamer

strenuous work schedule. They were also waiting for the appointed hour when the slave market opened. Now that all the slaves were assigned to the best job for them. They were working on granting the last remaining slaves their freedom.

He and Mordecai attended every slave auction and bought every slave. Doing this made it so that those needing slave labor would have to hire servants and pay them decent wages to get any work done.

Aseneth found herself in the same market as Joseph and Mordecai. She was enthralled with him. She was impressed with his accomplishments and though they had not spoken directly on the canal tour, she listened with great attention.

She was attracted to him and confused by him. Though Joseph was a beautiful man in the eyes of any woman in Egypt, she had the pleasure of meeting other attractive men. There was something about him besides his good looks that she was interested in.

Since she was not in a hurry, she decided to spy on Joseph. She was dressed elegantly, but not in her formal attire. She was able to blend in enough to get close enough to hear the conversation between Joseph and Mordecai.

"How many slaves over the last year have you been able to buy?" asked Mordecai.

"Eighty-eight," answered Joseph.

Eighty-eight slaves. That is much more than we have in our entire household and outdoor servants combined, thought Aseneth. *He must think a great deal of his stature. But then again, maybe he uses them on his work projects? I wonder . . .*

The Dreamer

"So you have freed every single one of those slaves?"

"Yes, every slave I buy goes free just as we planned," answered Joseph.

I wonder why I have never heard of this thing the Governor does, releasing his slaves and paying them. There is so much gossip, I cannot believe that this is not common knowledge and that everyone does not talk about it? Maybe they do not speak of it for fear other slaves will learn about it. That would not be good if they did.

Strangely, Aseneth felt something unfamiliar. She had grown up surrounded by slaves and servants. She had mostly treated them respectfully, but she treated them as though they were less than her even though there were no Gods that specifically promoted the use of slaves. She started to wonder at the morality of owning another person. That was a strange feeling, almost like she felt guilty. But she was born into a home of privilege and the slaves were born into slavery or in a lesser state that made them prone to slavery.

"You know, you are winning over people who have been opposing you. You built all those granaries and people laughed, wondering how they would ever get filled, then you had to build more because they filled so fast. There are fewer people opposing you now than in the beginning. You are truly blessed by the Lord. I am impressed."

"I have been blessed. That is true, however, I could not have achieved so much so fast if you had not been by my side. You have been a great help and a true friend Mordecai."

Their conversation was interrupted by the bells

The Dreamer

ringing to announce the start of the slave auction. As they left for the auction Aseneth wondered to herself, *how can a person be so good and not believe in the same gods I believe in? How can the Hebrew God be so bad, like Father has taught me, yet have someone so good as Joseph believe in him? It is confusing. Could father and mother be wrong*?

~

    The slave auction was over and Joseph and Mordecai's servants were escorting the new purchases back to the palace. Joseph and Mordecai were taking a leisurely pace to get home. They passed through the market on the way. Joseph noticed a fine-looking woman, striking in her beauty. There was something about her that was more than just beauty. He didn't understand what, but he was attracted to her. In spite of his great success and his winning ways, he was surprisingly shy when it came to women. He had kept an eye out for them, but had approached very few. This beauty was different. He wanted to approach her and learn a little about her. He didn't want to send Mordecai to talk to her like he had done in the past. But he was afraid. He knew he needed to summon up the inner strength to approach her, he wasn't sure how to do it. He offered up a prayer seeking help.
    He finally felt the courage well up in his heart. He approached her. As he got closer, he recognized her. She was dressed differently than when he first met her on the boat going on the canal. She was every bit as gorgeous as on the boat.

The Dreamer

"Aseneth, hello. I do not know if you remember me. My name is Joseph–"

"Yes, the Governor. Of course, I remember you," said Aseneth as she bowed before Joseph.

As she bowed before Joseph, other people in the crowded market looked at her and then Joseph and realized who was in their presence. Those nearby bowed to him as well. This flustered Joseph. He was used to power from his youth, but he wasn't used to the obeisance showed him by the people.

"Would you care to walk with me? Suddenly, I feel strange with all these people bowing to me," said Joseph

"Really? You are humble. That is very nice. Yes, I will walk with you."

They took off for a short stroll. Mordecai followed at a respectful distance. They had a friendly, but shallow conversation. They didn't know each other well enough to talk any other way. Their path wound back to the market.

"I will be in your part of the city soon as I am looking for more locations for silos' to build. I need to talk a little business with your father. Perhaps, I could call on you after that is done?"

"I do not think that will work. You are a Hebrew and, as you know, my father is the Priest of On. He does not look kindly upon you or your God. You can ask him, but do not expect much. I am surprised that I walked with you. I soon will become a Priestess and I am supposed to look down upon any god that is not in our pantheon."

Joseph looked upon her with indifference to what she said. She could tell he wasn't impressed with what she said. She wasn't sure what to think.

"Hopefully I will see you again."

The Dreamer

~

"Correct me if I am wrong, but the teachings of the God of Abraham do not allow marriage to a pagan. Hmm?" Asked Mordecai.

"You know very well you are correct. I know I should not have sought out her company. I have not been attracted to a woman like her ever. It was a powerful attraction. She is beautiful beyond description and very well educated and smart."

"Yes, but she will never be born a Hebrew . . ."

"Technically, she does not need to be Hebrew, she would just need to believe in the God of my fathers and have unyielding faith in him."

"So you can marry a convert then?" clarified Mordecai.

"That is correct."

"Maybe you should tell her that," suggested Mordecai.

"I think it is clear that she is loyal to her pagan gods. She said she would soon be a priestess. If she is that committed to her faith, then she would not entertain any other way of living," said Joseph.

"I guess you are right, unless she is committed to the truth more than her Gods?"

"I would not know, except for her talk of being a priestess, that is a big commitment. Enough of this talk. I am better off looking for a good Hebrew woman," said Joseph dismissively.

~

The Dreamer

    The time came for Joseph to tour the area where the Priest of On and his family lived. He contemplated making the trip, but decided to send Mordecai in his place. He was not interested in seeing what he had no chance to have, Aseneth. Furthermore, he had recently met a Hebrew woman he was interested in. She was no Aseneth, but she was lovely, well mannered and intelligent and the best part, she was single.
    He would have moved faster with the attractive Hebrew woman, but he was trying hard to overcome his attraction to Aseneth. If he were to commit himself to this lovely woman, he would have to do it honestly which would mean not having any feelings whatsoever toward Aseneth. Seeing Aseneth on this trip would just complicate things. Sending Mordecai is definitely the right thing to do. I will not have to try and avoid seeing Aseneth. Joseph gave Mordecai the assignment.

~

    Knowing that Joseph would be in her outlying community, Aseneth, knowing there was no future still kept a look out for when Joseph might visit. There was a high likelihood he would need to visit with her father. She was confused and a little annoyed with herself for wanting to see Joseph, but she did.
    What will I say to Joseph when he comes to our home? Will I make myself available to him? Why do I

The Dreamer

care?

    As she kept a watchful eye out for him, she also instructed many of her closest servants to be on the watch for him and they were to inform her if they learned of anything.

Chapter 25: Open Honest Heart

And he answered, Fear not: for they that be with us are more than they that be with them. 2 Kings 6:16

"Lady Aseneth," said her servant who was helping her prepare for the day, "there is a group of men meeting with your father right now. They are lead by a Hebrew."

"Is it Joseph? Why did not anyone tell me about this sooner?"

"It is not Joseph. I believe the mans name is Mordecai."

I thought Joseph was going to be meeting with my father? Hebrews coming and going through Egyptian society was a big deal and there were not many of them who could do that. It was a situation worth looking into. Aseneth came up with an excuse to leave her room and go through the big rooms in the house which would lead her past wherever her father and these Hebrew men might be. By the time she made her initial pass through the house, she found her father alone.

"Father, did I not hear correctly that there were Hebrew men speaking with you?"

"Yes, my child, you heard right, but they have come and gone. They will be building storage facilities within view of our property by royal order of Governor Joseph."

Hearing that, she knew she should be as irritated at the news as her father was, but hearing Joseph's name in an official capacity sent s thrilling sensation through her.

"Who did you meet with Father?"

"I met with an official delegation bearing the seal of the Governor."

The Dreamer

"Was Joseph himself not among the delegation?"

"No. The leader of the group was his assistant Mordecai."

Not wanting to reveal her interest in something she knew she could not have, she didn't ask any more questions. Instead, she went to the tallest place in their mansion and looked from the watch tower around their land to see if she could find where the building might be. Even though Joseph wasn't there yet, he could come by the construction site any day to check on its progress. She wanted to have a chance to accidentally bump into him.

A few weeks later with no Joseph in sight, she decided to take a stroll to the place of construction to check on it. Something that big, so close to her house created a suitable excuse to visit it. With her proper escorts she made her way to the site. *This is crazy. I am behaving like a child wanting to see Joseph.*

Mordecai was informed there was an official visitor on-site. Having learned a great deal from Joseph about how to deal with the naysayers and opponents of what they were doing throughout the land, Mordecai knew that being proactive was the way to handle them. He stopped what he was doing and met with Aseneth.

"Is there something I can help you with my lady?"

"I am just here looking over the construction of the granaries. Where is your master Joseph?"

"Joseph is not my master. I work for him as his assistant."

Aseneth considered herself a good and upright human, but she did have a fondness for the service of slaves and considered herself above the slave and servant class. With Joseph on the loose, the distinction between

The Dreamer

the slaves, servants and lower classes were getting blurred as so many servants were getting paid good wages and many Hebrew slaves were gaining their freedom.

"Well then, where is Joseph, whoever he is to you?"

"He is back at the capitol."

"He told me he was going to supervise this job. Why did he change his mind?"

Mordecai could honestly say that Joseph didn't tell him the reason, even though he suspected he knew. They had become increasingly close and Joseph was aware of Joseph's dilemma with finding a suitable wife.

"Joseph did not tell me the reason for giving me this assignment. I will be going back to see him in a few days. Is there a message I can give him for you?"

"No, of course not. Do not be ridiculous. Why would I have anything to say to the Governor?"

Mordecai was wise in his old age and could hear from Aseneth the words she couldn't say. He hoped that the opportunity would come up so he could tell her a few things might break down the barriers between these two impossible lovers.

"We are about to have our midday meal and devotional time," said Mordecai, "you are welcome to join us if you would like." His words were followed by the dinner bell.

"That would be something, eating with slaves and servants . . . Well, maybe I will stay and observe. I am not hungry, but I would not mind hearing a sermon about your Hebrew God. That might be interesting."

~

The Dreamer

Aseneth was stunned by the words she heard Mordecai speak. She really expected to watch the whole affair and smirk. She thought it would make a good story to tell around the dinner table. Instead, she was impressed that such powerful words could come from some lowly Hebrew servant, at least lowly in her estimation.

After the sermon and the midday meal, Mordecai made his way over to Aseneth and asked her again if she wanted to eat. After she declined the second time, he asked her what she thought of his message.

She found herself talking openly to him, "I was very impressed with what you had to say. I am shocked that someone with your background, a lowly sheep herder, then a slave could speak so eloquently about their God. How can you speak with such conviction and such certainty about your God?"

"That is a good question. I was exposed to Joseph and his teachings when we were both free men, then I was exposed to him while we were slaves to Potiphar. I knew his teachings, but I did not believe them at first. It was not until after Joseph got out of prison and we met up again that I truly started to believe what he had to say."

"What made the difference between believing and not believing?"

"Prayer. Joseph told me to pray about his teachings, to pray with an open and honest heart. His teachings felt good, just not good enough to change the way I thought. But then I took Joseph's words seriously and decided to talk to the Lord with the open and honest heart and that is when I felt a strong conviction come to

The Dreamer

me. I felt the truth of the words in my heart rather than in my mind. Once I really felt the spirit of the Lord, my mind followed suit."

What Mordecai said and how he said it rang true in Aseneth's mind, but not her heart. There was logic in feeling it in one's heart before one's mind.

Sensing that Aseneth was on the verge of having her moment with this new truth, Mordecai said, "Learn of the Hebrew God and compare him to your pagan gods. Do your pagan gods teach you to love your fellow man? Do they teach you to have humility and a contrite heart? Do they teach you to suffer long and have joy? Do your pagan Gods make you feel anything in your heart or is it all in your mind? Do they teach you to forgive the wrong others have done to you? Think about these things and pray with a sincere, open heart and see what happens."

Aseneth was feeling unstable in her faith for the first time in her life because she just realized that everything she knew and everything she believed was from her mind. Her mind was not a strong motivating force like her heart was. It was her heart that made her think she might be attracted to Joseph. It was her mind telling her it would never work. She knew when it came to Joseph, her heart was more in control than her mind. She wanted her mind to be as motivated as her heart in all things, including her spiritual life. She felt something change in her heart and her mind, she just didn't understand what that change was.

Until now Aseneth always looked down on Mordecai, but after listening to him preach and then the conversation they had, her estimation of him increased dramatically.

"Thank you kind sir. I appreciate the time you took

The Dreamer

to talk to me. I will leave now and go back to my house and think on the things we have talked about."

~

    Joseph was back home working on expanding some of the canals, pasture land and farmland. He was pleased with the way his efforts had been blessed by the Lord. Everything he did was successful and everything blossomed into much more than he expected. He couldn't keep enough silos built to store all the food. He had every reason to be happy except for his loneliness.

    His mind told him Aseneth was impossible to have. His heart told him something else completely. She was nearly a priestess. There was no way she would ever change her thinking or her faith in false idols. But there was something about her that challenged Joseph's commitments to living the way the Hebrew God told him to live.

    While part of his heart belonged to what he could never have, Aseneth. The bigger part of his heart belonged to the God of Abraham, Isaac and Jacob. He longed to be married to a righteous god-fearing Hebrew woman and raise children in the Lord. He wanted what his father Israel and his mother Racheal had. He was having a nearly impossible time finding a Hebrew woman. His heart wanted two opposite things. The part of his heart that belonged to his God was bigger than the part of his heart that belonged to Aseneth.

    He finally, after two days of agonizing over the whole affair decided to close the door of his heart on

The Dreamer

Aseneth and he made a vow to his God that he would live a life of loneliness rather than break the covenant and pursue Aseneth. After all, wickedness never was happiness. Somehow Elohim would turn his sorrow into happiness in his own due time. When he made that commitment in his heart he felt great peace and happiness, yet he still felt a sense of mourning, knowing that he would be forever alone in the flesh. He was sad yet grateful that the feelings of peace and happiness overshadowed feelings of despair and mourning.

The Dreamer

Chapter 26: Aseneth's Conversion

This is my comfort in my affliction: for thy word hath quickened me. Psalms 119:50

    The days grew into weeks and silos' continued to grow during the months that passed. Aseneth pondered daily on the question of the one true God of Abraham, Isaac and Jacob. There were many aspects of this God that appealed to her. It made sense that one God created and ruled the heavens and the earth. A god needs to be omnipotent and omniscient. But on the other hand, having a God for every particular thing is all she knew all her life. She had an emotional connection to those Gods, especially Ra.

    In spite of her lifelong connection to these Gods, her mind was starting to see weaknesses in each of them as she contemplated the Hebrew God who was supposed to be the one and only almighty God. She hadn't seen and even heard much about Joseph. She hadn't thought much about him. She was feeling as if her life had been tipped over by Mordecai's teachings. She was on the verge of becoming a priestess and she was now questioning her devotion. She couldn't spend the rest of her life living a lie.

    Her thoughts on life after death accepted the fate the Egyptian pantheon taught, but her heart soared when she thought about the continuation of life after death. She just wanted all of her beliefs to harmonize. If the Egyptian Gods proved true, she would never be with Joseph in this lifetime, but she would be with her family forever, at least as far as she understood.

    If the Hebrew God was indeed the one and only

The Dreamer

true God, then all those Egyptians that were mummified and buried in burial chambers or pyramids would have their spirits mingling with the spirits of all of God's children. That would mean she would see her family and her friends on the other side of the veil. That could mean she would see Joseph there as well. That thought pleased her greatly, but when it came down to it, it wasn't about Joseph and it wasn't about her family, it was about the one true God or the many Egyptian gods.

She came to the conclusion she would pray for three days and three nights to the God of creation for understanding as to which way she would trust, the Hebrew God or the Egyptian Pantheon.

She announced she was closing herself off for three days and all were instructed not disturb her. Since there was no idol to represent the Hebrew God, she cleared her room of all idols and statues. She put them all in a room adjacent to her bedroom. The room that housed all her idols, gold, jewelry and personal wealth had a window facing the street. The room she slept in had a room facing in the inner courts, pools and gardens.

She dressed comfortably and plainly. She wanted no distractions. She wondered if her father and mother ever did anything like this when they were young seeking answers? Did they ever doubt their belief? What would they think of the extreme measures she was going through to be sure of her faith? She started off kneeling in the middle of the room.

"I am praying to the God of Creation, whichever one that may be. I desire to know the eternal truth of which God is the God of Creation. Is it Atum of the Egyptian Gods or is it Elohim, the Hebrew God?

The Dreamer

I am willing and ready to devote my life to Atum or Elohim. Atum is the god of my parents and Elohim is the god of Joseph. At this moment in my life I do not care which god they worship. I will fully commit myself to becoming a priestess of the Egyptian gods if Atum is the God of creation. I will disavow my connection with the Egyptian pantheon and worship Elohim if he is the God of Creation. This is very important to me, I will give everything I have to the one true god. Please guide me divine God of Creation and lead me to that answer so I may know deep within my heart and within my mind both. Nothing else matters as much as worshiping the true god."

Aseneth paused the prayer and thought about what she had said. She was pleased with how it came out. She thought of the memories of pilgrimages to different halls in different cities to worship different gods. It was a time-honored tradition of her family. She remembered how good she felt when she announced to her parents she wanted to become a priestess.

The sacrifices made to the various Egyptian Gods were done as a family. She wondered if the memories of the feelings she had, were memories of being with her family and not so much from the actual communion with the gods they worshiped? That wasn't a bad thing at all, but was it something that could sustain her for the rest of her life as she committed herself to the one true God of Creation?

She had always known there was a Hebrew God Elohim, but she never knew much about him since his teachings said he was the only true God and there were no other gods but him. His teachings were inconsistent with Egyptian idol worship. Her mother and father spoke

The Dreamer

negatively about the Hebrew God.

She pondered over many of the things Mordecai had taught her about Elohim. She noticed the riches in her adjoining rooms, the gold and silver, diamonds and rubies, idols and gilded statues. Those symbols of extreme wealth would feed the poor and hungry people who lived below her in the street for weeks at a time. She could pray to the Gods, but that wouldn't fix the problem of hunger. She started to sense the emptiness of idols.

She felt herself stand up and walk into the room next door. It wasn't her idea, but she willingly followed along. She picked up two idols covered in gold and appointed with gemstones. She was holding two Egyptian Gods in her hands, whereas one could only hold the Hebrew God in their hearts and minds, not in their hands. She tossed the idols out of the room facing the street. There were poor working class Egyptians down below. She saw two people each picking up one idol. They didn't bow down to either of the idols, but rather went straight away to venders who accepted the idols as payment for an arm full of food. Those idols did not feed the heart or the soul, they only feed the stomach. Elohim belonged in the heart where it could not be sold or traded for anything.

Her heart felt better knowing there would be two families less hungry tonight and for the next several days. She thought about the sacrifices made to these gods and how an animal used in sacrifice could only be afforded by the rich, but could be used to feed the poor, but given as a sacrifice, did neither. She tossed out rings, necklaces and medallions to the crowded street below. Her heart felt aglow and warm inside to see how many fewer people would be hungry.

The Dreamer

She caught herself and remembered she was dedicating the next three days to prayer and pondering so she closed her window and went back into her bedroom where she was supposed to be praying.

"O God in heaven, please answer me and let me know how to spend my life in worship? I want to glorify thee with my life. I cannot bear to spend my time, energy and future worshiping a false god." She felt energized as she prayed on to the God of Creation. She felt like she was on the right path to her spiritual future. She just didn't know which path she was on yet.

A while later Aseneth woke up, not realizing she had fallen asleep. She had fallen to sleep while praying. She was not taking in any food during her time of prayer and she drank very little water. She wanted her every focus to be on her three days of prayer. The first day of prayer was winding up and she felt like she was making progress, at least in her heart she felt better, but her heart wasn't sure why, only that she was sacrificing to find the one true god.

She prayed well into the night before giving into her bodies demand for much needed sleep. She awoke in the morning of her second day of prayer by a large growl in her stomach. She sipped on some water and started in on prayer. She reminded whichever God, she was praying to she would give her all to that God as soon as he revealed himself to her.

She thought about what Mordecai had said about the Hebrew God and she thought of the way the servants and slaves responded to his teachings. She thought about the hope that was evident on the faces of those that listened to Mordecai teach them the gospel of the Hebrew

The Dreamer

God.

The various gods of the Egyptians didn't give hope as much as they demanded compliance. She felt a connection to the God she was praying to because she was feeling more and more in her heart that the God of creation would love what he created and since he created all mankind, he would love them as his own and she was feeling that connection. That feeling made sense to her, but it was a new experience for her.

During the day she found herself tossing out more rings, bracelets and idols to the streets below. She was feeling joy inside her knowing the excessive wealth she had was helping others less fortunate than her. She went through the second day of prayer feeling good and feeling closer to the God of creation. The morning of the third day she went into the adjoining room to give away more of her possessions and was surprised to see the room nearly empty. As her room was nearly empty, her heart was full of joy and peace.

She wasn't sure if it was a symbolic occurrence or if it was the answer to her three days of prayer. She emptied out the rest of her jewelry, idols, and statues that were small enough for her to handle alone. This time she felt bad because now she had given away all her wealth and she had no more to give to the hungry people below. On the other hand, she was grateful she had helped to feed as many people as possible. Then she realized as she had been feeding the poor people below her on the street, the God of Creation had been feeding her spiritually. She didn't notice her physical hunger because she was so filled with the spirit of God swelling up within her heart it seemed to fill her whole soul. She was overcome with

The Dreamer

peace, joy and love for the Hebrew God who was now her God. She also felt love toward her fellow man. Be they strangers or family. She loved all of God's creations.

The Dreamer

Chapter 27: Marriage

These things I have spoken unto you, that in me ye might have peace. In the world ye shall have tribulation: but be of good cheer; I have overcome the world. John 16:33

      Nearly two years had passed since Joseph had become Governor of Egypt. Many more canals had been built from off of the Nile increasing farmland to grow food storage. The tributaries that could, were extended increasing even more farmland. Many of the granaries over all the land were completely full.

      Joseph calculated at the current rate of expansion and how well the first two harvests had been, most of the construction time needed to be spent on building more silos and pasture land. The King was getting anxious to have his builders back building monuments and his pyramid.

      If it wasn't for the extreme success of the first two growing seasons the king would have taken his builders back, but he could clearly see Joseph's God was with him. Everything Joseph did, was blessed by the hand of his God. The King would daydream about what Joseph could do for him once the whole feast and famine time was over and they were back to a normal cycle of life.

      The king took every opportunity to praise Joseph and celebrate his successes. He often treated Joseph like he was a son. The Pharaoh called a celebration. It would serve a twofold purpose. It would celebrate the return of the Pharaoh's son from a four-year military expedition. The messengers had preceded the son's return with great news of military success. There had been more milestones

The Dreamer

passed in Joseph's construction projects, the last one was the biggest and last canal built from the Nile. It would open up half again as much farmland as was already under Joseph's control. He named this canal after Mordecai, his trusted assistant.

People were invited from all over the kingdom and had been arriving by ship on the life-giving Nile as well as by wagon and chariot. The first day of celebration started with the people lining the streets to welcome the army lead by Prince Maya as he marched through the main street to the royal courts in the Kings' palace where he would dismiss the Army, and he would be honored at an all-day event with entertainment and food.

The next day would be Joseph's turn to be honored. There would be more days of feasting and entertainment and then they would conclude with a final festival where both Joseph and Maya would be jointly honored as the future of Egypt.

The procession was over and the festivities were well under way when Joseph saw Aseneth arrive with her parents. He was talking to Mordecai when he first glanced at her.

"Did you happen to notice Aseneth just arrived with her parents?"

"Yes I did and she looks as radiant as ever," smiled Mordecai.

"She looks as if there is something different about her. Maybe a glow about her. I am not sure what it is, but there is something changed about her."

Mordecai nodded in agreement. He noticed it as well. He hadn't seen her since the time she visited the midday meal and preaching. He kept his eye on her

The Dreamer

because he was curious like Joseph; there was something new and unique about her countenance.

People were coming and going, and it was difficult to keep his eyes on her. Eventually, after greeting a few people, Mordecai lost sight of Aseneth. From out of nowhere, Mordecai felt a hand on his shoulder.

"Mordecai. Hello."

Mordecai turned to the voice of Aseneth. "Well, hello Aseneth. It is good to see you."

"It is good to see you as well."

"It has been a long time since we last spoke. How have you been?" asked Mordecai.

"I doubt I can possibly tell you everything that has happened or just how wonderful I am. But I owe a great deal to you and to Joseph. To you for your inspired words and to Joseph for being a wonderful example."

"What do you mean by that?" asked Mordecai.

"After pondering deeply on your words I prayed to the God of Creation for guidance to know which God to follow. I have felt his love and his inspiration in my life. I can say now I truly love the Hebrew God. He is my God now. I have given up my loyalty and allegiance to the pagan gods of the Egyptians. I feel the presence of my new God in my daily life. I cannot tell you how fulfilled I am inside. I feel at peace. It is a wonderful feeling."

"I am shocked beyond words," said Mordecai. "I am very happy for you. When I first saw you at the beginning of the party, I noticed something different about you. So did Joseph. We could not have known it was something so significant as this. It is remarkable how your countenance reflects your spiritual change."

Suddenly the blowing of horns interrupted their

The Dreamer

conversation and caught the attention of all the party goers. The feast was ready and everyone was to take their seats. Mordecai would sit next to Joseph, as was their practice. Joseph would sit next to the King. Maya, the king's son, would sit next to the king on his left side. Maya noticed he was on the left side of the king and not the right side. He was angry and wondered at the seating arrangements. He might have been more upset, but he was taken up with the person who sat next to him. It was Aseneth. She was something to behold and she took his breath away.

While his angst over the seating still simmered, he was more intrigued with such a beauty as Aseneth than he was about demanding an answer from his father. It had been so long since he last saw Aseneth. She was so much more lovely than he remembered her. After assuming his seat, Joseph looked across at Aseneth and his eyes lit up in spite of himself. His big brown eyes grew larger as he realized he was staring at her. Mordecai nudged him with his elbow. Joseph still stared. Then he caught Maya glaring at him from across the table. He heard the King starting to talk and that was what brought Joseph back to his normal self. He wondered again, what was it about Aseneth that was so different? She had always been beautiful. He wondered if it was possible that she could have become even more beautiful? She had a heavenly glow about her. She radiated peace and genuine joy.

The Pharaoh had spoken and Joseph had no clue what he said. He quickly turned to Mordecai and whispered to him. "What did the King just say?"

"The Pharaoh is going to announce the marriage of his son, Prince Maya."

The Dreamer

"Who is the Prince going to marry?"

"The King did not say. He is going to use the Pharaoh's prerogative and give him his wife."

"You are telling me," Joseph asked Mordecai, "that the King will give Maya whatever woman he wants regardless of the desires of the woman?"

"I doubt there are very many women in the social circles of the King and Prince that would be unhappy with such an arrangement."

"It does not seem right to force a woman into marriage against her will."

"Do not the Hebrews often arrange marriages?" asked Mordecai.

"Many do, but most of them would not force a union if one of the two did not want to marry that person," answered Joseph.

"Have you noticed Aseneth has been looking at you a lot since we sat down to eat?" Asked Mordecai.

"I have noticed that Maya has been staring at Aseneth a great deal."

"Yes, I have noticed that as well. It appears she is more interested in you than the Prince," stated Mordecai.

"It is too bad she is a Pagan. She and I can never be together," lamented Joseph.

"It appears you do not know her most recent developments?"

"About what?"

"Aseneth has converted her faith to our God, to the God of Abraham, Isaac, and Jacob."

"How do you know this?"

"I have spoken with her just this evening. I made her acquaintanceship during the construction project next

The Dreamer

to her parents' estate. I invited her to our midday meal and she heard some of my preachings. Apparently, that had an effect on her and sometime after that she came to understand the folly of false idols and became a true believer."

"That changes everything," said Joseph. "What if the King gives her to his son. I will never get a chance with her."

"You do not have much time– "

"I have no time left. No time to get to know her better, no time to talk to her, no time at all," lamented Joseph.

"Remember, you are Pharaoh's number two. You rank above his son. If you declare your intentions for her, you might just have a chance. But you would have to act now," urged Mordecai.

"What should I do?"

"Trust God."

"Trust God? I have not yet spoken to God about her. Until now there was no chance of us ever marrying and so I never brought it up with God for his help."

"He knows your heart," Mordecai reminded him.

Joseph bowed his head, ignoring everything going on around him. Mordecai recognized what he was doing, praying to his God.

Royal horns blew, calling everyone's attention to the Pharaoh. Once everyone quieted down the King said, "I would like to announce the marriage between– "

"Your Excellency," Joseph interrupted. Something he never did. Something he never had to do since he was always well thought out and well planned. His interruption carried a great deal of weight with the King.

The Dreamer

"Yes Governor. What do you want?"

Joseph got up from his chair and approached the King and whispered in his ear, "I want Aseneth for my wife. I am sorry for waiting so long before telling you of my intentions, but I must have Aseneth for my wife. I hope this does not create a problem for you and the announcement you were about to make."

By now Joseph and the Pharaoh had turned their backs on the audience and were able to talk softly with each other without anyone watching them

"I was going to give her to my son. What do you suggest I do now?"

"Let your son find someone he wants on his own."

"He wants Aseneth."

"Does Aseneth want him?"

"That does not matter what she wants."

"It should, after all, she is half of the marriage," said Joseph.

"The King has always had the right to give someone away in marriage."

"Then give her to me. You have blessed me so well your Majesty, would you deny me now after all of my faithful service?"

"Everything has been, as you said it would and I know your God blesses you and everything you do," the King was thinking out loud. "My son has served me well with the armies under him." There was a long silence after the King spoke.

"Is something wrong Father?" asked Maya, who had come up to the stand to join them.

"Joseph wants Aseneth for himself my son."

"But I am your son and a faithful servant to you am I

The Dreamer

not?" asked Maya.

"You are my son and you have been faithful for which you must be rewarded."

"I have two faithful people to please. One is my son, the Prince of Egypt and the other is Joseph, the Governor of all Egypt, but not my flesh and blood son. How shall I decide this matter to be fair and equitable to all parties?"

"Let us retire to your chambers. Then let us bring Aseneth before us and give her the opportunity to choose between the two of us," suggested Joseph.

"The Pharaoh has absolute authority over giving women in marriage," said the Prince.

"I am not disputing that law. I am suggesting a way to resolve this dispute and then the Pharaoh need not offend either of us. We agree to abide by the choice of Aseneth," said Joseph.

"I like Joseph's idea. It is wise and it is neutral. I will abide by whatever Aseneth chooses," decreed the Pharaoh. "Bring her into my chambers at once."

A few minutes later Aseneth and her parents, the Priest and Priestess of On, were in the King's chambers.

"How may we be of service my Lord?" asked Potipherah.

"Both the Prince and the Governor seek your daughter's hand in marriage. I was going to give her to my son, but Joseph informed me he wants your daughter Aseneth's hand in marriage."

"Surely a Hebrew is not worthy of such a prize," said Potipherah.

"Be he a Hebrew or Egyptian matters not to me. As Governor of Egypt, he is entitled to whomever he chooses for marriage," said the King sternly.

The Dreamer

"May we consult with our daughter before she makes a choice?"

"Yes, you may."

Aseneth and her parents were ushered to the back of the chambers by Potipherah so they could talk in private.

"My child. In case you are unsure of your choice, let me remind you of your exalted station in life. You may only choose Prince Maya. To choose a Hebrew, no matter his station in life is wrong."

"But I do not love the Prince. I am not attracted to him."

"My child," asked her mother. "Are you attracted to Joseph?"

"I am. I have been attracted to him from the first time I saw him. I did not think much of it at the time since I worshiped the Egyptian pantheon of Gods and he worships the Hebrew God. But I have had a profound change of heart and I too worship the Hebrew God."

Until now her parents had no idea of Aseneth's spiritual developments and were shocked at what she said.

"I do not like the fact I can be forced to marry anyone against my will, but if I must choose I will choose for the potential of love. I choose Joseph," Aseneth declared.

She walked away from her parents toward the King. Her parents were still dumbfounded and slow to respond. They followed some distance behind Aseneth.

"My King," said Aseneth, as she bowed before him. "My choice is Joseph, the Governor of Egypt."

Her parents were still in shock from what their

The Dreamer

daughter had said about the Hebrew God. Maya was furious he had not had the most beautiful woman in the Kingdom given to him as was promised. Joseph was both glad and shocked. He cared enough for Aseneth that he didn't want her to be married to someone like the Prince yet he wasn't sure how Aseneth thought about the Prince or even himself. Joseph smiled at what Aseneth said.

The King led everyone out of his chambers and he made his way to the stand where he stood until the royal horns sounded calling everyone's attention to the King.

I would like to announce the marriage between the Governor of all of Egypt and the daughter of the Priest of On, Aseneth. Aseneth, come forward."

Aseneth, in shock over the developments, but at least glad that she was marrying someone she was at least attracted to and respected as opposed to someone like the Prince who already had three wives. She stood before the King at the right-hand side of Joseph. The King married them and declared the next three days a celebration of their marriage.

The Dreamer

Chapter 28: Celebration

Likewise the Spirit also helpeth our infirmities: for we know not what we should pray for as we ought: but the Spirit itself maketh intercession for us with groanings which cannot be uttered. Romans 8:26

The celebration of the day was over and the palace intrigue was whispering that Maya was furious with Joseph for stealing his new wife. Joseph escorted his new bride into their royal chambers for their first night together.
"My dear Aseneth. I have no intention in consummating our marriage until we know each other well enough to be comfortable with each other. We need to get to know one another and develop a trust between us."
"That comforts me and I thank you for that," said Aseneth.
"I promise you two things," said Joseph. "One is to always be honest with you and the second is to do all I can, if and when I can, to absolve you of this marriage obligation if it is your desire once we get to know each other. I have no wish to burden you with an unwelcome marriage."
"Why did you marry me then?" asked Aseneth.
"Because if I did not do anything, you would be in Maya's chambers at this moment, instead of mine."
"For that, I am most grateful," said Aseneth.
"I think a woman of such substance would not appreciate being married to him. I am sure there are many who would desire it, I did not think you were one of them, especially after Mordecai told me you have forsaken your

The Dreamer

pagan gods in favor of the God of my fathers."

"Mordecai did not waste much time in telling you."

"No, he did not. He is a loyal friend to have."

"Was there no other reason for wanting to marry me?"

"I confess I am attracted to you, but there is much more than a physical attraction to have a joyous marriage. My desire is to find a wife that is as good as my mother was."

"What was your mother like?" asked Aseneth.

"I was young when she died giving birth to Benjamin, my youngest brother. But I remember the pure kindness and the most tender love you can possibly imagine coming from her. She was gentle and loving and kind and wonderful . . ." Joseph's voice trailed off with emotion.

"Your mother's memories evoke such emotion in you. I hope I can be such a mother as yours was. She must be special."

"She is."

"Oh, I thought from the way you spoke that she was dead?"

"Oh, she has passed on, like I said, she died when giving birth to my brother Benjamin."

"When you said 'she is,' it sounded as though she was still alive."

"Our God, the Hebrew God teaches us that there is a joyous life after death and that we will be with the ones we love if we live worthy of such a blessing. To me she is alive. Her body lies in a grave, but her spirit soars in the heavens above."

"What of your father and the rest of your family?"

The Dreamer

asked Aseneth.

"I do not know what state my Father and brothers and sisters are in. It could be that my aged father is dead. I have not seen my father or family since they sold me into slavery more than fifteen years ago."

"That is terrible that you were sold into slavery. You know the difference between being free and being a slave. Most slaves are born into it and have no idea about what freedom feels like. I have. . . Most of Egypt has seen that you have freed all the slaves that work for you. That is an admirable thing you do. Is it because you know what freedom is like?"

"Yes that is part of it. I cannot in good conscience be responsible for enslaving anyone for any reason. If someone does something wrong, they should face the consequences in jail, but never should his life be spent in slavery to another man."

"I grew up owning slaves and so that is what I am used to. It was not until I had my heart bathed in the redeeming love of our God that I started to feel bad about having slaves. Currently, I have four personal slaves. You must help me set them free. I do not know how to do such a thing. I would like to pay them and keep them in my employ though."

"If you free them, really free them, then they must have a choice to leave."

"What if they choose to leave even if I am willing to pay them for their service?"

"If you cannot make arrangements suitable for both you and them, then you must be willing to let them go."

"That does not sound as easy as I had hoped it would. I hope you will be patient with me as I learn how to

The Dreamer

live under the demands of a new God."

"I surely will. I hope you will be patient with me. I do not know much about married life except for the memories of my father and mother," said Joseph.

Aseneth took Joseph's hands in hers and squeezed them. "Let us then both pledge to each other our undying patience with each other as we grow together," Said Aseneth.

Joseph returned the gentle squeeze of her hands as she went on talking. "I must confess I am attracted to you. I know you to be a devoted man to the Hebrew God. I used to think it was terrible to be attracted to a Hebrew, but I already see that I was greatly mistaken. Of course, that is how I was raised."

Joseph smiled at what Aseneth said. He felt a little more relaxed in his heart. "It is late and I have an early morning meeting with the Pharaoh and the Prince. I would like to go to sleep, although I feel like I could talk with you all night long. Tomorrow's early morning meeting is very important."

~

Suddenly the horizon was filled with the Kings' enemies as they rode at breakneck speed toward the walls of the city. They all were riding under a white flag. The armies looked terrible, but all the staffers were waving white flags. Joseph and the Prince accompanied by a legion of chariot soldiers came out to the fields to meet them. Under the banner of peace, he conversed with the

The Dreamer

enemy leaders.

All the legions of enemies were unarmed, truly a strange sight. They were coming to purchase food from the Pharaoh. Four years of famine had spread throughout all the lands round about, and these enemies had no desire for battle. They were willing to pay for food and take it back with them to their cities and countries. Looking out at the vast display Joseph knew there was more than enough to supply them with food. He had an idea. He knew how to bring many years of peace to Egypt and the Pharaoh. That was strange that he had such a thought in the middle of a dream. It was as if he knew he was being taught in a dream state. Joseph then woke from the dream. It was nearly time for the meeting with the King and the Prince.

As Joseph got ready for his day and ate his morning meal, he wore a smile on his face. He had an idea on how to strategically use the vast stores of food they were stock piling.

Only one night had passed since Maya had lost Aseneth to Joseph and his temper was still flaring and his voice reflected it. Anything Joseph tried to say was immediately shut done by Maya. This was unusual because the King always respected everything Joseph had to say. The King was upset with the Prince as well, but understood his frustration. Finally, in an effort to bridge what appeared to be a growing gap between the Prince and the Governor, the King said, "While you were gone off to war I had two dreams. I will tell you the dreams Maya and ask you to interpret them for me. The first dream was when seven fat cows came out of the Nile, then seven poorly fed and starving cows came up out of the river and

The Dreamer

devoured the seven healthy robust cows.

The second dream was similar. Seven stocks of corn sprang up near the mighty Nile. They were full and plump and good. Then seven stocks of corn that were withered and blasted with the east wind sprang up and devoured the seven good stocks of corn.

I told these two dreams to all the wise men, priests and magicians and none could interpret them. What do these dreams mean to you my son? Speak and tell me," said the King.

Joseph smiled a big broad grin in his mind, but outwardly he appeared to be neutral. He was impressed at the wisdom of the King using his dreams to put the Prince in his proper place.

The prince didn't rush to answer the King. He thought long and hard about the two dreams. He was concerned that if he answered wrong, he would look bad, but if he didn't answer at all he would be no better than all the rest in the Kings' royal court. He had no idea and all the time he spent thinking about the dreams was really time thinking how to save face.

After considering how the priests, magicians, and wise men still seemed to be in good stead with the Pharaoh, he thought maybe saying nothing would be better than giving the wrong answer. If he did keep his silence, he would be admitting that there was something good and unique about Joseph. Was he ready to admit that there was something wise and good about the Governor? He was the only one to interpret the dreams and things seem to be going uncommonly well for Joseph. He continued to think about what to do. The sound of silence was deafening.

The Dreamer

"All right then. I concede that Joseph is uncommonly wise and is a gifted interpreter of dreams. Perhaps, Governor, you could prophecy about the future of me and my armies?"

"As a matter of fact, I do have some thoughts on the very subject. We are still in the seven years of plenty stage with just less than five seasons left to harvest. You will need to defend Egypt as you have done until the famine starts. Once it starts it will be widespread, affecting all the land's roundabout. Once word gets out that Egypt has plenty of food they will come from all around seeking the sustenance of our food that only we have. We will take their money for food, but that will not be enough. We will force treaties upon them for food. We will trade food for their weapons. We will render our enemies defenseless and honor bound to stay at peace with us."

Both the King and the Prince were very pleased with what Joseph had to say. For all of his faults, the Prince was unified with the King on protecting the safety of Egypt. He liked what he heard. It made perfect sense and displayed some cunning that he wished he had thought of.

~

Time had passed and Joseph was busy as ever. He and Aseneth had spent many nights talking into the early morning hours getting to know each other. Joseph shared the story of his dreams and how they lead to his brothers hating him and eventually kidnapping him. He told of how other evil travelers pulled him out of the well only to be

The Dreamer

sold into slavery.

Some of the story Aseneth knew, but not the details of any of the stories like how Joseph got thrown into jail on false charges and how he earned his release by staying true and faithful to their Hebrew God, trusting him along the way and interpreting the dreams of two of the Pharaohs' men.

As they took the time to get to know each other and often traveled together, they grew closer and in the process they fell in love. It was no secret they were attracted to each other, but they both wanted to learn about each other and develop a good relationship. They finally felt like they were at a point in their relationship where they could fulfill all the blessing of marriage and nine months later were blessed with a new baby boy they named Manasseh.

Joseph had never really known any personal peace, at least nothing profound. As a young man his brothers hated him and couldn't stand to be around him. He never had any real stretch of joy and peace. Now he was married to a righteous woman who shared his spiritual beliefs and now they had a son, the start of a righteous family.

When he was younger, he dreamed of having what his father had, a righteous woman that he was devoted to and raise children with. Joseph could hardly comprehend how great his life was. Two years later, another boy blessed their family. They named him Ephraim. Joseph couldn't imagine life being any better than when he was married to. Now that he had two sons he could not conceive life getting any better.

By the time Ephraim was born, there were only two more years left of the seven years of plenty. The silos and

The Dreamer

storage containers in all the land were overflowing. They had completed all the canals and long since finished creating more farm and pasture land. Each season the harvest was bigger than before. Joseph took all remaining builders and charged them with constructing twice as many granaries and pastures to hold the one-fifth of the taxes levied on the land as well as the government farms and pastures.

Joseph had given back enough builders to commence work on the Pharaoh's pyramid but kept the rest of the builders. Maya sent spies to spy on the countries surrounding the land of Egypt to find out how they were preparing for the coming famine. The spies returned with reports of empty silos and regular harvests, nothing spectacular like Egypt had. The various countries were making no effort to store against times of famine. The Pharaoh had made no secret of Joseph interpreting his dreams and he thought that other countries would at least try to store some food against the coming famine but they did not. They lived for the day, which also meant they were not planning any military action against Egypt, at least not soon.

The Dreamer

Chapter 29: Letting Go

Who shall separate us from the love of Christ? shall tribulation, or distress, or persecution, or famine, or nakedness, or peril, or sword? Romans 8:35

    The seventh season of the seven years of plenty passed. As it did Joseph and Aseneth were blessed with a baby girl they named Dinah after Joseph's older sister. They reaped the last of the great harvests and Joseph dismissed the builders to the Kings charge. Maya willingly posted soldiers around the government-owned pastures and storage facilities.

    The King called for a commemorative seven-day celebration in honor of Joseph for all he had done over the past seven years of plenty. Joseph didn't like such honors in his behalf. He requested that the celebration, honor the Hebrew God who was the one who blessed Joseph's efforts and the efforts of the thousands of workers over the past seven years.

    While King Sesostris and Prince Maya both respected Joseph and his religion, they had no desire to worship the Hebrew God. They struck a compromise and changed the seven-day celebration to honor all of the citizens of Egypt, who worked to build up crops and herds for the coming famine. While the celebration didn't specifically acknowledge the recently freed Hebrew workers and artisans, as free men and women, they were included in being Egyptian citizens who were being honored. Joseph felt satisfied at the compromise.

    For the time being, everyone had a full stomach and the crops had all been harvested. The herders and cattlemen still had to supervise the animals, and the farmers planned for another year of bumper crops even though the years of plenty were gone. The workers had a hard time accepting that another bounteous growing season would not come upon them.

The next spring came and all the farmers were looking for another flood where the life-giving Nile would deposit dark, rich mud to fertilize the desert for another bountiful year. The flood came, but it was much lower than the past seven years. Some of the tributaries managed to flood, but none of the canals could get full enough to overflow. There was not enough farmland to keep all of the farmers busy and with time those who worked the herds and cattle noticed a steep drop off in new livestock.

Some of the displaced workers joined Maya's armies, some sought for and became apprenticed to skilled artisans. Many of the free Hebrew workers sought after that which belonged to them and asked Joseph for the opportunity to travel back to their homelands. Joseph gave them their honest wages and provisions and happily sent them on their way honoring the promise to let any Hebrews who wanted to leave the opportunity to do so.

Joseph had much less work to do now that all construction projects for his project were completed. There was maintenance that needed to be done and he organized many labors and trained them so when the time came, they could efficiently share and sell the food they had in storage.

While all Egyptians were told about the coming seven years of famine, not all Egyptians stored their excess, while the government, under Joseph's leadership grew and expanded their crop land and pasture land as

The Dreamer

well as stored the one-fifth tax on all those who lived in Egypt.

It wasn't long when citizens and servants came to ask for relief. They were all informed that they should approach Joseph and his organization for relief. Joseph devised a plan. All servants were given enough food to last for one month. Then they would come back exactly one month later for another month supply. The families and estates that employed servants were given one month supply for their family and for their workers. Joseph sent some of his people around to check on the larger estates to make sure the servants were being well fed. Those not in compliance would be penalized, but not their workers.

Potiphar and others in the ruling classes like the Priest of On were still, in spite of all Joseph had done, opposed to everything he did. They were evil minded and jealous of Joseph. They did not heed Joseph's interpretation of the Kings dreams and put aside for the coming famine and now they needed food. They went to the King for assistance and the King refused to help them. They were commanded to go to Joseph for help or go hungry. In their fury they were humbled and forced to bow before the Governor for life-giving food. The King supported everything Joseph did or said.

Only six months had passed when people from tribes in the desert came seeking food. Joseph charged anyone who did not live in the land of Egypt for the food they received. Soon there were caravans from other countries coming into Egypt to inquire after food supplies. As yet, no official governments approached the King.

The Pharaoh held weekly meetings with his son the Prince and Joseph the Governor. The King presented a unique problem to Maya and Joseph at this meeting. "The treasury can no longer hold the wealth that has been steadily coming in from sales of the food stuffs. I am not sure what to do with this pleasant problem."

"Since my army is doing a lot of extra guard work, we could expand the army. That would take some money from the treasury," said the prince.

"I like that idea, it makes sense to increase the army," King Sesostris said.

"It is a good idea to ensure adequate protection of our food stores, but in the long run I think we need to build a much larger treasury to hold all the gold and silver that will continue to accumulate," said Joseph.

"I approve of both of your ideas. Let us implement both of them immediately. While Joseph is building a new treasury we will probably need more men guarding the new wealth," said the King.

Joseph also suggested using some of the surplus wealth to hire more craftsmen, artisans and workers for the Kings' construction projects.

~

In spite of the famine time passed. For those in Egypt it passed with little or no turmoil, but those coming to purchase food from the Governor of Egypt, were desperate. They willingly paid the price demanded for the food they bought and were grateful for it.

Soon, governments from nearby countries started to approach the Pharaoh about food and he, in turn sent them to Joseph for distribution. This was a situation they anticipated and had been waiting for. At first, Joseph

The Dreamer

charged these nearby foreign countries to pay with land that would be used as a buffer zone between Egypt and their country. When they became repeat customers for food, they were forced to sign treaties with Egypt promising never to invade Egypt. This pleased the Prince and the Pharaoh.

Things were going well for Joseph. Many of the ruling class and upper class of Egypt appreciated Joseph seeing that his interpretations proved to be true. Some still resented the fact that he was Hebrew, but none doubted his skill and talents.

Joseph was getting more and more busy with requests for food. He trained many of his aids on the methods he used to give and sale food supplies. He delegated all of the domestic requests to his aides. They were instructed to measure exact and keep records. Joseph only handled the requests from foreigners and other countries.

In one of their weekly meetings, Maya sounded an alarm, that because of the effects of the famine there could be spies sent in among those from other countries daily coming into the land for food.

"What information would they find? We are stronger than any other nation since we are the only ones prepared for the famine."

"That is exactly what I am concerned about. If they see our massive stores of food some countries might consider making alliances with other countries in order to come against us to do battle and take our supplies from us."

"What would you suggest we do?" asked Joseph.

"We could triple our guard at all food storage sights

The Dreamer

and we could have a bigger military presence in the city so when people come in for food they would see our military and think we are stronger than we are."

"I think that is a wise idea. Also, I've been taking their land and demanding treaties from them for their payment, but I could demand payment in the form of their weapons, horses and anything they could possibly use for war against us."

"That is a grand idea," said the King. "Between both of your ideas we should be as safe as we possibly can." Prince Maya agreed.

Chapter 30: Brothers

Praying always with all prayer and supplication in the Spirit, and watching thereunto with all perseverance . . .
Ephesians 6:18

    Joseph was on his throne overseeing distribution of food supplies to the foreigners when he noticed a group of men with long dirty hair and beards. Long scraggly hair and beards stood out in a land where all the men were clean shaven and well kept. They had big burly clothes compared to the fine linens Egyptians wore.
    Those men had an air of familiarity about them that Joseph couldn't quite figure out. The way they carried themselves and their rough exterior was trying to ring a bell in Joseph's memory.
    Then in a moment Joseph's heart stopped beating and time came to a standstill. There was an explosion of awareness that flooded the Governor's consciousness. There before him was his long lost older brothers, all ten of them. After more than twenty years there stood Reuben in the front of the motley group. Behind him were Simeon, Levi and Gad. Then Judah and Asher turned so he could see their faces.
    Joseph suddenly realized he needed to breathe. He opened his mouth and coughed in a little air. There was Naphtali toward the back. The last three of his brothers Issachar, Zebulon and Dan were partially turned so he couldn't yet see their faces, but he knew it was them.
    What are they doing in Egypt? What are they doing in my hall? After all this time what on earth are they doing here? Joseph thought in wonderment. There was a flurry

The Dreamer

of conflicting emotions coursing through Joseph's head. He was shocked to see his brothers, then there was a glint of excitement quickly followed by anger at what they had done to him all those years ago. He thought he had forgiven them.

For a few moments he wasn't sure if he was more glad to see his long lost family or if he was furious with them for their betrayal all those years ago. His feelings seem to give way to the hurt that their betrayal caused him. A sense of betrayal came flying to the foremost part of his mind. Betrayal was a deep wound in Joseph's memory. He had been able to overcome that wound by using a mental cane to help him along, but now that they were in the same building, under the same roof as Joseph he was feeling that old wound festering after all these years. He was confused. Why was he somewhat excited to see his brothers and yet he still felt that sting of rejection and betrayal?

He did not know what to think or how to feel. He was stunned. The line his brothers were in started to move forward.

"Governor? Governor? Joseph!" Mordecai whispered loudly in his ear. "Joseph. Are you all right?"

"What? Hmm? Oh yes, yes. Sorry about that. My mind was distracted."

"Are you all right Joseph?" Mordecai asked.

"Yes. I am fine. Like I said, I was just distracted. I am ready to see those who have come to purchase food."

After about a half an hour Joseph looked up to see that the next customer would be his brothers. He had been making mistakes that a thoughtful Mordecai and caught and corrected. That was not at all normal for the

The Dreamer

meticulous Joseph.

"Next," Mordecai called out.

Joseph was never flustered. Being frustrated was an unfamiliar experience. He wondered if he was sick, which was a rare thing. He was not sure what to say or what to do. There before him was his long lost ten older brothers. He stared at them for an unusually long time. They unknowingly stared back at him. Suddenly Joseph realized that they had no idea who they were looking at. He was positive that it was them, but why would they not recognize him after all these years? After all, there was a distinct familial look between them.

Why were they there? Of course they were there for the food. But in Joseph's mind his family was totally self reliant and depended on no one for anything. His brothers being there in the same hall as Joseph, the Governor of all Egypt, meant that things were not good for the family of Israel.

They do not know me . . . and I think I will keep it that way . . . At least for a while. Let us just see what is going on with them? Why are they here and what do they want?

He had been speaking through his interpreters all morning and he decided to continue using one as he spoke to them even though Hebrew was his native language. Once the brothers were officially introduced to Governor Zaphnath-paaneah, they all bowed before him calling to Joseph's mind the dreams he had of his brothers all those years before. Now the dreams of the tares and the stars were coming true, his brothers were paying obeisance to him, and they were humbly bowing before him.

The Dreamer

"Where do you men come from?" asked Joseph through the interpreter.

"From the land of Canaan," said Reuben

"Why are you here?" said Joseph through his interpreter.

"We come here to Egypt to buy food."

Again, those dreams of the grain and the stars were swimming around in Joseph's mind overwhelming his senses. He was overpowered by emotions and was still having a difficult time thinking straight.

I know I will not let my family starve. Surely I will provide them food. Why did not Benjamin come with them? Is he dead? What of my father Jacob? Is he still alive? If he is, then how is he doing? How can I find out that information without giving away my identity to them?

Then it came to Joseph what to say, "You have not come from Canaan to buy food. You are here to spy on us to see if we are strong or weak. You are spying on us to see our food supply and military strength."

"Begging your pardon, my Lord," said Reuben, "we are all brothers and have been sent by our Father to buy food for our very large family. We have no interest in your country except to buy food. We have heard from the Hebrews who have passed our way saying to us that Egypt has food enough to spare for sell to foreigners. That is the only reason we are here."

"I do not believe you. You all must be spies come to see what our conditions are like."

"Please Lord, we are ten brothers who come from a family of twelve brothers. We all have the same Father in the land of Canaan. Our father has kept our youngest brother back to himself in Canaan. The other brother is

The Dreamer

dead or perhaps a slave, we do not know about his station in life any longer," said Reuben. "It has been many years since we last saw him."

"I do not believe what you say. You must be spies," said Joseph as he saw Mordecai stare at him with a strange look on his face.

"My Lord, we are not spies, please believe us," said Simeon.

"Very well then. We will see if your words are true. I will place you all in prison for three days. During that time you will select one among you to go back to Canaan, if that is where you are really from. Then you will bring back the youngest brother. When I see that younger brother, I will know that you are not spies and I will deal with you and sell you food. Otherwise, you all shall spend the rest of your days in prison as spies."

Mordecai followed Joseph's command to place them in prison and stable their camels and donkeys while they were in prison. Once all the Governors commands were, executed Mordecai came to Joseph's home to report on what he had done. Joseph invited him into their main room to join in the conversation. Joseph and Aseneth had been discussing what had happened with his brothers earlier that day.

"Mordecai, those ten men that I sent to prison are my older brothers. The one brother they did not know if he was dead or alive is me. They think I may be dead. The youngest brother is Benjamin, my brother. We share the same mother Racheal."

"I thought some of those men looked vaguely familiar. Why would you send your brothers to prison . . . Oh, I see, you are getting even with them for kidnapping

The Dreamer

you and throwing you into the dry well?"

"I was so shocked, so startled, I was not thinking straight. I suppose, deep down I might be getting even with them, but what I was really trying to do was to learn about my father and my younger brother without them knowing who I am. That idea just came to me. I am still surprised about the whole thing. Aseneth and I have been talking about it ever since I got home."

"It has been a long time since you have seen your brothers and had to deal with them. Maybe you should just take some time and think about it and get used to the idea that they are here and back in your life," suggested Aseneth.

"I think that is a good idea," added Mordecai.

"Really Mordecai. Of all people I would think you would want to be a little harder on them as they have wronged you also back in Shechem."

"Well Joseph, is not this a perfect opportunity to practice the spirit of forgiveness?" Asked Mordecai.

"If anyone else suggested forgiveness, I think I would send them to Potiphar and have them executed. But you since you know what it is like to be wronged by them, well, I have to take your advice seriously."

"I do not presume to tell you what to do, it is just that the gospel that we learn from our God who teaches us to forgive and let go of the oppression of the offender and get on with our lives."

"I know very well the doctrines of our God and you are right. I do not know why it is so hard for me."

"Maybe that is why Aseneth's advice is so good, take some time and get used to the idea they are now back in your life and apparently need to be dealt with."

The Dreamer

"I feel so overwhelmed. I feel weak in body and weak in spirit," said Joseph.

"Are all the old emotions coming back to you?" asked Aseneth.

"Yes and I do not like those feelings. I am feeling nervous and afraid. I am feeling angry and confused. Maybe I do not know how I am feeling?"

"All the years I have known you Joseph, you have always sought to do the will of the Lord," said Mordecai.

There was a pause as that comment sank into Joseph. All this time and through all this shock, he hadn't stopped and considered what the Lord would have him do.

Aseneth and Mordecai noticed he was in deep thought and they gave him the space to think. After a few more moments Joseph asked Aseneth and Mordecai if they would pray with him. He wanted their support. They readily agreed to pray with him.

After a little more pause and thought Joseph began his prayer. "Dear God, the Father of us all, the creator of the heavens and the earth. I come before thy throne to seek thy help in this unexpected time of my life. I am grateful to have my brothers here with me and yet their presence also brings bad memories to my heart. I am confused between the love for them that I still surprisingly have, and the sense of their betrayal that I am reminded of. I do not know what to do. I do not know how I should feel. I do not want to do anything to offend thee, my dear Father and Creator. Please guide me to know what I should do and how I should do it to bring all reverence and glory to thee. Amen."

"Amen," said Aseneth.

"Amen," added Mordecai.

The Dreamer

"If I may Joseph," said Mordecai. "I remember when we met up again after we were sold into slavery, we talked about the circumstances that brought us into slavery. We both had run-ins with your brothers. We talked about how they beat you and kidnapped you and how you were eventually sold into slavery. I remember you saying something about how you needed to let go of the hatred and anger you were feeling. You needed that energy that you might otherwise spend holding a grudge toward them. You had a new life to adapt to and you needed to focus your emotional and physical efforts on your new life. And remember how you were so dramatically blessed by the Lord?"

Joseph took the time to let those comments sink in also. He let out a sigh and said, "Maybe that is the problem. I need to not let their presence afflict me and change who I am and what I've become, no thanks to them. I have a great thing going and they are no longer in a position to hurt me. The strange thing is that I thought I had let go of them and the evil they inflicted on me and gotten on with my life. Then here they come back into my life and throw me for a loop that I was not prepared for. They show up and here I am all a flutter and unsure of myself or what I should do."

"In the past you have let go of the many wrongs that have been done to you throughout your life and got on with living a happy and productive life, you can do it again," suggested Aseneth.

"In spite of what has been done to you, you have been so richly blessed that it is hard to believe so many terrible things have happened to you. You are such a strong individual. You have not let go of life. You have

The Dreamer

forged on with life and made something good out of something so bad in spite of all the bad that has happened," said Mordecai. "You have been a blessing to many around you, and you have been a wonderfully rich blessing to me in my life."

"Whatever you do, do not let them have any more control over your life by letting them hurt your relationship with God." Said Aseneth.

"My thanks to you, both of you. I knew that you both would be a big help and you have been. Now I think I need to be alone and ponder on what you both have said. I think you two have been inspired in the words you have given me."

The Dreamer

Chapter 31: Judgement

But I say unto you, Love your enemies, bless them that curse you, do good to them that hate you, and pray for them which despitefully use you, and persecute you. Matthew 5:44

Over the next three days, Joseph spent a great deal of time alone thinking about what to do with his brothers. Should he really keep all but one of them? He wondered if he overdid it by saying they all had to stay in prison, allowing only one to go free. After all, there were several brothers like Simeon and Levi who might run for home and never come back. If they picked one of the brothers inclined to run away, they would all be stuck in prison.

His primary goal was to get them to bring Benjamin back so he could be reunited with his younger brother and know more about his father without giving himself away. He explained himself to Aseneth and Mordecai and what he wanted to achieve.

"One thing worth considering," said Mordecai, "is the safety of that one brother going all the way back to Canaan by himself."

"That is a good point," agreed Joseph.

"Maybe you could keep six and let six go back together for safety?" asked Aseneth.

"If you let all the brothers agree on who to stay behind that might ensure that they would come back for him, then you could release the rest. There is safety in numbers. Safety is more of a concern now that the famine has started," said Mordecai.

If only one brother was allowed to go free, they

The Dreamer

could be robbed and killed and never make it back to Canaan.

After three days Joseph had his brothers brought before him. Speaking through his interpreter, he said to them, "I have decided that I will only keep one of you as a prisoner. The rest of you will be sent on your way with your bags full of grain and corn that you may bring them to your houses to help feed the hunger they are suffering from. The one among you I will keep will remain a prisoner until your younger brother is brought before me. If you do not return with your younger brother, I will know that you are indeed spies."

Not knowing that Joseph could understand what they were saying, they spoke among themselves.

"This must be punishment against us for what we did to young Joseph all those years ago," said Dan.

"Our Father has lost Joseph and we will return with one less brother again, all because of what we did to Joseph," said Judah.

"Remember the look in his eyes when he was begging us not to hurt him when we threw him into the pit," said Naphtali.

"We could see the anguish and sense of betrayal he felt and we went ahead and hurt him and caused that he would disappear from our lives forever," said Judah.

"We have brought this on ourselves. This really is our punishment for the evil we have done against our Father, against Joseph, and against our God," said Issachar.

"Remember. I told you all not to do anything to him. I told you not to kidnap him and I told you not to kill him," said

The Dreamer

Reuben. "None of you listened except that you did not kill him. Now we are being punished like Judah said."

After hearing their interaction with each other Joseph felt overcome with emotion. He got up off his throne and walked down off the dais and with his back turned away from everyone he silently wept, letting out the pent-up emotion inside of him. *There may be hope for them, some of them are actually expressing sorrow for what they did to me and some of them seem to feel sorrow for the sins they committed against God.*

Mordecai was left to supervise the situation in Joseph's absence. "Select from among you the brother that will stay behind in prison before my Lord returns."

The sons of Israel spoke among themselves. Everyone was talking and no one was listening. It was chaos among them. Mordecai glanced behind the throne and saw Joseph standing down from the platform that the throne rested upon. Joseph wasn't making any effort to return and the ten men were all in an uproar. Mordecai decided to approach Joseph. He walked behind the throne and walked down the stairs down to where Joseph was.

"Joseph, is something wrong?"

"No . . . Well, yes. I am just overcome with feelings of doubt, sadness, and a little hope. All this time and they still do not recognize me. I deliberately did not identify myself to see just how long it would take to recognize me and still, to them, I am just the Governor of Egypt," said Joseph as he turned and climbed the stairs back to the dais. "At least some of them seem to have a degree of remorse and are concerned about their standing with God that is something, not a lot, but it is perhaps more than I could have hoped for. I am confused with the swell of

The Dreamer

emotions going on inside of me."

They were standing just behind and to the side of the throne still talking to each other.

"Do you think someone will return with Benjamin?" asked Joseph.

"I do not know. The way they are arguing among themselves to see who will stay makes me wonder if they do not trust each other to return to them."

"What shall we do?" asked Mordecai.

"I am beside myself. I am filled mostly with doubt. At this point I would just as soon send them on their way and be done with them, then perhaps I will regain my confidence."

"If you give me a name, I can bind him and send the rest on their way," offered Mordecai.

"Keep Simeon behind, but before you do that have some of our servants fill their sacks with corn and other grains. Then, once all of their sacks are completely full, put their money on top of the grain and then fasten their sacks closed. Give them each a bag of food and provisions for the journey back to Canaan. Then, once that is all done keep Simeon and send the rest on their way."

"Why return their money?" asked Mordecai.

"While we have been talking, I have also been thinking about the dreams I had all those years ago, about them kneeling before for me. Then I thought of how my Father bestowed the birthright on me . . ." Joseph trailed off and was silent for a few moments before Mordecai interrupted him. "Joseph, are you all right?"

Joseph answered with his voice soft and wavering, "I have a very strong feeling that the birthright still rests on me and with that comes a great responsibility. I cannot

The Dreamer

charge my family for life-giving food."

"Why take their money at all?"

"I do not know. I am trying to make sense of all this. Just do as I said please." Joseph sounded frustrated.

"Very well, my Lord."

Mordecai had all their sacks filled with corn and gave them a bag of provisions for the journey home. As instructed, he placed the money each had paid, back in their sacks on top of the grain. After finishing those tasks Mordecai came back into the receiving hall and had Simeon bound and escorted off to prison.

After watching their brother be escorted out of the hall, the nine remaining brothers thanked Mordecai with gratitude in their heart and in their voice. Then departed Egypt for Canaan.

~

Reuben led his eight younger brothers out of Egypt on a road in the desert. They were now in familiar surroundings, leaving the gilded lifestyle of Egypt behind. They were wealthy men, but they came from a far different culture.

They had nice homes to live in and they had a nice and efficient estate with many buildings for their servants and their servants' families. Their estate was so big that it resembled a small city. None of them were especially comfortable in the Egyptian excess. It was nice to visit, but not a place to live in, and if they were going to spend three days in prison they would just as soon skip Egypt altogether.

The Dreamer

They stopped only twice for water on their day-long journey. They rode hard in an effort to bed down for the night at a traveler's inn along the way. They didn't mind sleeping in the desert, but they preferred the small luxury of the inn.

They made it to the inn with a little daylight to spare. They were in the stables taking off the saddles and burdens on the camels and donkeys when Gad opened his sack of grain and saw the money he paid for the supplies were resting on top of the food. He was shocked with no idea how the money got there.

"Reuben, come and look at this," said Gad as he pulled out the coinage from his sack. "This is the same amount of money we each paid for our grain." Reuben was shocked. He opened his sack of corn to see the same thing.

"Asher, Dan, and Naphtali open your sacks and see if your money is there," demanded a nervous Reuben.

"Yes, every bit of my money is here," said Dan.

"Every bit of the amount is here," added Naphtali.

"Mine as well," added Asher.

"What is going on?" Asked Judah, who was now looking in his sack.

"Is this a blessing or a curse?" asked Levi, "to have our money restored to us. What we have here is free food—"

"Or it is a huge mistake and we could be in a lot of trouble," Issachar finished his sentence. "They may think it is stolen."

"What should we do? Should we go back and give the money to Mordecai or the Governor?" asked Zebulon.

Reuben let out a long sigh and shook his head. "I

The Dreamer

do not know. It is a long days journey back to Egypt and we are three days overdue. We had no idea we would be in prison. Everyone is at home and on the verge of going hungry."

"Father Jacob and the rest have little food left and the small ones will be getting hungry any day now," Judah thought out loud.

"We know we have to go back with Benjamin somehow and retrieve Simeon so we will buy more food when we do. We can bring this money with us and tell them what happened and return this money. I think we need to push on first thing in the morning," said Reuben.

"I agree," said Judah and the rest nodded in agreement.

~

The sky was clear and brilliant blue. The air was dry and hot and the clouds of sand kicked up by the donkeys and camels was scorching and irritating. Reuben and Judah lead the caravan as they meandered their way along the trail to Canaan.

"What are we going to tell our Father? He sends us out to buy grain and we are accused of being spies and then we lose Simeon and now we have to bring Benjamin back with us to rescue him. Father will not like that. Not one bit," lamented Judah.

Wiping beads of sweat from his forehead, Reuben said, "We have to do something, we cannot leave Simeon in prison forever."

"I agree. I just do not know how Father will respond

The Dreamer

to it all. He loves Benjamin more than the rest of us now that Joseph is gone," said Reuben.

"I wonder whatever became of Joseph?" asked Judah.

"We agreed not to ever bring Joseph's name up, remember?" Said Levi who was within earshot.

"It has been more than two decades since we threw him in that pit. We cannot deny what we have done. We may be paying the price for what we did. God could be punishing us for that evil deed," Judah shook his head.

"We do need to talk to everyone and decide what to say to Father and how to handle this situation," said Reuben.

"Let us go talk to everyone and see if we can come up with a good idea," suggested Judah.

"That is a good idea. We only have until tomorrow afternoon before we arrive home. We all need to agree to the story we will tell Father. If we are going to have any chance of Father letting us go back for Simeon we have to have a persuasive story," said Reuben

"I will talk to Issachar, you can go talk to Zebulon behind you. Maybe we will have a good idea of what to do by the time we break for camp tonight," said Judah.

After talking to Issachar, Judah went over to where he could ride his camel next to Levi. "Reuben and I are going among all of you to see how to handle Father if we are going to have any chance of getting Simeon home. What are your thoughts on this terrible situation we are in?" asked Judah.

"I assume we are not going to talk about God punishing us for what we did to Joseph."

"No, no mention of Joseph unless Father brings it

The Dreamer

up," said Judah

"After all that did come up when we were talking to the Governor," said Levi.

"I agree. When we tell Father what happened, we will leave that out of the story," said Judah.

"Do you have regrets for what we did to poor Joseph?" asked Levi.

"Yes, I do. I have thought long and hard about it ever since we told Father Jacob that Joseph was killed by a wild animal. To see the hurt and anguish in his heart and soul. I would hardly wish that grief on my worst enemy, and that is saying a lot," declared Judah.

"I do have regrets, but on the other hand, it was infuriating to hear what that little viper was saying. It was hard to handle how he set himself above us. I never dreamed Father would take it so hard. He still mourns Joseph to this very day. I remember the look in Joseph's eyes when we were beating him and throwing him into the pit." Shaking his head Levi went on to say, "I do not really know. This whole thing is confusing to me."

~

That evening, just before the last rays of the sun went down beyond the horizon, the nine brothers stopped on the side of the trail and made camp. They had all been thinking about what to tell Israel and how to get him to agree to let them take Benjamin back to Egypt.

Once a fire was made and the animals were fed and taken care of they gathered around the fire to eat and to talk. The smell of the fire and the smell of the food they were cooking was filling the dark air around them. They

The Dreamer

talked among themselves for a while before Reuben took over. "We need to all agree on what we tell Father. We all need to be unified with our story if we are going to have any chance at getting Simeon back."

"Why would the governor think we are spies?" asked Naphtali.

"I have been wondering that myself," said Gad.

"That spy thing . . . None of it will matter if we're able to bring Benjamin back with us. That will prove our innocence," said Zebulon.

"So getting back to the matter at hand, how do we approach Father Jacob so he will allow us to take Benjamin back with us?" asked Judah.

"We have a lot of grain, enough to last us several months. We could just tell father what happened and then when it is time to go back for more grain we tell Father that either Benjamin comes with us or we cannot go back for more food," said Asher.

"That is true. We have no choice. If we want more corn then Benjamin has to come with us. Father will just have to let him go or else we will all starve," said Gad.

"Meanwhile Simeon is in Egypt rotting in that prison," said Levi.

"So then we tell him everything that happened, just like it happened without bringing up Joseph. We will tell him the need to bring Benjamin back as soon as possible to rescue Simeon. Father will likely refuse initially so we will let the idea simmer in his mind. Then a month or so later bring it up again. If he says no, and he probably will, then we will wait until we are desperate for food and try one more time," said Issachar.

After talking a little more they were all in agreement.

The Dreamer

Issachar took the first watch and they all went to sleep.

The Dreamer

Chapter 32: Obeisance

And unto him that smiteth thee on the one cheek offer also the other; and him that taketh away thy cloak forbid not to take thy coat also. Give to every man that asketh of thee; and of him that taketh away thy goods ask them not again. Luke 6: 29-30

    The next day was slow going at first due to an unseasonably windy day. The sand was blowing everywhere and the animals didn't want to move very fast as they had to walk directly into the wind. Shortly after midday the wind died down and they were able to push on faster.

    A few hours later they looked over the valley of Canaan and could see their father's estate. It was dry all over. The pasture was brown with a few green meandering lines representing the small stream that ran through part of their grounds. The sheep were let loose over the hill near the river that was flowing much lower and going much slower due to the drought that plagued the entire countryside.

    "It is hard to look at that brown and dry country and wonder how long we can live without purchasing food?" said Judah.

    "At least we have food for a while," offered Issachar.

    "Indeed," said Gad as he spurred on his camel.

    They were coming down from higher ground when Benjamin saw their caravan. He got on his camel and loped after them. They met each other long before they got to the main house where Israel resided.

    Reuben and Judah rehearsed everything that

The Dreamer

happened testing their story on Benjamin. He surprised them a little when he volunteered to go immediately to rescue Simeon.

"I am ready to go with you right now to prove your words to the Governor and to bring our brother back," said Benjamin with a courageous tone.

"Surely you must realize that Father will not be so anxious for you to leave his side," said Reuben.

"That is true. But he will want Simeon back. Right?"

"I hope so," said Judah.

Benjamin tended to the animals so that his brothers could immediately go inside and tell Father Jacob what had happened in Egypt and why it had taken three extra days. Reuben rehearsed in detail all that had happened. Father Benjamin tore the tunic that he was wearing in anger and sadness as he went on to lament the turn of events.

"First I lose my Joseph and now my son Simeon is captive in an Egyptian prison. Why does the Governor think you men are spies?"

"We have been wondering that ever since it happened and we do not know," said Gad.

"Did you talk to the Pharaoh?" asked Israel.

"He would not see us. We, like everyone else seeking to buy food had to go through the Governor," said Issachar.

"All we have to do is bring Benjamin back with us and that will prove to him that we are not spies," said Levi.

"I cannot allow that to happen. He is my only son left from my dear wife Racheal. If Benjamin goes and does not return to me then I will surely die in my great mourning," said Jacob in a doleful tone. "I can scarcely

The Dreamer

find the will to live as I mourn the loss of Joseph."

They all knew not to push the matter and to let Father Jacob think about if for a while. For the time being they had enough food and there was no great rush to push Jacob. Benjamin came in from tending to the cattle. He carried in a sack of grain and put it down before Israel and his brothers. When he opened the bag some of the grain fell out along with their money onto the floor.

"What is this? Why is your money in the sack of grain?"

"That happened to every sack of grain we bought, the money was put back in the top of each sack. We intend on bringing that money back when we go buy more food. We thought about returning it that very day, but since we were already delayed by three days, we were afraid you and the rest may need the food so we hurried home," said Judah.

~

Time passed slowly for Jacob. After all these years he still grieved for Joseph and now he also grieved for the absence of Simeon. Time passed slowly for the animals for they had less water and food from which to feed on. They grew lean and weak. Time passed slowly for the brothers, their families and their servants. They had enough water to drink and enough food to eat, but they had the unpleasant burden of knowing that their brother Simeon was dwindling away in a foreign prison.

For the brothers themselves, they also grieved for

The Dreamer

their younger brother Joseph. Not as much for his absence, but for what they had done to him those few decades ago. Many of them felt remorse.

They wondered if this whole spy thing was a punishment from God. They felt bad for what they had put their father through and now he was going through it again for Simeon. As time went on so did the famine. The house of Jacob's food supply was growing low, requiring the brothers to get ready for another trip to Egypt for more grain.

Father Jacob called Reuben and Judah into to his house so they might discuss going back to Egypt for food.

"The Governor told us that without Benjamin we would not be able to have an audience with him. It is a waste of time and effort to make the trip if we do not have Benjamin with us," said Judah.

"Why did you even mention that you had a younger brother?" asked bewildered Jacob.

"He accused us of being spies and we were only trying to explain who we were. We had no way of knowing it would turn out like this. We simply were explaining that we were a part of a bigger family," said Reuben.

"Father," said Judah, "please send Benjamin with us and I will take full responsibility for him. If we do not go then we will all eventually die. We cannot make it through this drought and famine without food from Egypt. I will do everything in my power to ensure Benjamin's safe return to you."

"Why is this happening to me?" Lamented Father Jacob. "Very well, you may take Benjamin with you. Also, gather from among the best fruits in our land to take with you. Also take presents of balm, honey, myrrh, and

The Dreamer

almonds to present to the Governor to try and gain his favor."

"We will do that and we will take the money that was returned to us and enough money for a larger purchase. We will do whatever we can to gain his favor," said Reuben.

Before Reuben, Judah and the other eight brothers left for Egypt, they had a prayer with Israel and he blessed them that God Almighty would give them mercy to gain Simeon and keep Benjamin from harm that they both might return to Father Jacob.

~

Joseph had decided to share with Mordecai the duty of selling food and provisions to the foreigners. The only people Joseph would see were representative of the various countries in the nearby lands. The only reason for seeing them was he was the only one with authority to work out treaties and demand weapons and other instruments of war as payment for the grain.

As his family grew with the new arrival of a baby girl, he felt the need to spend more time at home. Mordecai was very reliable and a perfect substitute for Joseph.

On a hot summer day while Joseph, Aseneth and their children were enjoying family time together on the hillside with shade trees, Joseph saw a caravan coming from the direction of Canaan. He, Aseneth and Mordecai had all been wondering when his brothers would return for

The Dreamer

more food and their brother Simeon. It had been several months since their departure.

Joseph knew they would have to return for food and he assumed they would want to come back for Simeon, but so much time had elapsed that Joseph began to wonder what might be happening with his family in far off Canaan. Now, seeing a caravan coming from that direction, Joseph wondered if that might be his brothers. It was a bigger caravan than they had the first time they came to Egypt.

Wherever Joseph or his family went, they were escorted by guards and a few servants. He sent a servant to bring Mordecai back to him.

Less than two hours later Mordecai arrived. He got down off of his camel and he was breathing hard because he had ridden the camel hard to get to his friend as soon as possible.

"What did you want to see me about my Lord?"

"Can you see that caravan on the horizon? Look toward Canaan. See it?"

"Yes, I do."

"Do you think it could be my brothers finally coming back?"

"They are coming from the right direction, that much is sure. The caravan seems bigger than the one they had when they were here first," said Mordecai.

"I noticed that as well. It is just that this caravan is coming from the right direction and they have got to be short of food. Maybe it is just wishful thinking . . ." Joseph trailed off as he looked in the direction of the caravan with his hand, creating a visor for his eyes.

"I will assign two of my best men to keep an eye on

The Dreamer

that caravan to see if it proves to be your brethren," offered Mordecai.

"Thank you. I appreciate it. If it proves to be my brothers contact me immediately and let me know if Benjamin, my youngest brother is with them."

"I will follow your directions with exactness," said Mordecai.

~

It was later in the morning when Mordecai rushed up the hillside on his camel looking for Joseph. He was able to find him quickly and he gave word that the caravan was, indeed, after all this time, Joseph's brothers and they had a man with them that they supposed was Benjamin. Joseph instructed Mordecai to kill two fatted calves for a celebratory feast. He instructed that his brothers be brought before Mordecai.

Mordecai was skilled at anticipating Joseph's needs and desires and already had the two men who were looking after the caravan go to them and escort them to Joseph's private hall away from the public hall where the grain was sold to foreigners.

As the caravan was being escorted to Joseph's private hall Judah commented to Reuben, "I am a little nervous at our reception. We are being directed somewhere less public. That cannot be good."

"We have no choice. If we want to be reunited with Simeon we have to do what they say," responded Reuben.

"Maybe they are taking us to prison because of us

The Dreamer

not paying for the food when we were here last," suggested Zebulon. "Maybe they will throw us in prison and take our camels and donkey's and our menservants."

"I hope not, but what choice do we have? We are strangers in a strange land. We do not understand their traditions and customs. We just have to go along having faith the we will be delivered with our brother," said Reuben.

All ten brothers with their caravan followed their escort until they came to Joseph's private hall. They secured their animals and followed the escort into the great hall where they met Mordecai. They recognized him as the Governors' assistant from their last trip to Egypt.

As they entered into the foyer of the great hall, they were asked to remove their sandals from their feet. While these tired and dirty men were coming in and complying with the instructions Reuben and Judah spoke privately with Mordecai.

"My Lord," said Judah. "When we came to your country the first time to buy food we paid for our grain and food in full. When were on our way back to Canaan we discovered the money we paid for our food was in our sacks of grain. Since we were running three days behind and our Father and little ones were in need of the food we had, we decided to forge on intending to bring the money back to you on our next trip to Egypt. We have the money on us and intend on paying you now for the food we first received."

Reuben and Judah, each held out four large bags full of gold coins. Mordecai smiled and said, "I remember taking your money and you paid in full. We balance our records nightly and there was no sign of any money

The Dreamer

missing so please do not concern yourself over the money. The God of your Fathers must have blessed you with the coins." Reuben and Judah stood there dumbfounded shaking their heads in disbelief.

"I trust that younger man over there," Mordecai said as he pointed to Benjamin, "is he the younger brother you spoke of to the Governor?"

"Yes, indeed. His name is Benjamin and he is the younger brother, we spoke about," said Judah.

"Very well then, you have fulfilled what was required of you. I will bring Simeon to you forthwith," said Mordecai. "Please sit down and wash your feet while you wait to be reunited with your brother."

Mordecai sent five men out to tend to their animals and he sent two men to fetch Simeon from prison. By the time all this was done and the brother's feet were washed, they saw Simeon with two guards come through the main door. They dared not react to his presence until instructed to do so because they did not understand the Egyptian customs or the wishes of the Governor.

Mordecai came into the room to check on the progress of events to see the men standing and staring at their brother. "Do not be a stranger to your brother. Be reunited with him. You will be seated in ten minutes for the midday meal with the governor. Clean and prepare your brother for the midday meal."

The brothers took turns hugging Simeon and helping him clean up and wash his feet. They reached into their individual packs and brought out the gifts they had brought to give to the Governor of Egypt.

They were barely done reuniting with Simeon when Mordecai ushered them into the great Hall of Joseph.

The Dreamer

Joseph stood just inside the doorway to greet each of the brothers. Each one, starting with Levi, bowed down before Joseph and presented a gift to the governor before getting up and moving into the hall.

Judah kept back until all but Benjamin had bowed before the Governor. He approached the Governor and said, "Behold, this is Benjamin, our youngest brother. He is the one you wanted to see."

When Joseph laid his eyes on Benjamin, his heart skipped a beat. "God be gracious unto thee, my son," said Joseph as he grabbed Benjamin's shoulders and he looked into his eyes. Joseph could feel tears fighting their way toward his eyes. He let go of Benjamin and quickly made his way to one of his private chambers alongside the north wall of the great hall.

Joseph, while weeping thought to himself, *I did not expect such feelings, I cannot show emotion, not yet anyway. He looks so much like me. My favorite brother is finally here, we are finally reunited.* Joseph was at first unsuccessful when he tried to stop crying. He decided to let the tears work themselves out. *Everyone else can wait, I have waited more than twenty years for this moment, they can all wait.*

Joseph relived what few memories he had with his younger brother as he muddled through his emotions. Finally he regained his composure and he washed his face in a basin of cool water. Once he dried his face he drew in three deep breaths and verified that he had fully regained his composer. He came out of the private chambers to see his brothers standing and talking among themselves as they waited for him. Silently Joseph directed Reuben to stand in front of the first plate, then he found Simeon

The Dreamer

huddled with some of his brothers and placed him next to Reuben. He then directed Levi to stand next to Simeon and Judah came next. This he did until every brother was lined up around the table in the order of their birth until he got to Benjamin, the youngest of all the brothers. He then directed them to all sit.

Joseph then motioned for all the invited Egyptians to sit in their order at their own table. Finally, Joseph sat at a table of his own where only he and Mordecai sat.

Naphtali thought to himself, *how strange . . . That the Governor would arrange us in the order of our birth?*

Judah whispered to Dan, "Look at the way the Governor has arranged us, it is as if he knows the order of our birth."

Once they were all seated Mordecai motioned for the servers to bring the food. The servers gave each brother the same amount of food, one after another in the order they were seated except for Benjamin. They sat before him five plates and filled them full of food.

How strange? Why does Benjamin get so much food? Wondered Issachar.

Joseph offered a prayer before eating. He offered the prayer in Hebrew without an interpreter which further amazed Reuben and his brothers. Then the Governor held up his favorite ornate ceremonial silver cup motioned to each brother from Reuben to Benjamin and then took a sip of it and held it high once more to signal that all within the hall could start to eat and drink.

Keeping a close eye on the Governors table, the sons of Israel waited until Mordecai started to eat before they joined in eating and drinking.

Chapter 33: Silver Cup

No weapon that is formed against thee shall prosper; and every tongue that shall rise against thee in judgment thou shalt condemn. This is the heritage of the servants of the Lord, and their righteousness is of me, saith the Lord. Isaiah 54:17

By the time the midday meal and merriment were over it was late in the afternoon. The Governor invited them all to stay as his guest for the night so they might get an early start for Canaan the next morning.

Mordecai met with Joseph, later on, to see how he was doing after having spent the afternoon with his brothers.

"Why did you not sit with your brothers?" asked Mordecai.

"I was not prepared to. I was feeling uncertain. I needed not be with them right away. I feel as though I have forgiven them all for their abuse toward me and for kidnapping me and having me sold into slavery. I just . . . Well, I am not ready to mingle with them. I am not comfortable around them just yet."

"What about Benjamin, he was never a part of the mistreatment and abuse? You could have had him sit with us," said Mordecai.

"That is true. I was so unsure of my feelings that I did not think of that."

"You are far more spiritually advanced than I am, but I wonder . . . When you forgive someone, how are you supposed to treat them? I am not so sure you are treating them right, but I am not judging, I am just wondering?"

The Dreamer

Joseph was grateful for his wife Aseneth and his dear confidant Mordecai. They were the only two people that could talk to him without any pretense. It was nice to have them around.

"I do not hold on to those terrible events that my brothers put me through as defining moments in my life anymore. I try not to use them as an excuse for my behavior. I am over that, I think. I do not think I am bitter toward them. After all, the Lord has blessed me greatly with Aseneth and my three wonderful children. I just do not really know how I should interact with them. You are a closer brother to me than they will ever be. I have a sense of family obligation to them, but right now that is all."

"Do you wonder if they have changed much in the past twenty-something years?" asked Mordecai.

"I do wonder that very thing. I feel like I have forgiven them, but I do not know who they are anymore, it has been so long since I have interacted with them."

Joseph went off with Aseneth for the rest of the evening. They had their evening meal with their children and after the kids went to sleep they sat out on their balcony and watched the stars and talked to each other. Joseph told her what he and Mordecai talked about earlier.

"I hope our children love each other and always get along with each other," said Aseneth.

"I hope they are loyal to each other in doing the right sort of things," added Joseph.

"Do you think your Father did anything wrong in raising your older brothers that would explain the way they treated you?"

"That is a good question. I have never thought of it before. From the best I can recollect, I would tend to think

The Dreamer

he raised us all the same."

"How did you turn out so much better and so much different from your brothers?" asked Aseneth.

"I can only think that the real difference between them and me is that I loved the Lord from very young in life. I grew up wanting to please God in all I did. My older brothers made fun of me in my efforts to please God. I think the real difference is that they chose not to follow the God of Creation and I did, that made us very different," said Joseph.

"Do you think our children will desire to please the Lord, the way you do?"

"I sure hope so. It would break my heart if they chose to follow after worldly things at the exclusion of God."

"It would break my heart as well," added Aseneth.

Their conversation came to a lull as they stared at the night time stars.

~

Joseph and Mordecai woke early the next day to plan the day's activities while eating their morning meal together. Manasseh and Ephraim were running around the room playing while they were talking.

"I have a thought. I was talking to Aseneth last night and we came up with an idea. I think one of my problems like you suggested last night was knowing if my brothers are the same after all these years or if they have changed. Like me, Benjamin has the same mother and father and

The Dreamer

where my Father favored me he now favors Benjamin. I need to see if they hated Benjamin like they hated me. I need to see how they treat him when the situation is dire. That should tell me a lot about who they are now. Have they changed or are they still the same?"

"So what would you have me do?" asked Mordecai.

"I will bid them goodbye and then you have all their sacks and containers filled full of grain, corn and other foodstuffs. Like before, put their money back in each sack."

While Joseph was pausing in his instructions Mordecai asked, "Why not tell them there is no charge for the food rather than the extra work of refunding their money without them knowing?"

"I am not ready for them to know who I am and I do not want to give them any reason to wonder. I still cannot believe they do not recognize me."

"Very well then, I will put their money back in their main sacks."

"In Benjamin's bag also put my ceremonial silver cup in the mouth of his sack. Then have their animals brought to them and send them on their way."

Curious, Mordecai asked, "What plan have you worked out?"

"Well, give them enough time to travel out of the city, then take twenty guards with you and go after them swiftly and stop them. Accuse them of stealing my ceremonial cup. Play it up well and make a big deal out of searching their sacks and make sure Benjamin's sack is last. When you discover the cup in Benjamin's bag, arrest him and bring him back."

"What do I do with the others?" asked Mordecai.

The Dreamer

"That is the whole point of this charade. They will either leave him behind or follow you back into the city."

"Oh, so if they follow us back then they are concerned for Benjamin and if they go on and leave him, then we can see they have not changed much in all these years?"

"Yes, that is the plan. I am not sure if I should be doing this," said Joseph. "I know I will now be able to save them from starvation during this famine . . . But at least after that test, I will know fairly well just who they are now and whether they have changed for good."

Joseph's brothers were sent on their way and after they left Mordecai assembled the twenty guards. At the appointed time they took off after the Hebrew caravan. They made sure not to catch up with them until they were outside of the city walls.

Once Mordecai saw them a short distance outside the city walls, they took off in a gallop to overtake them, which they did rather quickly. They surrounded the caravan and they all came to a standstill. Mordecai approached Reuben the eldest and said, "a silver cup is missing. The ceremonial silver cup of the Governor. I have been sent by the Governor himself to arrest whoever has the cup and bring the cup and the offender back with me."

"My Lord," said Reuben, "why would you suspect us of doing this thing. When we discovered the money in our sacks, we brought it with us to make sure that our grain was paid for. This is a testament to our honesty and loyalty to the Governor. Please, do not accuse us of such a thing."

"I have my orders," demanded Mordecai."

"I am so sure of our innocence that we will allow

The Dreamer

you to examine every sack of grain that we have on us. If you should find the silver cup on one of us then that person should die and the rest of us will be your servants."

"I will abide my Lords' direction," said Mordecai. "Whoever has the cup will be the Governors' servant and there will be no blame or obligation on the rest of you."

In an effort to be done with this distraction and get on with their journey, every brother and servant quickly pulled down the sacks of grain and opened the sacks as Mordecai came along expecting the mouth of the sacks of corn and grain.

Mordecai started with Reuben and went down through the rest ending up lastly with Benjamin. Benjamin opened the first of his sacks and there was the ornate ceremonial silver cup.

"What is this we have here?" asked Mordecai as he picked up the cup and dusted it off before holding it high for all to see.

Reuben, Levi, Judah and the rest of them rent their shirts and Judah cried out in anguish, "What is this evil you have done Benjamin?"

"I have done nothing wrong," said Benjamin. "I do not know how that silver cup got in my sack. I did not put it there, nor did I put any money in the mouth of the sack either."

Mordecai ordered two of his guards to bind Benjamin and escort him back to the city to the Governors' hall.

"Do not worry Benjamin," said Judah, "we will follow along shortly and see to this madness. The rest of his brothers reloaded the many sacks of grain. They sent the servants onward with most of the grain and they followed

The Dreamer

the guards back to the city.

They lost the trail of the guards by the time they got there, but they were able to remember the way to the great hall where they stayed with the Governor.

"Why would Benjamin do such a thing?" asked Issachar.

"I do not think he did anything wrong, but I cannot explain how that cup got there," said Naphtali.

"All of the money we paid for the grain was returned in our sacks as well, let us not forget," added Gad, "to return the money."

"These are certainly strange things happening to us," said Naphtali.

Once they made their way to the great hall, they secured their camels and approached the entrance when they were met with Mordecai.

"The Governor will see you," said Mordecai.

They came into the hall single file and one by one they gave obeisance to the Governor. Once they were all kneeling before the Governor, he said, "What is this that you have done? Did you think you could slip away from me with my ceremonial silver cup and I would not notice such a thing?"

"What can we possibly say unto to my Lord? How is it possible for us to clear our brother of this charge? While we are guilty of much iniquity, we are not guilty of this, nor is our younger brother guilty," said Judah. "We all will be thy servants along with Benjamin, who had the silver cup."

"No. Only Benjamin, the one who had the cup will be my servant. The rest of you can return to Canaan in peace," said the Governor.

"Oh Lord, let thy humble servant approach thee to

The Dreamer

speak without making thee angrier than you already are," said Judah.

"Come forward," said the Governor.

"When we were here the first time seeking to buy grain from Egypt, you said we were spies. We said we were not spies, but we were all brothers from the same father. We told you we had a younger brother and another younger brother who we have lost touch with and fear that he may be dead. You said we needed to prove what we said by bringing our younger brother to you which we did. Our father feared that he may lose Benjamin, who is his youngest son and only son left of his favorite wife Racheal. We fear that if we show up without Benjamin our father would surely die in mourning for the loss of Benjamin and he has not stopped grieving for the lost son. I told my father I would be responsible for Benjamin's safe return, but what matters most of all is that he will die if we do not bring Benjamin back to him. We cannot return without him."

"What would you have me do? Benjamin is guilty of taking my ceremonial silver cup. Justice must be served. I am sure in the land of Canaan you have laws regarding thieves just as we have here in Egypt?"

"I am responsible for Benjamin's safe return so please let me take the place of my youngest brother and let him return home to our Father Jacob and let me be thy servant in his place."

While Joseph was grateful that his brothers returned to seek Benjamin, he was overwhelmed by this unexpected turn of events. He was watching the other brothers as Judah spoke and he could discern which of the brothers were supportive of what Judah said those

The Dreamer

who were not. He was overwhelmed by emotion and had Mordecai send everyone out of the great hall except his brothers and Mordecai. Once the hall was empty except for the twelve sons of Israel and Mordecai, Joseph said to them all, "I am Joseph your younger brother. The one you sold into slavery. Is my Father well?"

The world stopped spinning and time stood still for Reuben, Simeon, Levi, Judah, Issachar, Zebulon, Gad, Asher, Dan, Naphtali, and Benjamin as they gazed at the Governor of Egypt. Was this man the young Joseph who they had abused, beaten, kidnapped, and allowed to be sold in Egypt? Could Joseph still be alive and standing in front of them right now? Is this the boy that some of them once wanted to kill?

Joseph got off his throne and stood right in front of all eleven of his brothers and said, "Do not let your hearts be troubled at this turn of events. Do not feel anger for what you have done to me. I have forgiven the hurt you have caused me. God used this experience by blessing me that I might still protect you from this great famine. Because what God has done with me, I am able to preserve your lives, Fathers' life and the rest of our family."

Joseph was overcome with great emotions and finally broke down in front of his eleven brothers and cried aloud. His lamentation was so loud that all the Egyptians and the Pharaoh that were nearby heard his crying.

Hesitant at first, Benjamin stood up and walked near Joseph as he cried. After a few moments of hesitation, Benjamin put his arms around his older brother Joseph. Joseph put his arms around Benjamin and they both felt much of that long lost love they had for each erupt into pure joy.

The Dreamer

One by one some of Joseph's other brothers stood up and came to where Joseph and Benjamin stood, and they all took turns placing their arms around Joseph. Buoyed up by the love of his brethren, Joseph was able to regain his composure.

"The famine still has five long years before it will end. It will destroy many lands and many people. Go to Canaan and unto Father Jacob, and tell him I am alive and well and ruler over all of Egypt. Gather the family and your flocks and herds and come up to Egypt to a land we call Goshen. This will be a fertile place for you and your families to dwell during the famine and we will all be close by."

By now the Pharaoh, having heard, Joseph's public weeping was in the great hall observing the events as they unfolded. After a while, Joseph dismissed his brothers and told them to spend the night and they would share the evening meal together.

Joseph was off to the side of the great hall, sitting by himself still regaining his composure and meditating. The Pharaoh approached him and they spoke for a while as Joseph told him the entire story from the beginning until the present time. The King was overwhelmed with this epic story.

The Pharaoh added to Joseph's command by telling his brothers to take many wagons back with them so that the women and children would have a much more comfortable mode of transportation. Only bring what is dear to you for when you settle in Goshen you will have all the good of the land at your disposal. They were given the best provisions available for their journey to Canaan and their return trip to Goshen. The provisions included much

The Dreamer

more than corn, they included ten donkeys to carry the best foods Egyptians could provide. Ten additional donkeys carried corn, bread, and meat for Father Jacob to enjoy on his way to Goshen on the return trip.

All of Joseph's brothers were given a change of clothing except Benjamin. He was given five changes of clothes and three hundred pieces of silver. Joseph saw them off the following morning and wished them well.

~

Reuben and Judah lead the caravan back home. They were filled with joy as they plodded along the hot dusty road back to Canaan. As they got nearer to Father Jacobs home, they wondered aloud how they would break this great news to their father. They hoped that the good news wouldn't be too much for him to handle. In the end, they decided to start from when they arrived in Egypt and then left with the silver cup all the way to the present.

Reuben and Judah left the caravan and rushed the last couple of miles to Jacobs home. They found him in the main room of his home. They told him of the grand news and ended the story by saying, Joseph is yet alive, and he is governor over all the land of Egypt. And Jacob's heart fainted, for he believed them not.

And they told him all the words of Joseph, which he had said unto them: and when he saw the wagons which Joseph had sent to carry him, the spirit of Jacob their father revived: And Israel said, It is enough; Joseph my son is yet alive: I will go and see him before I die.

The Dreamer

Book Club Discussion Questions

1. How do you think it would feel to be sold as a slave?

2. Joseph was betrayed by his own brothers. How would it feel to be betrayed by someone close to you?

3. How would you feel if you were Joseph and your master was blessed with great wealth because of you, yet you didn't benefit from the wealth?

4. How do you supposed Joseph felt when Zeleakia tempted him?

5. The narration of the book mentions life giving benefits of the Nile river and also of the sun. How do they compare to Joseph?

6. Once a person has victimized you, how can you let go of their influence?

7. Does a person have the power to fight back against the one who has victimized them? Where does that power come from?

8. Does it take energy to nurse a grudge toward someone who has wronged you?

The Dreamer

9. Is it possible to grow from the experience of being victimized? Did Joseph grow through the many times he was victimized?

10. How often was Joseph victimized? In what ways was Joseph victimized?

11. How can we stop someone from victimizing us a second time?

12. How was Joseph blessed in the middle of all his trials?

13. In the scriptural account of this story it says that Jacob loved Joseph more than his other sons. We know from other verses in Genesis that Jacob was a Prophet and Patriarch and a very good man. Would he really love one son above the others? If Yes then why? If no then why not?

14. In your opinion what are the top two or three lessons taught in this wonderful story?

15. Did Joseph make the most of the various situations he was in? How can you make the most of the situations you are found in?

16. We know that God can do anything, so why didn't he deliver Joseph from the various hardships he went through?

17. Why would God, who can do anything, not deliver

The Dreamer

you from your trials?

18. What have you got to live for? Make a gratitude list and mention everything you are grateful for.

The Dreamer

Personal Study Guide For Genesis 37, 39-45

This novel is considered historical fiction which means it is based on historical events, in this case the history comes from Genesis in the Old Testament. In the novel there is a great deal of both fiction and historical fact. Some characters like Mordecai are made up for purposes of telling the story. Reading through these chapters is a great way to understand the truth of the story as opposed to the fiction of the book.

Read the story of Joseph in Egypt, Genesis 37, 39-45, and use these questions to help you learn the beauty and power of this story. Do not use the novel to answer question, but rather get the answers from the Bible.

While studying these chapters ask yourself how they apply to you and your life? Note: for many of these questions there is no right or wrong answer. Some of the questions are designed to make you think about particular a particular issue of that chapter.

Genesis 37

1. Why did Joseph's older brothers hate him?

2. What did his dreams mean?

3. Who actually sold Joseph into slavery?

Genesis 39

1. What lesson can we learn from how Joseph

The Dreamer

responded to Zeleakia's advances?

2. Who was greatest in the house of Potiphar?

3. What happened to Joseph after he was falsely accused?

Genesis 40

1. What Kind of man was Joseph while he was in prison?

2. How did Joseph interpret the dreams of the baker and butcher?

3. What did Joseph tell the Butler after interpreting his dream?

Genesis 41

1. Who was responsible for the interpretation of the Pharaoh's dream?

2. How did Joseph interpret the Kings dream?

3. Do you think Joseph was married to Aseneth immediately after Joseph was made governor or did some time pass?

4. Why didn't Benjamin go with the older ten brothers to Egypt?

The Dreamer

5. Joseph named his first two children Manasseh and Ephraim. What is the significance of these two names?

Genesis 42

1. Why didn't Joseph make himself known to his brothers?

2. Why did Joseph go to the trouble of accusing his brothers of being spies when he knew who they were?

3. Was Joseph getting even with his brothers or was he testing them when he kept one brother behind and sent the others on their way?

4. Does Genesis 42:21 show remorse on the part of some of the brothers?

5. Why do ye suppose the Joseph commanded that they get the food they came for along with provisions for the trip home and did not charge them for any of it?

Genesis 43

1. How did Father Jacob feel about sending Benjamin with his the rest of his sons to Egypt?

2. What kind of gifts did Jacob tell his sons to take as a gift to Egypt?

3. What did Joseph first say to Benjamin?

The Dreamer

4. Why do you suppose Joseph sat the brothers in order of their birth?

Genesis 44
1. Why do you suppose the Joseph had his silver cup hid in their sacks of grain?

2. Why did Joseph send away the brothers only to have them brought back on trumped up charges?

3. Which brother offers to stay in place of Benjamin?

Genesis 45
1. What does Joseph tell his brothers after he identifies himself?

2. What does Joseph tells his brothers to do after talking to them?

3. What does the Pharaoh tell Joseph to do in regards to his brothers?

Made in the USA
Columbia, SC
21 February 2019